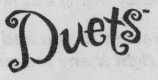

**Two brand-new stories in every volume...
twice a month!**

Duets Vol. #67

Delightful Holly Jacobs serves up
a very special Double Duets this month with kids,
chaos and, of course, rollicking romance.
"Ms. Jacobs' exceptional talent for penning
extremely humorous and captivating romances is
clearly evident..." says *Heart Rate Reviews*.

Duets Vol. #68

Bestselling author Elise Title returns
with a screwball comedy that will keep you
chuckling. This prolific, versatile author has written
over fifty books for Harlequin! Joining her is talented
Darlene Gardner, who always "spins a delightful tale
with an engaging set-up and lovable characters,"
asserts *Romantic Times*.

Be sure to pick up both Duets volumes today!

Ready, Willing and...Abel?

"I'm attracted to you and I can't fight it any longer!"

Hannah couldn't believe Abel was telling her this. Especially in the kitchen at midnight, with a piece of pizza in one hand and his best friend's kids asleep upstairs. Those kids—Hannah recalled how well he'd cared for them this weekend. Abel had insisted he'd never make a good father, but she knew otherwise.

However, she only wanted him to father her baby.

"What are you thinking?" he whispered softly.

"That you're thinking I'm no troll will make having a baby together a lot easier," she replied with a smile.

He was no troll, either. Not by a long shot.

"I'm attracted to you despite the fact that you want my baby. That's saying something," he said half-jokingly.

"What's it saying?" she asked.

"That maybe it's time I tried this...."

As soon as his lips touched hers, she knew she was done for. *Get the license,* she thought, *rent the hall, book the church.* There'll be no going back now, she knew...not ever.

For more, turn to page 9

Raising Cain

"Kiss me?" Lucy squeaked.

She was trying to concentrate on her driving, but Woody's flirting was frying her brain.

"Yeah," Woody continued. "I'd start slow and gentle, to make sure you wanted to be kissed. You would, wouldn't you?"

"Want to be kissed? If I wasn't driving, and if I didn't remember the ninety-nine reasons why we shouldn't and if the kids weren't around, then yes, I'd want to be. But that's a lot of ifs."

"After slow and gentle, I'd pull you even closer and kiss you harder and more intimately. I'd want to memorize your lips. I'd want to see if you really tasted like sunshine. And while I was doing that, my hand—"

"Woody!" Lucy pulled the minivan over to the side of the road. "That's enough."

"Funny. Because I was thinking as hot as it was talking about kissing, it could be even hotter trying it. And you're no longer driving. And there are no kids around. And for the life of me I can't think of a single reason in the world why I shouldn't kiss you. *Can you?*"

For more, turn to page 197

HARLEQUIN DUETS

ISBN 0-373-44133-9

Copyright in the collection:
Copyright © 2002 by Harlequin Books S.A.

Excerpts from the children's story used herein
with kind permission of the author.

The publisher acknowledges the copyright holder
of the individual works as follows:

READY, WILLING AND...ABEL?
Copyright © 2002 by Holly Fuhrmann

RAISING CAIN
Copyright © 2002 by Holly Fuhrmann

Ready, Willing and...Abel?

Holly Jacobs

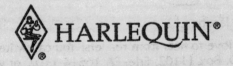

HARLEQUIN®

TORONTO • NEW YORK • LONDON
AMSTERDAM • PARIS • SYDNEY • HAMBURG
STOCKHOLM • ATHENS • TOKYO • MILAN • MADRID
PRAGUE • WARSAW • BUDAPEST • AUCKLAND

Dear Reader,

I have to include a disclaimer for this book. The fact that I have four children—three girls and a boy—should not in any way lead you to believe I've based the demon-spawn, whom Hannah and Abel baby-sit, on them. Absolutely not. I mean, the demon-spawn in the story are three boys and a girl. So that *definitely* means they can't be my children. I just needed you to know that fact as you're reading the term demon-spawn in this story. These fictional children are exactly that, and they're especially not related to me. Oh, and they're not actually demons either, just truly inventive children.

Now that we've got that clear (see, kids, I made sure there was no confusion), I hope you enjoy my second Harlequin Duets novel. Hannah and Abel's story was so much fun to write. I must confess I have a fondness for children (even the truly inventive ones), for dogs and for men who don't realize how cute they are when cuddling both.

Happy reading!

Holly Jacobs

P.S. I love to hear from readers! You can write to me at P.O. Box 11102, Erie, PA 16514-1102, or visit me online at www.HollysBooks.com.

To D. Jacob Fuhrmann, whose name was accidentally left off the dedication of my first Duets novel. Thanks for inspiring me at every turn. Though you might resemble the children in this story on occasion, they're not based on you or your sisters, I swear. (Maybe your uncles, though.)
You're the best son any mother could ask for!

1

SPERM "R" US.

That's what the catalog should be called.

Number 325. Six foot four, one hundred seventy pounds, chestnut hair, brown eyes. Studying for a degree in history.

Or there was Number 5571. Six foot, one hundred sixty pounds, blond hair, blue eyes. Master's degree in chemistry.

Or...

Hannah Harrington continued flipping through the pages of the catalog, but after reading the first few descriptions she was overloaded with information.

It seemed she could pick any number of attributes for her baby's father. It was sort of like visiting a toy store when she was little and picking out just the right Barbie doll. Only this time she was shopping for a Ken.

As much as she wanted a baby, finding the father in a catalog of sperm donors just didn't feel right. But, even though she was a Certified Nurse Midwife and worked with mothers and babies everyday, try as she might, Hannah just couldn't figure out any other way to get a baby of her own. She'd spent months wrestling with the problem, but she was no closer to an acceptable answer than when she started.

She wanted a baby.

When she was young her foster mother, Irene, had had a parade of babies come through the house and Hannah learned to love everything about them. She loved their smell. She loved the feel of holding them. Okay, she didn't love messy diapers, and wasn't overly fond of spit-up, but those were minor annoyances that didn't even begin to negate how wonderful babies were. And she'd always known that she wanted a baby of her own.

Hannah thumbed through the sperm bank catalog.

But as much as she worried about the ticking of her biological clock, she just didn't think this was the way to go about having a baby before it stopped ticking altogether.

Hannah's intercom buzzed, which pulled her away from her baby dreams.

"Hannah, there's an Abel Kennedy here to see you?" There was more than a small question in Sharon's, the receptionist's, voice. An office with obstetricians was a place where men did not abound, especially men with their own appointments.

"Send him in."

Hannah wouldn't have confessed it to Sharon, but she was just a little curious herself about Abel Kennedy. The males who visited Stephanson and Associates Obstetrics were either drug reps or were partners of patients. Mr. Kennedy had stated he was neither when he made the appointment. He said he had personal business with Hannah. But Hannah couldn't place the name, and couldn't imagine what *personal* business they could have together.

"You'll tell me all about it later?" Sharon asked.

Hannah laughed. "No promises."

"Okay, you'll tell me if he's pregnant though, right?" Sharon pressed. "I can supplement my income by selling the story to the tabloids."

Hannah laughed. "Oh, show the man in."

She slid her catalog under a stack of files. It might be one of the only options open to her, but she just didn't think it would work. Clinical and impersonal. Hannah wanted more than that for her baby...if there ever was going to be a baby.

There was a slight rap on the door and Sharon ushered in a gentleman. "Hannah, this is Mr. Kennedy."

Mr. Kennedy was dark haired, dark eyed and was utterly gorgeous. Not too tall, she realized as she stood to shake his hand. But it didn't take much to appear tall to Hannah's five-four frame. Mr. Kennedy's upper five-foot range looked plenty tall enough to her.

"Mr. Kennedy, please have a seat." He had that long, lanky build so many athletes had. Did he play a sport? If he did it would almost be worth sitting through a game just to watch him move, even though she was anything but a sports fan.

Yeah, she'd suffer through just about any type of sport if she got to watch this man in action on a court or field.

Hannah noticed that Sharon lingered at the back of the room. "Thanks for showing Mr. Kennedy in, Sharon."

"No problem." The receptionist made no move to leave the office.

"You can go now," Hannah said bluntly.

Sharon heaved a put-upon sigh and left, shutting the door behind her.

"Mr. Kennedy, I'm not sure what I can do for you..." Hannah just left the sentence hanging, waiting with almost as much curiosity as Sharon for his answer.

"I guess obstetric practices don't get many men with appointments?" he asked with a killer smile on his face.

The man just looked better and better.

"Well," she said hoping he didn't notice she was noticing him, "men certainly do come with their partners, but solo males? No, we don't see many of those. So what can I do for you today? I'll confess, I'm curious."

"It's about some property you own." He paused, then prompted, "Irene Cahill?"

There went Sharon's story for the tabloids, Hannah thought as she smiled. "I know the property you're referring to. Irene gave it *to* me, but it's not really mine."

Irene Cahill had been Hannah's foster mother. She'd raised Hannah, and her friend Lucy, as well as caring for many babies who were waiting to be adopted. When she'd moved to a Florida retirement community, she'd given Hannah the three small lots downtown, knowing Hannah's dream of building a health center.

"I know about the health center," he said. "Irene told me about it."

"I'm sorry, I'm not sure I understand."

"I went to her to buy this property and she told me that she'd given it to you, and told me about your health center," he continued. "I'm here to offer to find some other property nearby for it, if you'll sell me those lots."

"I see."

"I don't think you do. I need that property. I can find you some other location that will more than suit your needs. I have to have these lots."

"What's so important about three small plots of property in an old neighborhood?"

"My partner and I are planning to bring new homes to that area. The new census figures show Erie needs new, more modern, housing in the city.

The city is losing too many citizens to the suburbs. It's time to bring them back into downtown Erie..."

Hannah half listened as Abel Kennedy jumped right into a subject that was obviously near and dear to his heart. He spoke at length about developing blocks of land, pushed figures at her about the viability of attracting young professionals to stay in the city. He talked about tax bases and investing in the city's future.

Hannah heard very little of it. Instead, she studied him. Abel Kennedy was exactly what she wanted in a father for her baby. Too bad she hadn't found someone like him in that catalog.

He spoke with passion. Passion was a good thing.

Hannah watched his movements. Graceful. In control. He was gorgeous. Tongue-hanging-out-of-the-mouth gorgeous. Eye candy, pure and simple.

And after listening to him talk it was clear Abel Kennedy had a brain. A good one. So intelligence was no problem.

He looked healthy enough. A healthy father was important. The sperm people tested their donors. Abel Kennedy would more than likely pass his physical with flying colors.

Did he have a sense of humor? Not that it really mattered.

From a fantasy standpoint, Abel Kennedy would be a perfect candidate for fathering her baby. All she really needed was a living, breathing, healthy, intelligent male. Humor was just a bonus.

Abel Kennedy seemed to fit all her *absolute* requirements.

His spiel had ended and the floor was Hannah's. He sat back in his chair, obviously waiting for her response.

"A subdivision in the city, rather than in the suburbs? Well, yes, that has merit," she managed, thankful she had caught that much while she indulged in her baby-fathering fantasies.

"And if we can buy up the *entire* nine-block section, city council will let us close off some of the through streets. A real subdivision with no through traffic. We need your property to make that happen."

"Mr. Kennedy, I'll have to think about it."

"Ms. Harrington, I sell real estate, so I know that I should play it cool here, but I'm going to lay it on the line. I need this property and I'll do whatever it takes to get you to sell. I'll find you new property for your health center. I'll even make a healthy contribution to its building fund. I'll pay a better than fair market cost for this property. Just tell me what it is you want, and I'll do my best to see to it you get it."

He paused, focused his complete attention on her and asked, "What is it you need?"

"Want and need. Two very different things. The

only thing I want right now is a baby, and the only thing I need is someone to father it.''

Hannah's mouth snapped shut. What on earth had she said? Maybe she'd only imagined she'd said it out loud.

"What?" Abel's tense scrutiny gave way to surprise. No, more than surprise. Shock.

Nope, she had definitely said the sentence out loud. Airing her fantasies wasn't what she'd planned. She chuckled nervously and tried to think of something to say.

But her laughter died abruptly as she realized that, though she hadn't meant to say the words, Abel Kennedy *was* a perfect solution to her baby-making problem. He was a perfect daddy candidate.

The sheer insanity and audacity of the thought hit her. She wanted to laugh again and assure the poor man that she'd just been joking.

But being sane and unassuming would never get her what she wanted. And Hannah Harrington wanted a baby. So she sucked in a fortifying breath and—before she could change her mind—blurted out, "I'd like you to consider fathering my baby."

This time it was Abel who broke into laughter. In fact, it was uncontrolled laughter that showed no sign of ebbing.

Hannah realized she'd been right. Abel Kennedy fit her father requirements to a Tee. He was a living, breathing, apparently healthy, intelligent male. And as she listened to his laughter she knew he met her last *optional* requirement, as well.

The man had a sense of humor.

"Mr. Kennedy, it's not funny," Hannah said over the sound of his amusement. "I'm quite serious about having a baby. I've been studying this stupid sperm bank donor information," she pulled out the catalog and waved it about, "but the whole idea just doesn't feel right."

She set the catalog down and pushed it toward him. "Listen, I don't expect you to agree to my proposal. I didn't mean to say what I did. It just slipped out—just a wisecrack. Or maybe it was a Freudian slip. You did ask what I wanted, what I *needed,* after all. Well, I want a baby, and in order to get one, I need someone to father it."

Abel's laughing died suddenly mid-ha as he apparently realized she was serious. "Ms. Harrington—"

"Please, let me finish," she said. "If I don't say it now, I'll chicken out and never get it all said."

Abel, no longer laughing, sat back and silently waited. He looked rather shell-shocked.

Hannah knew this was a spur-of-the-moment proposal, but she didn't have anything to lose so she forged ahead. "I don't have a significant other, and don't see any hopes of being in that type of relationship soon. And a relationship based on simply the need to have a baby wouldn't stand much of a chance, so that's out.''

She ran through the options she'd explored, trying to outline her problems to this stranger. ''I could trick a man, but I won't. That idea doesn't even bear consideration. So that leaves me finding someone to father my baby. Someone I'm not in a relationship with. Someone I don't expect to be in a relationship with. And that's where the trouble starts.''

She nervously toyed with the edges of the catalog. ''I could ask a friend. But a friend is someone who's in your life. Even if he thought he could let me raise the child on my own, he'd have his own ideas and suggestions. We'd fight and that would be the end of the friendship. It could be as messy as a divorce. In my case my only close male friend is also my partner. We work together. I don't have enough friends to go around losing them. So friends are out.''

She continued in a rush, as if she could say it all fast enough and have it make sense. ''That leaves acquaintances and strangers. The problem is, the men who would consider fathering my baby are men I wouldn't *want* to father my baby. And the men I would want would never consider it. It's a conundrum of epic proportion. That leaves sperm banks. I can't tell you how much I don't want to go that route.''

"And so you're asking me?" Abel asked, no humor left in his voice, only shock.

"You did ask what I wanted. I want a baby. And you asked what I needed. Well, I need a father for that baby."

"Why would you even think I'd consider something so ..."

She filled in the word for him. "Crazy? Because I have something you need."

"You'd hold it over my head? That's blackmail."

Hannah sighed. He was right. But she was desperate.

"Listen, I know this suggestion came as a shock. I was surprised to hear myself say the words out loud. But I'm not asking you to father the baby now."

A mental image of Abel—long, lean and luscious Abel Kennedy—holding her, leaning her back onto the desk flitted across Hannah's mind, but she quickly unflitted it. She wasn't proposing this because Abel had her hormones running in overdrive. This was business.

"I'm simply asking you to consider it. Get to know me, and let me get to know you. You seem to fit all my requirements, but you may have some huge character flaw I wouldn't want passed on to my child."

He paused a moment, eyes narrowing as he studied her.

"What do you suggest?" he asked slowly.

The fact that he even asked what she had in mind surprised her. She really had no idea herself, so she simply blurted out, "We spend time together."

Abel leaned forward, still examining her intently, as if he was trying to figure out a difficult puzzle. Finally he said, "The only reason I'd spend time with you is to convince you to sell me that land and to forget about babies."

There was a frankness in his statement that Hannah admired. "Okay, that's fair. The only reason I'd spend time with you is to convince you I can't forget about babies and you should help me have one."

"Ms....?" He paused, searching for her name, as if her proposal had wiped everything else from his mind.

"Harrington. Hannah," she filled in gently. He seemed so befuddled and she felt a spurt of sympathy. This was an ill-conceived plan to conceive, but...

There it was, that *but*. But having a flesh-and-blood male she'd at least met father her baby seemed so much less distasteful than dealing with an anonymous donor at a sperm bank.

"Ms. Harrington, you don't know me."

She knew Abel Kennedy could help her realize her dream, and that was enough.

"And you don't know me," she said. "But let me tell you a little about myself. Other girls dreamed about careers and high-powered jobs. I dreamed about babies.

"And though I work with babies every day, my dream went deeper than that. I want my own baby. Last year, I realized that time was slipping by and I was no closer to that dream. I'm closing in on thirty and I realized that one of these days it will be too late."

"Ms. Harrington, I don't think—"

"I didn't think it would prove this difficult to get pregnant. But it's been more than difficult, it's been impossible." She wasn't sure what to say. "This is so awkward. But the more I considered it, the more I think it's was worth a try."

She opened her top drawer and pulled out a well-worn sheet of paper. "Here's the list I made. I don't think my requirements are all that tough. I just want a living, breathing male who's intelligent—not a rocket scientist, but I want someone who'll pass on a good mind. And he has to be healthy. Those are the absolute requirements. Humor is a bonus. But with the way you laughed when I told you what I wanted, it's obvious you've got that, too."

"I don't want kids." He ran his fingers through his dark hair, leaving little spikes standing on end.

Hannah had a sudden urge to smooth that hair back in place while she tried to soothe this man. Then his statement registered. "You don't want children? Even better. I don't know why I didn't think of that before. A man who doesn't want children is perfect for my needs. You'd leave me alone to raise the baby.''

"Let me get this straight. You don't know me, but that's a good thing. All you need to know is that I'm a living, breathing, intelligent male. Plus I don't want kids. So I'm your idea of a perfect father?"

"Father candidate. I can't base a decision this big on just one meeting," she clarified. "And you forgot a sense of humor. It was negotiable, but it's obvious you possess one."

She paused, trying to think of a way to make her odd proposal sound at least a little sane. "This is the new millennium and these things are done more and more. I'm not asking you to say yes, I just want you to just consider my proposal. We'll make it all nice and legal. No child support, no visitation."

"Are we talking making a baby the old-fashioned way, or just my donating—"

Hannah cut him off even as she felt her face heat up. "We can talk about that later if you decide to do it," she stammered as her courage nearly deserted her.

Making a baby with Abel the old-fashioned way?

A little tingle ran down her spine at the thought. It wouldn't be such a hardship.

"Do you honestly think I'll go along with this idea?" His fingers tapped a frustrated beat against the desk.

The tingle faded and Hannah's heart sank as she admitted, "Probably not. I know it's a long shot. But I have something you want—something you need. And you have something I want."

Oh, how she could want Abel Kennedy. That furrow in his brow that deepened as he listened to her offer only made him look more…just *more*.

"And if I agree to consider fathering your baby, to spend time with you, you'll sell me the land?"

"If I sold it to you this minute, there's no way you'd ever talk to me about this again. I'm not stupid. That land's my bargaining chip. I'm holding on to it for now. We can get to know each other. Maybe you're not as perfect a candidate as you appear to be."

Abel studied the small blonde. What on earth had just happened? He'd come into her office, confident in his ability to buy the property he needed, and now she was asking him to father her baby?

"This is ridiculous," he said. He should get up and walk out of her office right now but he needed the property she now owned. So, instead of walking out he found himself saying, "But maybe…"

"Maybe?" she repeated, tentative hope in her voice.

If he agreed to getting to know her, to considering this plan, it would be a lie. There was no way he'd ever truly consider fathering a baby then walking away from it and its mother.

He *should* get up and just walk out of her office now, but Abel couldn't force himself to just walk away from his dreams, even if it meant stringing her along until he could come up with another plan.

"Maybe," he said again. "You're right, you hold all the cards. So maybe I'll play along for now. We could start with dinner."

"Dinner?" she stammered.

Suddenly the tables were turned. It was obvious Hannah hadn't expected him to go along with her plan.

"Dinner. You try and convince me to give you a baby, and I'll try to convince you to sell me that land." He watched her sit as if in a daze. This is what she wanted, so why was she taking so long to respond?

The woman was cute, in a pixieish sort of way with her short blond hair and slight stature. Cute and definitely crazy. But who was crazier? She'd come up with the plan, but he was suggesting dinner.

"Fine. I'm done with work at seven-thirty. I can meet you."

"It's okay. I'll pick you up here." He stood. "But I don't want you holding out too much hope. I'm just doing this for the property."

HANNAH SAT DAZED at her desk. What on earth had possessed her to even suggest something like that to a stranger? Granted, the man spiked her blood pressure, but so did any number of movie stars, and she hadn't asked them to father her baby.

Not sure what to do now, Hannah called Irene. She wanted to know what her foster mother knew about this Abel Kennedy. But all she got was Irene's answering machine.

"Hi, this is Irene. I'm not in right now, but if you're male and over sixty, I'll get back to you as soon as possible. If you're not…Well, I'll get back to you when I'm done with him."

Hannah couldn't help smile despite herself. Irene was living out her retirement to the fullest.

"Irene, it's Hannah. I had a visitor today. Abel Kennedy? He said he'd talked to you about the property you gave me for the health center. I wanted, uh…" she paused, not knowing what she wanted. "Anyway, just call me when you can."

She hung up, no closer to understanding what had just happened. She wished she could call her best friend. Lucy would be able to help her sort things out. Unfortunately, Lucy was in Europe on business.

Part of Hannah wanted to simply give up and let the man have his property. Those lots were a key to his dream and at least one of them should see a dream come true.

She'd go out with him tonight and next week she'd tell him the property was his. Keeping it wasn't an option after hearing his speech about this project. She couldn't imagine taking his dream away. But for now she was going to hold on to her dream. Maybe he'd reconsider.

"Sharon told me you had a male visitor. So what's up with that?" Rick Stephanson, her partner, asked as he walked unannounced into her office.

"He wanted to buy that property Irene gave me. He said she was all for it, but I couldn't get a hold of her. You know Irene," Hannah said. Had she just honestly asked a man to father her baby?

"What about the health center?" Rick asked. He took the seat Abel Kennedy—the potential father for her baby—had just vacated.

"That's what I asked. I guess he's been talking to Irene, because he said he had other properties for me to consider in that same area."

"So did you sell?" Rick asked. "How much did you get?" Rick took care of the financial end of the practice.

"Well, let's just say we're negotiating."

"Hannah, I've known you too long not to realize there's something you're not telling me."

Hannah saw the exact moment he spotted the catalog on her desk. He snatched it up.

"You're not going through with it, are you?" he asked.

"Let's just say that I may have other options opened to me now."

He tossed the catalog onto the desk and his eyes narrowed as he studied her even closer.

"What do you mean?" he asked slowly.

"Remember my list of requirements?"

He nodded slowly. "How could I forget. I keep telling you to dismiss the entire idea." Rick had been less than impressed with her idea of having a baby on her own.

"Maybe I've found someone who fits every requirement."

"Who?" Suddenly, the answer dawned on him. "Oh, Hannah, tell me I'm wrong."

"Okay. You're wrong," she said with little conviction.

"No, I'm not. You're just telling me what I want to hear."

"You're right, I'm telling you what you want to hear. And I'm hoping Abel Kennedy will tell me what I want to hear."

Rick started in on all the reasons why this was ridiculous, why having a baby with a stranger would be a disaster. Hannah didn't argue. She couldn't believe she'd approached Abel about fathering her baby anymore than Rick could. And yet, as long as there was a chance Abel might say yes, Hannah was prepared to be a little ridiculous.

RIDICULOUS.

Abel left Hannah Harrington's office, muttering about midwives with ridiculous proposals. He could almost hear her blurt it out again. She'd looked as shocked to say it as he was to hear it. She'd looked even more shocked when he suggested dinner, staring at him with those big blue eyes. There was an honesty reflected in them.

There was honesty in her proposal, too. If it wasn't for her proposition, Abel could be interested in Hannah Harrington—not in a baby-making way, but in a totally carnal way.

She must know men would fall over themselves to be with her. She was short in stature, but long in physical attributes. Any man would notice that, and certainly any number of them did.

How easy it would be to have a little *accident.* Instead, she'd offered him this absurd deal. A deal that Abel knew he couldn't take no matter how tempting Hannah Harrington was in a non-baby-making way.

She could talk herself blue, but he'd never father a stranger's baby. But if they talked he could convince her to sell the property. He was a good salesman.

In addition to convincing her to sell the land he needed to talk her out of having a baby. The thought of Hannah propositioning some other man made his blood run cold with fear. But worrying about her wasn't his concern. He needed to talk her out of a baby because if she didn't want a baby there would be no reason for her not to sell the property.

But how could he convince her that she'd be better off without a kid? He needed a plan.

He was good at making plans. But as he got in his truck and backed out of his parking space, he couldn't come up with one single, solitary idea. His mind was spinning.

A midwife certainly knew about babies, but what did she know about kids? He had to convince her that cute, cuddly babies grew up to be difficult, cuddle-less kids.

He flipped on the radio and an advertisement floated over the airwaves. *Playtime Pizza…where good times and good food come together.*

An idea began to form. It was cunning. It was devious.

It was perfect.

2

"PLAYTIME PIZZA?" Hannah asked as they walked
toward the restaurant entrance that evening.

"It has the best pizza in town. I come here all the
time."

Hannah glanced at Abel as she followed him into
the loud restaurant. Screaming, laughing children,
beeping video games, music… It was controlled
chaos.

She glanced at the tall, dark and handsome, but
not very sly, man next to her. He wore a satisfied
grin, as if he had it all figured out.

Well, she could see right through Abel. He
thought coming here would intimidate her, maybe
even convince her to give up her plans for a baby
and just sell him the land.

Oh, yeah. Abel might fit all her criteria for a father
for her baby, but he was still a man. A man with a
plan that was bound to fail.

"How many?" the host asked.

"Two," Abel said.

"You know the rules," the host said, plainly waiting for something.

Abel looked clueless, and Hannah delighted in clueing him in. "You have to sing."

"Sing?"

"Sing for your supper at Playtime Pizza," she said with a commercial narrator's inflection. "You know, it's their new promotion. Come on, I'll help."

The host pointed to a poster on the wall.

Hannah started singing with gusto, ignoring the fact Abel wasn't helping. "Playtime Pizza's really neat. Playtime Pizza's quite a treat. I could eat here every day, eat my food then run and play."

The host gave Hannah a nod of approval that didn't extend to Abel.

"You must not have eaten here since the new promotion," Hannah said, trying to hide her amusement.

"Yeah, it's been a while," he muttered.

When the host led them toward the video game section, Hannah was even more amused. She could have told Abel there would be little conversing in this particular part of the restaurant, but she wasn't about to make anything easier for the not-so-tricky Abel Kennedy tonight. He'd made a huge tactical error.

She slid into the booth and waited for the fun to start.

"So what do you want?" He practically had to shout to be heard.

"What?" she asked, even though she'd heard him the first time.

"What do you want for dinner?" he said even louder, enunciating each word with care.

"You picked a pizza place, so I think that's what I want. You're right. It's great here."

"You've eaten here before?" Even though she could barely hear him over the video games' beeps and blips, his disappointment was evident in his expression.

"Oh, yeah," she continued merrily. "All the time. My best friend Lucy has a son. They live in Pittsburgh, though they're both in England right now. But when they're in town, this is the perfect place for a night out. He gets to play, we get to talk, or rather shout at each other."

She paused a moment, then as innocently as she could, added, "I'm surprised that you'd want to eat dinner here, though."

"The pizza is the best in town" he said quickly. Too quickly.

"Really?" Hannah asked, letting her tone imply her doubt.

"Really. Now, about the land—" A particularly loud shriek interrupted Abel. "What the hell?"

"Watch your language. There are kids around," Hannah scolded.

"Are you ready to order?" the waitress asked in

a booming voice that was probably a prerequisite for the job.

"A large pizza," Hannah said. "Abel here says it's the best in town."

"Toppings?" the waitress asked.

"Abel?" she asked, perfectly willing to follow his lead, as long as that way eventually led to her baby. "What do you want?"

"Pepperoni, mushrooms and cheese," was his rather terse response.

"Drink?" the waitress asked him.

"Something strong. Make it a double."

"This is a family place, Abel," Hannah reminded him. "No alcohol."

"I knew that. I was just kidding."

She could see a rosy stain creep into his cheeks. He was blushing? Better she shouldn't tease him about it. Abel was having a tough enough time as it was.

"Cola?" he asked the waitress.

"Sure." She scribbled on her pad and turned to Hannah. "And you?"

"Just ice water, with lemon, please."

"I'll be back in a jiffy."

Abel dove right back into his attack. "About the land—"

Another piercing scream interrupted Abel. For the next half hour she listened to his abortive attempts to discuss the land he wanted to buy as they ate their pizza. It *was* some of the best pizza in town, but she wasn't sure Abel would agree.

She was having so much fun watching him try to convince her amidst the noise of the restaurant that she almost felt guilty. After all, Abel wasn't having fun. No, he looked ready to give up.

That was okay with Hannah. Maybe if he gave up he'd *give it up* and she'd get her baby.

A little girl whizzed by their booth, her blond hair had escaped her ponytail and flew wildly behind her. If Hannah had a baby would she have her blond hair, or Abel's darker hair? Would her baby look like this little girl?

The child climbed on a chair and started punching buttons on a video game. Since she hadn't put any money in the machine, the screen just rolled along its merry way, trying to entice someone to play, but the child obviously thought she was actually playing because she continued to energetically press the buttons and hoot with glee as the machine blipped and beeped.

"Hannah?"

She realized that she'd been so intent watching the little girl that she'd forgotten Abel. She studied the man across the table. Despite the fact his plan obviously hadn't worked, he was being a good sport.

"Sorry, I drifted off for a moment. What did you say?"

"What were you watching?"

"Not what, who. See that little girl? If we had a daughter, she might look like that, at least if she got my hair. If she got yours," she scanned the children and found a likely candidate, "she might look more like her."

"And if it was a boy?" He pointed to a toddler with dark, dark curls playing in a pit of plastic balls. "Maybe him?"

"Maybe." She sighed. Her troubles flooding back. "But I guess it doesn't matter since you're not willing to father my baby."

"About that—"

Out of the corner of her eye Hannah saw the little blonde she'd been watching earlier topple off her chair. The child screamed. Not the happy scream they'd heard throughout their meal, but a scream that spoke to every mother in the bustling restaurant.

Hannah sprang from the booth and raced across the floor to the crying child and took her into her arms.

"Did you get hurt?" she asked, as she did a quick assessment.

The little girl shook her head, the blond strands of hair flew left then right.

Relief flooded through Hannah's system. "Why don't you go find your mama and tell her about it."

Sniffing, the child gave Hannah a hug and went across the dining room.

ABEL WATCHED Hannah and the little girl. She was giving the child her complete attention. Everything and everyone else in the building had ceased to exist for her. What would it be like to have that kind of intensity focused on him?

The thought caused a sharp blood-pressure spike. The image of Hannah staring at him as if he was the center of the universe, as if nothing else existed but the two of them...

The little girl hugged Hannah and for a moment Abel felt a spurt of something that could have been jealousy. Hannah Harrington was an attractive woman.

Who was he kidding? She was more than attractive. If she wasn't out to get Abel into her bed, it was very likely he'd be trying to talk her into his. But not to become a father. Not to have a baby.

That was their impasse.

Abel was an only child and he had never been around kids. He avoided them. They made him nervous. He felt no dire biological need to produce one of his own.

The little girl toddled across the floor and Hannah returned to the table.

"Is she okay?" Abel asked.

"Just a fall from a chair. She'll survive." Hannah glanced at the direction the child had gone in. "If we had a little girl I'd cut her hair. It's safer that way. It makes it harder for the boys to pull it."

"Did they pull your hair when you were little?" he found himself asking.

"Actually, they did. It was long when I was little and there was this one boy, J.R., who used to pull my pigtails all the time. I cut it when I was eleven. I've kept it short since. No hair pulling and no hassles."

Abel generally liked long hair, but Hannah's cut made her look like a pixie—full of laughter and high jinks. He'd like to run his hand through it and see if it felt as soft as it looked. He'd like—

What was he thinking? He didn't bring Hannah to dinner to start fantasizing about her. He'd come to convince her she didn't want a baby and she did want to sell him that land.

Coming here had been a mistake. "We should go. We really need to talk—"

"Oh, no we don't. We really need to dance." She was looking at something behind him.

"It's Partying with *Pete Za* time! I think he wants you to be his first pepperoni slice!"

Abel turned and there was a huge slice of pizza directly behind him. A man's head was visible in the center of the slice. He handed Abel a huge piece of pepperoni and moved on to the next table.

"Oh, gee, you're so lucky," Hannah crooned. "Cain always loves being the pepperoni."

Abel just held the pepperoni-shaped felt hat.

"Come on, Abel. You picked the restaurant, now be a good sport."

"You can't actually think I'm going to wear this, can you?"

He waited for her response. Maybe she did. A woman who would ask a stranger to father her baby probably wouldn't see anything peculiar in a grown man wearing pepperoni on his head.

"They're starting," she shouted.

The pizza slice, like some triangular-shaped Pied Piper, was leading a whole line of writhing children through the restaurant as they danced to the absurd song Hannah had sung.

"I'm not—" Abel was cut off by Hannah shoving the pepperoni slice on his head, as she grabbed his hand and led him to the dance. She hopped right in line and began gyrating along with the rest of the kids and a surprising number of adults.

Abel stood for a moment, captivated by the sight of Hannah's swaying hips. They were as mesmerizing as any swaying cobra...and probably just as dangerous. At least to Abel.

A small hand patted his back and shook him from his reverie. "Hurry up, mister," a small girl prompted.

Hannah must have noticed he wasn't following, because she turned around, grabbed his hand and pulled him along with the line.

Abel comforted himself with the fact he didn't

dance. He merely walked behind Hannah. But since he had pepperoni on his head, it wasn't much comfort. He expended all his energy trying not to let Hannah's uninhibited dancing get to him. When the line started to disperse he eagerly headed back to their table. A few moments later, Hannah followed him.

"Are you ready to go?" he asked.

This evening hadn't gone the way he planned. Instead of scaring her out of having kids, Hannah had him joining in her fantasies about what her daughter would look like, and dancing with pizza.

"I'm ready to leave anytime you are."

Walking out of the building into the balmy, summer evening was a relief. The quiet was soothing after an hour of unremitting noise.

"That was louder than I—" he started to say *thought it would be,* but remembered he'd claimed to have eaten there before, and said "—than I remember."

"It didn't work, you know," she said softly.

"What?"

Hannah laughed. He liked the way it sounded. Soft and inviting. As if she found the world to be a joyous, wondrous place. Abel couldn't quite remember the last time he looked at the world like that. Lately his world had narrowed to real estate and his project with Woody. Try as he might, Abel couldn't remember the last time he'd laughed just for the joy of it.

"You don't play poker, do you?" Hannah asked.

"No." He was having trouble following the twists and turns of this woman's conversations. They paused next to his truck.

"Good. Even in the dark I can see you well enough to tell you that you don't have a poker face. You'd end up losing everything."

She paused a moment and continued, "I know you think that I haven't thought this baby business through. But, like I said before, that doesn't mean I'm stupid. I know you brought me here thinking I'd decided I wanted a child on the spur of the moment and that the chaos here might convince me otherwise. It didn't work. Actually, it didn't stand a chance of working. I know about kids, I know about babies. I know how much work they are, how they can tear at your heart.

"I also know about the kind of joy they can bring to your life, how they can enrich it and teach you things you never knew you knew. Well, I want to learn all about it firsthand. I understand your hesitancy, truly I do. But I am going to have a baby. Since you're not willing to help, I'll just have to settle for less than the man of my dreams."

"I'm the man of your dreams?" he asked softly.

Hannah paused and stared at him. Even in the dim evening light Abel felt exposed, as if she was looking at places he didn't even see himself. "You're possibly the man of my baby dreams. But there are other men."

The thought of Hannah propositioning another man didn't sit any better now than it had earlier. "Listen, I'll admit I brought you here hoping you'd change your mind."

"I didn't," she said quietly.

"I know. And I saw you with that little girl and maybe my mind started to change...at least a little. You'd make a great mom, I think."

"Are you saying you'll do it?"

There was such hope in her voice, that for a moment Abel was tempted to blurt out *yes* just to see her reaction. But he wasn't a man who gave in to temptation, so he simply said, "I'm saying you'd make a great mom, but I don't know if I'd make a great dad."

"That's okay, I don't want you to be my baby's father. I just want you to...well, put the bun in the oven. I'll do the baking and the rest."

"Hannah." He paused. He should simply tell her that she was crazy, and to keep her land, that he'd find a new site. But instead he said, "I want to get to know you. I need time to think this through, to consider all the ramifications."

"Really?"

He shrugged. "Really. I don't know anything about you except that you're a midwife with Stephanson and Associates, that you own some property, and that you want a baby.''

"Let's see. I love the water, though I'm not much of a swimmer. I like to build sand castles, and watch the sun set. I like feeding the seagulls. I like to read. I like to laugh. And I believe in family. I might not have a big biological family, but I believe family is more than biology. It's people who will always take you in, no questions ask. They'll stick by you, whether or not they believe in what you're doing.''

She paused and thought of Rick's disapproval of her baby-making plans. He might not approve, but he'd stick by her. Of that she had no doubt.

"Now you know a little more." She started to walk around his truck to the passenger side.

"You mentioned health on your list. A healthy father. I know there would be tests," he said as they both opened their doors and started to climb into the truck. "How long do they take?"

Hannah didn't say anything. She took her seat and slammed the door. Abel followed suit. "I meant it, how long would it take to get a complete bill of health?"

"You have preliminary results back in about a week, and then there's another part of the AIDS test, so all told, about two weeks."

"What if I were to make the appointment and get that physical. While we waited for my test results we could…"

"Date?" she asked.

"Not in a romantic way," he hurriedly clarified. "But in a get-to-know-each-other sort of way. I mean, I don't want you to think I'm saying yes to giving you a baby by having the tests. I'm just saying that I'm open to being convinced."

"So I have about two weeks to convince you?"

"And while you try to convince me to give you a baby, I'll keep trying to convince you to sell me that property."

Hannah stuck out her hand. "Deal."

Abel took it. She had a surprisingly strong handshake for such a small woman. But it wasn't just her strength that surprised him. It was the feeling that accompanied touching her, even in this very casual way. The feeling was something akin to desire and it snaked its way through his body, reaching every corner in an instant.

But of course it wasn't desire. Hannah Harrington was a kook who only saw him as a sperm-mobile, nothing more. And he saw her as...?

Before tonight he simply saw her as a means-to-an-end, but now? Hannah Harrington was something more than just that.

Abel didn't have a clue just what that was, but it looked like he was going to have two weeks to find out. Two weeks to convince her that she didn't want a baby.

Playtime Pizza was a good idea, but he needed

something more drastic to convince her. Something worse than a restaurant full of screaming kids. Something so scary that having children would be the last thing on her mind.

Suddenly Abel knew just what he had to do.

"WHAT DO YOU MEAN?" Woody Pembrooke bellowed.

Woody was Abel's childhood friend. Abel had gone into real estate and Woody had gone into construction. When they'd hit on the idea for a subdivision within the city limits, they'd jumped at the chance to work as partners. So far it had been a partnership made in heaven.

Oh, they had their differences.

Woody's office was a mess. It drove Abel, and his need for orderliness, absolutely crazy whenever he visited. But today his mind wasn't on the chaos of Woody's office. No, his mind was on a short blonde with bedroom eyes and a hankering for a baby. Abel tossed the stack of papers from the chair onto the floor and sat.

"I didn't tell her I'd give her a baby," he said patiently. "I only agreed to get tested for disease in order to stall her. I have two weeks to convince her to sell us that property."

Abel ripped the bandage off the inside of his elbow. He hated needles, but the tests required a blood sample.

Woody's eyes narrowed. "How do you plan to convince her?"

"That's where you come in."

"Oh, no. I'm not coming anywhere near that lady. I've already got four kids. Even if she doesn't want a father figure, but just a baby-maker, I refuse to bring another baby into the world. Four is my absolute limit."

The thought of Woody and Hannah made Abel's stomach clench. He didn't want to question his reaction, instead he ignored it and tried to reassure his partner. "I didn't want—"

"I can't believe you'd think I'd agree to something this bizarre, no matter how much we want that property. I mean, I know I don't shoot blanks. An accurate shot every time." There was more than a hint of pride in Woody's tone.

"But I'm off the market." He thumped his desk for emphasis and sent a couple pens skittering off the edge.

"Woody, that's not—"

Woody again interrupted. "I've got fourteen years of raising kids ahead of me, and what sane woman would sign on for something like that? No, I'm a confirmed bachelor, and I'm not donating my stud services just to get that property, no matter how much it would mean to you, me and the project."

The idea of Woody and Hannah had honestly never crossed Abel's mind, and now that it had he needed to uncross it fast because he could feel his blood pressure spiking. "Calm down."

"Calm down? When you're pimping for me? I don't think so."

"I'm not pimping for you!" Abel wasn't even pimping for himself. He was stalling.

"What would you call trying to sell me to the highest bidder?" the big man insisted.

"Woody, would you keep quiet. What I'm trying to say is I want to baby-sit your demon-spawn for the weekend."

"You what?" Woody froze midtirade, suddenly all ears.

Abel knew he was going to regret this offer, and before he could change his mind he blurted out, "I need to convince Hannah that she really doesn't want to have kids. She delivers babies and knows all about them. And she's got a friend who's got a kid, so she knows about Playtime Pizza. She even knows the song by heart—"

"Playtime Pizza?"

"—but she's a single lady. What does she know about what happens with kids day in and day out?"

"Nothing?" Woody guessed.

"Right. And your bunch is enough to make anyone consider permanent sterilization."

"Hey, I resent that. They're not bad kids, just," Woody paused, obviously weighing his words, "just high-spirited."

"Too *high-spirited* for most of the human race to deal with. Most of the time I avoid them like the plague. So does anyone with half a brain. How many sitters have you had in the last six months?"

"Five," Woody said with disgust. "But who's counting?"

"Me. That's who. And five is wonderful. They've scared that many sitters away in the last six months. They'll scare Hannah off in less than a day."

"So, let me get this straight. You're offering to baby-sit for a whole weekend in order to scare this Hannah off her idea of having a baby?"

"Yeah." Abel allowed himself a self-satisfied smile. "Once she's done with this baby nonsense, she'll sell me the land." He might not know Hannah well, but this much he knew was true.

It was a brilliant plan. He couldn't believe it had taken him so long to think of it. Playtime Pizza was a step in the right direction, but baby-sitting Woody's kids for a whole weekend? That was jumping into the parenthood pool with both feet. And if things worked out the way he planned, Hannah would be begging for a life jacket before the weekend was over.

"And what if she leaves in one day?" Woody asked. "You'll still keep them from Friday night until Sunday night. Right?"

"I thought maybe you'd stay someplace close by and when, *not if,* she leaves, I'll call."

"Oh, no." Woody shook his head vigorously. "I love my kids, but I haven't had a weekend off in over a year. I'm not giving this up if she leaves. You want my kids? You've got to keep them until Sunday, no matter what."

"Fine." This wasn't quite what Abel had planned, but he'd take it. After all, a weekend with the demon-spawn was worth it if he and Woody got the land.

"It's a deal then," Woody said quickly, as if he was afraid Abel would try to back out. "This Friday, six o'clock. I'll see you then, bud."

Abel reached across the cluttered desk and shook his hand, realizing he'd just made a pact with the devil. But it was worth it. Woody's kids weren't really children in any traditional sense. They were monsters. Pure and simple.

They were horrible.

They were perfect.

3

"It's JUST Braxton Hicks contractions, Tammy." Hannah took Tammy's hand and helped her sit up.

The young, mother-to-be sighed. "I was worried it was too soon, and yet I was hoping it was over. I know being on my own isn't the ideal way to have a baby, but I can't wait to hold him or her. And I'm so ready not to be pregnant."

Hannah chuckled. "That's a normal reaction at this point."

As much as Hannah was looking forward to being pregnant and having a baby, would she get tired by the end of her third trimester? She'd be on her own, just like Tammy.

Feeling a spurt of empathy for the mother, she said, "Are you doing okay? I mean, last time we talked you were worried about your job."

Tammy shrugged. "My boss finally agreed that I could try working out of the house. I mean, I'll have to go into the office one or two days a week, but most of my work can be done from home, which means I won't have to leave Squiggy here at day care too often."

"That's great."

Hannah had worried about what to do with her baby with her hectic hours, but she'd decided to cross that bridge when she got to it.

"If you need anything else, if you think you're in labor, or just need to talk, call me."

"I'm so embarrassed I dragged you here," Tammy said. She clutched the back of the hospital gown as she got up off the table.

"Don't be," Hannah said. "Braxton Hicks contractions are common at this point in your pregnancy. And I was here anyway. I have a mother in labor."

"Well, thanks."

Hannah waited while Tammy dressed, then walked her to the elevator, feeling a strong connection with her patient. Tammy had been left on her own, and she claimed she was better off that way.

Hannah was musing over their similarities as she checked charts at the nurses' station when one of the nurses, Kristin, called, "Hannah, phone. Line three."

She moved to the small office just off the nurses' station and picked up the phone. "Hello. This is Hannah Harrington."

"Hannah, it's Abel."

She felt giddy with excitement. This week had been a comedy of errors. They'd planned to have dinner Monday night, but she'd had an emergency about ten minutes after sitting down to the meal. Tuesday was out because he had an appointment to show a couple some houses after work. Last night she'd been on call and two of Rick's patients had needed her. So here it was Thursday.

"Abel, what can I do for you?"

"I have an idea that I'd like to run by you. I'm afraid dinner's not going to work out tonight for me. Any chance you can break free for lunch?"

Another night that wouldn't work? If they couldn't connect to date, how would they ever connect to…*connect?*

Hannah tried to sound blasé as she answered, "I'm not in the office today. I just saw a patient and have another patient in labor."

"The hospital has a cafeteria, right?" he pressed.

"Right." Could he be as anxious to see her as she was to see him? Hannah's spirits lifted at the thought.

"How about I meet you there in a half hour?" he asked. "We really need to talk."

A sense of hopeful possibilities filled her. Maybe he'd decided to give her a baby. She tried to contain her excitement as she answered, "Fine. Unless this mother progresses faster than I expect, I should be able to make it."

"Great. See you then."

She wondered how she was going to wait thirty whole minutes. She wondered what she was going to do if he said no. And conversely, she wondered what she'd do if he said yes. Myriad emotions tumbled over one another. Fear, excitement, fear, anticipation. Over and over they mixed together, leaving Hannah wondering which way was up.

Needing to do something for the next thirty minutes, and knowing she'd never be able to concentrate on paperwork, she dialed Irene's number. They'd played phone tag all week long maybe this time she'd actually touch base.

"Hiya," came Irene's voice over the phone.

"Irene! Finally. I didn't think I'd ever get you at home." Hannah sagged against the back of the chair.

"I've been busy, sweetie. I've got a new man in my life. And between Sal and my classes—"

"What classes are you taking now?" Hannah interrupted.

"Belly dancing. Sal helps me study every night, which is probably why I'm on top in my class. Hell, I'm on top with Sal, too. A bad back, don't you know."

"Irene!"

She chuckled. "Oh, don't be such a prude. Now, we've bounced half a dozen messages back and forth this week, so I figure something's up. And since you mentioned Abel Kennedy in that first message, I have a sneaky suspicion I can guess just *what's up.* Is it?"

"What?" Hannah asked, choking on absolutely nothing.

"What's up between you two?" Irene clarified. "I mean, I never met him in person, but he sounds as if he's gorgeous."

"I wouldn't know about that," Hannah said in her primmest manner.

"No? He didn't sound like a troll."

"He's not. I mean, that doesn't matter. He wants to buy the property."

"That's what he said. So are you going to sell?"

"That's why I wanted to talk to you." Hannah twirled and untwirled the cord on her finger. "I need to know you won't mind if I sold it and put the health center somewhere else."

"Of course I don't. That Abel said he had another area in mind. But that's not why I sent him to you. He sounded your age, and he's male. You need to get a life, Hannah."

"I have a life."

"Work," Irene said with a snort. "You need more than that."

"Don't start."

"How are you going to have a baby if you don't find a father?"

Hannah hadn't mentioned her plan to Irene, and couldn't seem to bring herself to say anything now. As free-spirited as Irene was, Hannah doubted she'd approve any more than Rick did. "I, ah, I've got to go, Irene. I've got an appointment. I just wanted to make sure it was okay with you if I decided to sell."

"I just want you to be happy, Hannah," her foster mother said.

"Have fun with your classes, and with Sal."

"Oh, I will," Irene said with conviction. "Don't forget, we leave on Friday for that cruise. I'll be back in a few weeks. You can fill me in on what you've done with Abel then."

"Done with Abel?" Hannah asked, sure she wouldn't fill Irene in on all she hoped to *do* with him.

"About the land."

"Oh, about the land. I'll let you know when you get back."

What was she going to do about Abel? Better yet, what was he going to do about her proposition?

Hannah wasn't sure what she'd hoped Irene would say, but she still felt at loose ends as she went down to the cafeteria to wait. She was eating—or at least pretending to eat as she moved pieces of lettuce around in her salad—when Abel came in and sat across from her.

"Do you want to get something?" she asked.

"No. Actually, I just came here to talk to you."

The fact that he planned to avoid the cafeteria food only made her more convinced of his intelligence. He'd make a perfect father for her baby.

But she forced herself to tamp down her excitement. First she'd wait to hear what he had to say. "And what you needed to talk about couldn't have waited?"

"I've got a meeting tonight and tomorrow is going to be nuts. I wanted to talk to you about this now before I chicken out."

Chicken out?

He was going to do it?!

Hannah's heart leapt. He was going to say yes and donate sperm. Or maybe he'd suggest doing it the old-fashioned way.

A mental image of Abel in her bed kissing her—and then more than kissing her—left her breathless. Making a baby in a traditional way with Abel wouldn't be a hardship.

Afraid to say anything, she simply waited for him to say the words.

"I want you..." he started, then paused, as if the words were difficult to get out.

He wanted her?

"I want you to baby-sit with me this weekend," he said in a rush.

Baby-sit—that wasn't some new slang for wild sex was it? "Baby-sit?" she asked.

"Yeah. A friend needs some help and I thought it would be perfect for us. You told me you want a baby."

He grabbed a slice of green pepper off her plate and munched on it. "And I'll grant that you obviously know a lot about babies. You even deal well with kids at a restaurant. But I need to know you can handle a kid day in and day out. I might not particularly want children, but I wouldn't want one of mine raised by someone who can't handle the stress. And having kids is stressful.''

''I know all about stress,'' Hannah muttered, resisting the urge to stab his hand with her fork as he snagged another pepper.

''Maybe. But I need to be sure,'' he insisted while crunching.

''What do you suggest?'' she asked. ''There's no written test for parents. Parenting is a learned skill. You grow into it.''

''You can start growing this weekend.'' He looked pleased with himself. ''Like I said, I want you to baby-sit with me.''

Hannah sensed a trap. Abel was just too pleased with himself. ''Who are we baby-sitting?''

''My partner, Woody's kids. His wife left him last year, and other than work, the guy has no social life. I thought we'd give him a weekend off, and I'd get to see how you handle kids.''

''Kids?'' Plural. Hannah knew this wasn't good. Abel was far too excited about baby-sitting. ''How many children are we talking about?''

''Four.'' He took a cucumber this time.

''Four? That's not a fair test. I don't want four kids, I just want one.''

"Yes, but you'll be handling all the parenting stuff yourself. That's got to be as stressful as two of us handling four kids," he insisted.

Hannah's eyes narrowed as she studied the annoyingly pleased man. "How old?"

"I figured you'd ask, so I checked. Robbie's twelve, Shane's ten, Lynda's eight and Brandon's the baby. He's four."

"And what if I pass the test? I mean, what if I can handle four kids for a weekend? Are you saying that you'll believe I'm serious, and that I'm capable of single-parenting a child? Are you saying you'll father my baby?"

"You still don't know me," he said.

"You can teach me whatever else I need to know this weekend. Plus I know enough." She added salad thief to the list of things she knew about Abel Kennedy. But since she doubted that was a genetic trait, he was still her best option.

"Yeah," he sighed. "I'm a living, breathing male."

"You forgot funny and intelligent. And even though the doctor's reports are still out on the healthy, I don't think that's going to be a problem."

"If, and it's a big *if,* we live through this weekend, and *if* you still want kids after two days with Woody's demons, er, kids, then I'll give up trying to scare you off and really consider your proposal."

"I'll do it. I did promise to let you try to convince me while I tried to convince you, so I'm in."

"Well, okay," he said. He stuck out his hand, as if he wanted to shake on it.

Hannah wondered what he'd do if she suggested they kiss on it.

Abel had kissable lips, she'd decided. No living, breathing female could miss that fact. Very, very kissable lips. But she wasn't going to experiment with how kissable in the hospital cafeteria.

But maybe this weekend? It would be good practice for their baby-making.

Hannah ignored his hand, and ignored her fantasies about kissing. This was business. "I have another patient on the verge of delivering. They seem to come in clumps. So I can't promise the whole weekend."

"You don't know that she'll go into labor this weekend, do you?" he asked.

"No. It could be twenty minutes from now or it could be any time in the next two weeks. Babies don't come by appointment."

"Then if she goes into labor and you miss time, we'll deal with it. We're scheduled from Friday at six o'clock until Sunday at six o'clock."

"Deal." Hannah said.

"Deal," he echoed, then pushed back his chair and walked out of the cafeteria.

Hannah watched him leave, admiring the view.

Abel thought he could scare her out of wanting a baby. He still didn't know her at all.

But he would.

She closed her eyes and thought about his lips. Lust. That's what she felt. She was lusting after her baby's potential father.

Lusting wasn't what she'd planned. She wasn't doing this because he was sexy, she was doing this because she wanted a baby and Abel Kennedy was just her means to an end. There was no room for lust.

No matter how lustable Abel Kennedy was.

ABEL GLANCED AT his watch. Were they ever going to finish up? The Andersons had asked to walk through the house one more time. Normally it wouldn't matter, but Abel was supposed to be meeting Hannah at Woody's in an hour.

"Well, folks?" he asked, hoping to hurry them along.

"We'll take it," Mr. Anderson said.

"That's great. You can come to my office tomorrow and sign the papers."

"Actually, we wanted to do it tonight. Julie could go into labor at any time, and we want this house."

"Let's have a seat at the kitchen table then," Abel said, bowing to the inevitable. The sooner he filled out the paperwork, the sooner he'd get to Woody's.

He watched as Michael Anderson helped his wife

lower her expanded girth into a chair before taking his own. Unconsciously, the man's hand rested on her stomach in a possessive, protective way.

As Abel filled out papers and passed them to the couple for their signatures, he realized that if he did give Hannah her baby, he'd never get to do anything as simple as helping her in or out of a chair. He'd miss everything. He'd miss seeing her stomach expand with his baby. He'd miss its first kick.

"And this one," he said, handing another paper to the couple.

"Oh," Julie said.

"Oh, what?" Abel asked. "Is there a problem? That was your bid, right?"

"Just oh," she said, her hands clutching her stomach. "I think that was a contraction."

"What do you mean, a contraction?" her husband asked.

"What do you mean, a contraction?" Abel echoed.

"I mean, I think it's a good thing we're filling out the papers today because it looks like it won't be long until we're kind of busy." She smiled then.

Abel had never understood why people felt pregnant women *glowed,* but now he knew. Julie was glowing.

"We should go to the hospital. Call the doctor. Call an ambulance," Mike said.

"Mike, it was just one contraction. We probably

have hours and hours to go. Let's just finish this and then we'll go."

"I can fill these out and bring them to you," Abel said, no longer worried about being late, but worried about babies born on kitchen floors. What would the current owners think?

They'd probably want him to foot the cleaning bill. But even the thought of the cleaning bill wasn't as nerve-inducing as the thought of Julie Anderson delivering her baby now.

"Let's finish," Julie said.

"But—" her husband said.

"But—" Abel echoed.

"Let's finish."

In his lifetime as a real estate agent, Abel had never processed a bid so quickly. "There," he said triumphantly as the last paper was signed.

"Oh," Julie said again.

"Let's go," Mike said.

"I'll let you know if they take your offer, you let me know if it's a boy or a girl," Abel said.

He watched Michael hurry his wife out of the house and probably right to the hospital.

Who would drive Hannah to the hospital when she gave birth? Who would turn pale and look like he was going to pass out when she went into labor?

No one.

Abel found the thought distressing. Then he glanced at his watch and became even more distressed. He was going to be late. Now more than ever it was important he convince Hannah how insane her plan was.

HANNAH GLANCED AT her watch. Five fifty-eight. She was two minutes early. How on earth had she come to be in such an absurd situation? She was looking for a satisfying answer as she raised her hand to ring the doorbell when it hit her...literally.

Splat!

She looked up in time to see a neon yellow plastic bucket retreat inside a second story window. She wiped the water from her eyes, ran her fingers through her dripping hair and rang the bell.

The door flew open and a man said, "You must be Hannah."

"Yes." She might have been awed by the size of the man who opened the door, if she wasn't so preoccupied by her recent soaking.

"Is it raining?" he asked, peering at the crystal blue sky.

"Only on me it seems. And only when I'm on your sidewalk with a bucket hanging out your upstairs window."

"I'll kill them." There was enough ferociousness in his tone that Hannah was concerned for *them*, despite the fact she was soaked.

"I don't think that's a good idea. Last I heard people went to jail for that sort of thing."

The big man sighed. "Well, come on in." His voice was deep and pleasant. "You're not going to win Abel's services standing out here dripping."

It took a second for Hannah to register what Woody had just said. "Abel…he told you?"

She'd never been so humiliated. Okay, maybe she'd felt this embarrassed when she'd blurted out her proposition, but she certainly didn't expect Abel to make an announcement to the whole world.

Abel Kennedy thought baby-sitting four kids was going to kill her? Well, he'd better watch out because *she* was going to kill *him,* the tongue-waggling, vegetable-stealing, living, breathing male with a sense of humor, blabbermouth.

"He told you?" she repeated.

Woody led her into the entry and shut the outside door. He looked chagrined as he said, "I didn't mean to say that. I was thinking about killing my kids and it just slid out. And Abel didn't have a choice but to tell me. The minute he asked to baby-sit I knew something was up. I mean, Abel volunteering to watch my kids? He generally avoids them like the plague."

"According to Abel the plague might be preferable, and at the moment I might agree." Hannah clapped a hand over her mouth, realizing what she'd just said. "I'm sorry. I didn't mean—"

"Don't worry. They are a…" he paused, as if searching for a good word. "Rambunctious group."

"Let's start over. Hi! I'm Hannah Harrington, Abel's baby-sitting partner for the weekend." She thrust her hand forward.

The big man extended his hand and engulfed hers in it as he shook. "And I'm Woody Can't-Keep-My-Mouth-Shut Pembrooke, Abel's partner and friend. Now, come on in and I'll find you a towel."

Woody was well over six feet tall, with hair that could use a trim and a face that hadn't seen a razor in quite awhile. He had a certain bearish quality about him. And yet, despite his rather disheveled appearance, there was an aura of warmth as well.

Hannah followed him into the rambling house. From the outside she'd admired the sleek wood siding and stonework that emphasized the unexpected angles of the house. Expecting more sleek, modern styles on the inside, Hannah found chaos instead.

"I meant to get things cleaned up," Woody apologized as he looked around the room, then back at Hannah. There was a basket sitting in a corner. He dug through the clothing in it and handed her a towel.

She prayed they were clean and just not folded clothes, as she took it. It felt dry and didn't smell offensive, so she decided to be optimistic and started toweling herself off. From beneath the cover of the towel, she surveyed the mess. Clothes covered almost every inch of the living room. Dishes littered the coffee table. Hannah didn't even want to imagine what the kitchen looked like.

"Hey, kids!" Woody boomed.

She heard them before she saw them. Four boys ran down the stairs and burst into the room. They stared at her expectantly.

Hannah didn't say a word. She didn't have to. Woody no longer seemed like a warm fuzzy bear. He seemed quite grizzlyish as he growled, "You're in trouble."

"It wasn't me," the second to the smallest one hollered. "It was Robbie."

"This one's Robbie. And I believe he has something to say to you," Woody said.

The dark-haired boy looked a lot older than twelve, probably because he was so tall. It was obvious that he'd had inherited his father's height and strong features. He stood, silently staring at Hannah.

"Robbie," Woody prompted. "You water-bombed our guest and want to apologize, right?"

"I'm sorry," the boy said. "I didn't see you down there when I tried to water my flowers."

Water his flowers? Hannah decided not to point out there were no flowers in front of the house. "No problem."

Woody didn't look entirely satisfied, but Hannah said, "Really, no harm done. It was only a little water. Why don't you introduce me to everyone else?"

Woody nodded at the slightly younger clone of Robbie standing next to him. "This is Shane. He's ten."

The third boy didn't have the heavy-boned features of the other two and instead of the dark brown, bordering black hair of his siblings, he had light blond hair poking out from beneath a baseball cap perched precariously on his head. He snapped a huge bubble.

"And this is Lynda," Woody said. "She's eight."

"Seven, Daddy," Lynda said with a heavy adult-sounding sigh. "I'm seven."

"Sorry." Beneath the scraggly beard the giant man looked contrite.

A girl? Thank goodness her features were finer than the boys. Hannah wondered what Lynda would look like if she scraped a layer of grime off the girl's face and put her in a dress. Studying the rough-and-tumble child, she didn't think she was going to get a chance to find out.

"And this is Brandon. He's four." The dark-haired little boy also had the finer bone structure of his sister. Hannah wondered if it had to do with his age, or if he and his sister took after their absentee mother.

"I'm pleased to meet you all," she said, wanting to add something more, but unsure where to start.

"Yeah, that's what they all say at first," Robbie said. "They're saying a lot of other things—"

"Things Daddy won't let me say," Lynda interrupted.

"—when they leave," Robbie finished.

"Well, I'll try to watch my language," Hannah promised. "And then you're welcome to repeat whatever I say when I leave."

"Are you going to marry Daddy?" Brandon asked, inching closer to his father as if to protect him from a marriage threat.

Hannah knelt by the littlest, juice-mustached, Pembrooke. "No. I just met your daddy. I'm a friend of Abel's and we're going to baby-sit this weekend."

Woody leaned down and picked up the little boy with ease. "Why don't you go pick up your rooms." The three oldest ones scampered back up the stairs. "I'm sorry about that," he said to Hannah.

"Don't be. Kids will be kids."

Woody, still carrying Brandon, took a nearly vacant seat on the couch, mindless of the clothes he sat on.

"I owe you an apology for the mess. I told Abel I'd lost five sitters in the last month. I lied. As of yesterday I've lost six."

"I'm sorry." Hannah pushed a pile of coloring books over and sat on the edge of a chair.

"I'm getting used to it," the big man said with a sigh. "The kids really aren't bad. They're just high-spirited. I—'' Whatever else Woody was going to say was lost when Abel burst in the front door.

"Sorry. I'm running late." He tossed a duffle bag next to hers, and gently set a second bag on a pile of clothes on the couch. "I'd showed clients a house and they decided to make an offer right there on the spot, so I had to write up the paper work, she went into labor, and…'' He paused and finally looked at Hannah. "What happened to you?"

"A freak shower," was all she said. She wasn't going to give him ammunition to use against her. "And don't worry about being late. Woody and I were just getting to know each other."

"And now that you're here, I'm out of here," the big man said. "See you both Sunday night."

Woody grabbed his bag—though how he found it in the midst of a pile of clothes would forever remain a mystery to Hannah—and walked past Abel into the hall.

"Hey, kids?" he called.

The noise was even louder than the first time, as they thundered down the stairs.

"I'm going. I just wanted to say goodbye."

Watching the big man lean down and pass out a generous supply of kisses and hugs, impressed Hannah. He was a caring father.

"Mind Hannah and Abel and watch yourselves," he said. "I'll see you all on Sunday. Now go finish those rooms."

The kids clattered their way back up the stairs and Woody stopped next to Abel and whispered loud enough for Hannah to hear, "Better watch yourself as well, buddy. I don't think you have a clue what you're in for."

"Just one good friend doing a favor for another. That's all I'm in for."

Woody glanced over his shoulder at Hannah, winked, then walked out the door.

"So, you met the demons?" Abel asked.

She could see that he was searching for some hint of fear and tried to resist laughing.

"I met the children." Hannah said with all the primness she could muster. "They seem wonderful."

"Oh, yeah. Wonderful." He started to sit down on the couch Woody had vacated.

"Oh, no you don't," Hannah scolded, grabbing his hand and pulling him back to his feet. The feel of him was electric, sending a jolt skittering throughout her body.

A jolt of *what* was the question she'd been mulling over since their handshake yesterday. Hannah searched for an appropriate word. The other day she'd thought it was lust.

Lust? It wasn't the first time she'd thought of the word in reference to Abel. She weighed it silently.

Lust was close, but not quite on the mark. She'd already decided that Abel Kennedy was a fine-looking man and it would be very easy to fall in...lust with him. But her reaction to him wasn't quite lust. It was—

"Hannah?"

She jerked back to awareness. "What?"

"Are you going to stand here holding my hand all night, or are you going to tell me what you have planned?"

She dropped his hand as if it burned. "Sorry. I was...I got lost trying to plan where to start."

"Where to start what?" Abel asked. His voice sounded deeper and huskier than it normally did.

Could that be desire in his tone?

No, Hannah was sure it was just wistful thinking on her part.

"Cleaning this place," she said. She tried to forget the odd way Abel affected her and concentrated on making this house at least livable.

She surveyed the living room. "I know we're only here for the weekend, but I can't handle staying in this kind of mess. Plus, Woody could definitely use the help. So we're going to start our weekend by having a pick-up party."

"I'm not cleaning Woody's house. Let him do it himself."

"The poor man's juggling four kids and a business on his own. And another housekeeper just quit. So, the two of us are going to pitch in and give him a hand."

"Hannah." There was more than just a hint of stubbornness in Abel's tone.

"Hey, this is your idea," she felt obliged to point out. "You can't wiggle out of it."

"Baby-sitting was my idea, not cleaning."

"Well, I can't stand a pigsty, so cleaning in this case, goes hand in hand with baby-sitting." She glanced again at the living room. "I'll change into some dry clothes and then start the laundry. And you take the kitchen."

"Hey, I've been in Woody's kitchen before," Abel protested. "I don't want to clean the kitchen."

"The kitchen or the bathroom. You pick."

While he mulled it over a noise from the couch caught her attention. "What was that?"

"What was what?"

There was something odd here. Abel looked…too innocent. "That squeaking noise," Hannah said slowly, watching him.

"Oh." He went to the duffle bag and unzipped it. "That was my dog. I couldn't leave her home alone all weekend."

As if on cue, a small head peeked out of the bag. A head that would have looked more at home on a rat than on a dog. A head with a small pink bow sitting jauntily on top of the small tuft of hair that pretty much made up all the hair the dog possessed.

"That's your…dog?" She hesitated assigning the animal that designation. It looked more like a rat, but there was a certain doggishness about it, if it was examined closely enough.

Abel held his arms open and the rat-dog jumped into them. Hannah could see the rest of the dog resembled as much of a rat as its head. A rat with a pink bow on its head and painted pink toenails.

"Do you have a problem with her?" Abel asked, as he stroked the rat-dog.

Other than the fact that an exterminator would be tempted to exterminate the pet, Hannah had no problem. "What's its name?"

"*Her* name is Marigold."

Laughter was bubbling in her, but Hannah valiantly held it inside. From his stance, it was clear Abel was ready for a fight. "You have a dog that wears nail polish and bows, and her name is Marigold?"

"Yeah." And though he didn't say it, Hannah could sense a *do you want to make something of it* tone in that one single syllable.

"Well, she's just lovely," Hannah said, proud that she hadn't even stuttered over the blatant lie.

And though the dog wasn't quite lovely—actually not even cute—Abel was. In fact, he looked very cute cuddling the ugly dog as if she was a princess and not some dog-rat hybrid.

Cute or not, Hannah wasn't going to forget Abel set out to sabotage her plans by making her baby-sit with him this weekend. She wasn't about to forget, or forgive.

"Now, back to the cleaning," she said, resisting a smile as he groaned. "Kitchen or bathroom?"

"The kitchen," Abel muttered, still cradling Marigold as he walked to the kitchen, with all the enthusiasm of a man heading to his execution.

4

THIS WEEKEND HAD just started and already wasn't
going the way he expected it to. Abel had hoped that
Hannah would take one look at Woody's crew and
decide that she had better things to do than baby-
sitting and getting pregnant.

Better things like selling him those lots.

He surveyed the kitchen. It wasn't as bad as he'd
feared. The fact that the last housekeeper had just
quit was obviously the reason. A couple more days
and he wouldn't have dared set Marigold down.

"You sit right there, and don't move," he said to
the dog. Marigold sat with a tiny plop in the middle
of the floor.

"What are we doing here?" he asked her. The
great thing about Marigold was she just listened, and
tilted her head in that very sympathetic way of hers.

He stared at the pile of dishes in the sink. "Yeah,
I know why we're here, but I still don't believe this
is happening to me."

Abel rolled up his sleeves and went to work. The
sooner he started, the sooner he'd be done with
Woody's toxic waste dump of a kitchen.

"Don't you eat any crumbs off the floor. It could be dangerous, fatal even."

Who knew what Woody's gang ate. If she ate one wrong crumb, Marigold would be in mortal jeopardy.

Jeopardy. That's how Abel felt, as if not just years of work on the subdivision plans were hanging in the balance, but as if his very way of life was as well.

If he went through with this absurd idea, and gave Hannah her baby, his life would change. He would be a father, even if he didn't have an active part in his child's life.

And could he actually go through with it? Could he give Hannah a baby and then walk away? He didn't think he had it in him. As much as he couldn't envision being a father, he also couldn't envision walking away from a child he helped to create.

And yet, when he thought about the yearning he saw in Hannah's face, a part of him knew he couldn't just walk away and leave her childless.

"What am I going to do?" he asked Marigold who was too busy sniffing a glop of something on the floor to answer him.

"Yeah, that's what I thought." He was in Woody's kitchen doing dishes and seriously considering becoming a father. And if he examined his motives, he had a growing fear that the desire to please Hannah had absolutely nothing to do with the project.

"Hannah said I should help you," a voice that Abel knew couldn't be Marigold's, said.

Suddenly all worries about babies faded and he concentrated on the child in front of him. Woody's kids were dangerous.

"Robbie?" he guessed.

The dark head shook so violently, Abel wondered how it stayed on the boy's neck.

"No, I'm Shane," the boy said.

"If you're here to help, why don't you clear the table?"

"Even the cookie jar?" Shane asked.

"No, I think that's supposed to stay on the table." It sat with a matching group of accessories, like the salt, pepper shakers and the sugar bowl.

"I mean, do you want to clean it out as well?"

"What's in it?" Abel asked. "Leftover cookie crumbs?"

"You think Dad makes cookies?" Shane laughed.

Okay, Abel couldn't see Woody making cookies. "Maybe your sitters did."

"Nah. Most of them were too busy with us to worry about cookies."

"Maybe you should have been nicer to them. And if you weren't nice to them, why are you being so helpful to me?" Abel became suspicious. "What's going on?"

"Nothing." Shane shrugged, and avoided looking Abel in the eye.

He scanned the kitchen and didn't see anything out of place except all the stuff that had been out of place when he walked into it. "What are you up to?"

"I don't know what you—"

It hit him what was wrong. "Where's my dog?"

"What dog?" Shane looked innocently around the kitchen, but he didn't fool Abel.

"The dog that was sitting here a minute ago when you walked into the room." They'd kidnapped Marigold. He'd heard so many horror stories about Woody's kids that he hated to even think about what they might have done to his dog.

"I didn't see no dog. Are you sure you have one?" Shane asked.

"Listen, kid, if you did anything to my dog, I'll…" He left the threat hanging.

"Here," Shane said, handing him a note as he turned and ran from the room.

Abel read the paper and bellowed, "Hannah!"

A moment later she came scurrying into the kitchen in a different, much drier, outfit.

"What's wrong?" She looked around the kitchen. "Wow, what a mess."

"They kidnapped her."

"Who's *they* and who's *her?*"

"The demon-spawn have kidnapped my dog." He

thrust the paper at her. "They have ransom demands."

Hannah had the nerve to actually smile as she read the note. "I don't think these should be hard to meet. We had to do something with them tomorrow anyway."

"I absolutely refuse to reward those...those..."

"Abel, watch your language," Hannah warned.

"I won't reward those demon-spawn by paying ransom on my dog."

"They're simply kids out to have a good time. I'm sure Marigold's fine." Hannah felt a sense of triumph that she didn't even smile when she said the dog's name. "And I love the beach."

"But—"

"Kids!" she called.

Four innocent faces appeared in the doorway. "Yes?"

"Bring Abel back his dog."

"What about the beach?" Robbie asked.

"I think that's an easy enough request to fulfill. You didn't need to hold Marigold for ransom in order to go."

"Your dog's named Marigold?" Robbie, who didn't have Hannah's superior willpower, laughed.

"I like him," Brandon said.

"Her," Abel mumbled. "Go get her."

They scampered out of the room.

"You're letting them bribe you," he said, accusation in his tone.

"Sure I am. They've been tossed about for months, from one sitter to the next. They just want to feel as if they have some control. The beach is a small enough thing."

"They kidnapped my dog."

"Like I said, it's a small enough thing." This time she didn't hold back her laughter.

Lynda came to the door with Marigold in her arms. "She likes me."

"She does, eh?" Hannah asked.

"We wouldn't have hurt her," Lynda said.

Abel didn't say anything, so Hannah said, "We know that. It was a cute joke."

"Shane talked to Abel and I snuck in and took her. She came right to me 'cause she likes me." The little girl stared at the two adults as if she was challenging them to disagree with her.

"Maybe you could watch her for me while I finish cleaning the kitchen?" Abel said, surprising Hannah with the suggestion.

Lynda's face lit up. "You mean it? I'll watch her real good, I promise. I won't let the boys touch her, except maybe Brandon. He'll be real careful."

"She looks like she's comfortable with you. And I've got the kitchen to clean, so yeah, I mean it."

"Great." She could see the little girl was aglow, even under the layer of grime that covered her face.

"If we're going to the beach tomorrow, you've got to finish cleaning your room," Hannah reminded her gently. "Tell your brothers too, okay?"

"Sure. I'll tell them. Oh, and don't forget the cookie jar." She turned, dog in hand, and left the room in a hurry, as if she was afraid Abel would change his mind.

"That was nice of you," Hannah said softly.

"Not really." Abel looked embarrassed by the compliment. "I figure if Lynda has her, those boys won't try and kidnap her again."

"Still, it was nice," Hannah insisted.

"You know, that's the second time someone's warned me about the cookie jar." Abel walked over to the table and opened the brown jar. "Ugh."

Hannah peeked in and grimaced at the well-past-their-prime, fuzzy remains of dinners past. "That's just gross."

"The only thing making cleaning this kitchen palatable is I know you have the bathroom."

"Yeah, but I bet there's not a week's worth of vegetables hidden anywhere in there." Thank goodness. It was a smelly, disgusting looking mess.

"No, but there's three little boys using the toilet. You'll love seeing what kind of aim they have."

"Oh."

"Kids are messy, Hannah. Changing your mind yet?"

"Not on your life."

TWO HOURS LATER, the house was clean. Hannah had whipped four kids and Abel into a cleaning regiment. The two older boys disappeared as soon as she announced the work was over and the two younger ones were cuddled next to her on the couch, Lynda still cradling Marigold.

Hannah had opened a book she'd brought and started reading.

Abel watched this woman who had stumbled into his life.

What was he doing? The entire situation was ludicrous. There was no way he was fathering her baby. And yet, as he watched her with Woody's kids, he couldn't help but feel that she'd make a good mother.

Though he was pretending to read the paper, he couldn't help but watch the small blonde as she read to Lynda and Brandon.

"*...she even made up a little song to the tune of 'This Old Man,' which was Belinda Mae's favorite song. 'B-E-L-I-N-D-A M-A-E that is me. With a Belinda Mae then Sophia can not win, Belinda Mae begin again. A-B-E-R-N-A-T-H-Y now you can say, Belinda Mae Abernathy you really have begun, with this song you've learned to sung.'*

"*Belinda knew that learned to sung wasn't quite right, but it rhymed, so she left it and sang the whole song all day long.*"

Hannah sat between the children. Lynda on one

side curled in the crook of her arm, and Brandon on the other side. The little boy was snuggled as close as he could get to her. Lynda was a bit more aloof, but Hannah didn't seem to notice as she read.

"The entire class watched, their faces solemn, as Belinda Mae Abernathy and Sophia Tonya Bumpersnipe carried their great big pieces of paper to their table. Belinda started humming 'This Old Man' and began to write her name."

"Can she do it? Can she write her whole big name?" Brandon asked. "I can write Brandon, but Pembrooke is long."

"So's Abernathy," Lynda said, leaning closer, forgetting, at least for the moment, that she was trying to remain aloof.

That's just what Abel was trying to do, remain aloof. But there was something about Hannah that drew people to her. Brandon and Lynda had already succumbed, and he had no doubt that before the weekend was over Hannah would conquer Robbie and Shane as well.

And what about him? Abel could feel himself slipping under her spell, even though he was trying to avoid it. But the longer he was with her the more he wondered why he was resisting when so much of him didn't want to resist.

"Ms. O'Neil just smiled and said, 'This is excellent Belinda Mae Abernathy.' The whole class clapped.

Sophia Tonya Bumpersnipe looked like she might cry as she carried up her paper. 'I couldn't make my S's,' she said softly to Ms. O'Neil.''

"Serves her right," Lynda said. "She's mean."

"S's are hard," Brandon argued. "It wasn't fair."

"What does Ms. O'Neil do?" Lynda asked.

"Well, it's not really Ms. O'Neil who does it," Hannah said softly. *"Belinda Mae thought about S's. Those squiggly little letters were very hard to make. Belinda Mae had never been able to make one just right.*

'I'm sorry, Sophia,' Ms. O'Neil said.''

"Oh, poor Sophia," Brandon cried.

"Wait," Hannah said. *"Suddenly Belinda Mae didn't feel so good about being Belinda Mae Abernathy. It almost wasn't fair. After all, Belinda Mae Abernathy didn't have any S's.*

'Ms. O'Neil?' she asked.

'Yes Belinda Mae Abernathy?'

'Being called Belinda Mae Abernathy every time is kind of silly. Maybe you could just call me Belinda Mae and I'll give my Abernathy to Sophia and she can be Sophia Tonya?'

Ms. O'Neil smiled a very big smile that made Belinda Mae feel good all over.''

Abel knew just how Ms. O'Neil felt praising Belinda's kindness. Sitting in front of him was a woman whose heart was every bit as big as the fictional little girl's. Here was a woman who deserved to share that heart with someone.

Hannah was right, she should be a mother.

But Abel wasn't the man to father that baby for her. Hannah deserved more than just a baby, more than just a short-term man.

She deserved a real family. She deserved a man who loved her. A man who would give her more than just a child, but could give her a family. She deserved to be part of a couple like the Andersons. She should have the family she longed for and deserved.

And though he might be falling under her spell, he knew that he wasn't the man for Hannah. He didn't know anything about kids, and he knew even less about making a relationship work. His focus was work. He had his real estate agency and this new project with Woody. That was enough for any man.

And Hannah deserved a man who could put her first. Abel had proven to himself, over and over, that for him work was always first.

No, the man of her dreams wasn't him. She just wanted him as a sperm donor.

And for some reason, the thought sat heavily on him.

HANNAH COULDN'T SLEEP—a situation that had become almost commonplace since she'd met Abel Kennedy.

At Abel's insistence she'd taken Woody's room and he'd taken the couch. Thankfully Woody's room was far more orderly than the rest of the house. He'd even put clean sheets on the bed. But lying in the king-size bed trying to sleep was an exercise in futility.

It was all Abel's fault. Every time she closed her eyes there he was. Studying her. He'd watched her all evening, as if he was weighing her every action.

Well, she'd done okay tonight.

With those dark eyes following her every move, Hannah couldn't help but feel exposed. As if Abel could read her every thought and fantasy.

And tonight, lying in Woody's bed with all four kids safely tucked in and Abel sleeping on the living room couch, all her fantasies featured Abel Kennedy. And every time she wished he would just sweep her into his arms.

And then…

What happened next in her fantasies might be necessary if she wanted a baby, but her dreams had nothing to do with that and everything to do with Abel Kennedy himself.

Baby or not, she wanted him.

Darn.

Falling in lust with Abel wasn't what she had planned. Falling to sleep was, and realizing there was no way she was going to close her eyes for some time to come, Hannah got up and tossed on her robe.

Maybe a quick raid of the refrigerator would help. She wouldn't trust anything Woody had in the house, but she knew the pizza was fresh and edible since they'd ordered it after the pick-up party.

She tiptoed through the dark living room. Thank goodness Abel was asleep, tucked safe and sound under a sheet, with Marigold lying across his chest.

Hannah had spent at least a half hour trying to decide what Abel wore to bed. And though the question had niggled at her, she didn't want to find out firsthand. She wanted to forget about him, not reinforce her fantasies.

The small light over the sink was still on, so she didn't have to turn on any bright lights. She took the pizza box out of the refrigerator and, standing at the counter, helped herself to a slice.

"The good thing about tonight's pizza is it doesn't dance," Abel said from behind her.

She whirled around and practically ran into Abel's chest...Abel's bare chest. "What are you doing up?"

Hannah couldn't seem to help looking down to see what Abel wore. Long, grey sweatpants, with bare feet sticking out at the bottom. Sweatpants shouldn't seem sexy, after all sweatpants were the epitome of nonsexy, but on Abel they were hot. Very, very hot.

And he had nice feet. Hannah had long ago decided that feet were one of the ugliest body parts, but Abel's were very nicely shaped.

Rats. She was really in lust if she thought his feet were cute. She realized Abel was talking but had a hard time tearing her gaze away from his sexy bare feet.

"I'm up because I heard someone creeping around and thought I'd better check that it wasn't one of the kids," he said.

"Oh," was the only response she felt capable of making. Monosyllabic words didn't require much thought, and thinking was definitely a problem right now, with a sexy-footed, bare-chested man in front of her.

Hannah forced her gaze upward. But she got stuck mid-torso. She couldn't help but notice the light sprinkling of hair that covered Abel's chest. There was just enough to make her wonder how it would feel pressed against her bare skin.

No, she lectured herself, she wasn't going to think about Abel's chest, his feet, or how he could make even sweatpants look sexy.

She was going to think of something to say. But nothing came to mind. No, what came to mind was the half-naked man standing in front of her. And she liked it.

"Hannah?" Abel asked. "Are you okay? Or don't you want to share the pizza?"

Pizza. Oh, pizza was a much safer topic than how

Abel's half-naked body, or how his totally naked chest would feel if she reached out and ran her fingers over its hard lines. "Pizza. Sure, help yourself to a piece."

Help himself to a piece? Realizing what she'd said, she contained a groan.

"A piece of pizza," she clarified.

"Want something to drink?" he asked. "I think I spotted a bottle of wine in the back of the refrigerator. I'd say a brand and year, but I'm pretty sure Woody's wine taste runs toward screw-on lids."

"Screwing is fine." Oh, it was getting worse and worse. She sounded as if she was asking for something other than a glass of wine so she hastily added, "A screw-on-lid is fine. Sure I'll take a glass."

He brought two glasses and his pizza to the island and sat across from her.

Needing something new to focus on, she said, "Abel, can I ask you something?"

"You can ask, but I won't promise to answer until I hear the question."

"In my office, that first day, you said you didn't like kids. Why?" When he didn't immediately answer, she continued, "I mean, I know it has nothing to do with our deal, but I'd like to know."

"It's not really that I don't like kids. It's just that I'm not sure I'm cut out to be a father. Kids make me nervous."

"Again, why?" She took a steadying sip of wine.

"Well, they make me nervous and uncomfortable because I've never been around them."

"That could change, if you had some of your own, not just some borrowed..." she paused a moment, looking for the word Abel used, "borrowed demon-spawn."

"Did I ever mention my parents to you?" he asked abruptly.

She shook her head.

"You'd like them. Actually, they'd probably like you. They were the best. I mean, Dad was a cop and he worked odd shifts, and yet despite that, I was his priority and I knew it. At the end of every month he'd sit and work out the next month's schedule— work, extra security jobs, and whatnot. But before anything else went on that calendar, I did. He'd write in my basketball games and whatever else I had going on. Then, he'd make out the rest of his month's schedule. I don't know if I could do that, if I could be that kind of a dad and put a kid first. I mean, work is my priority."

"And you're not sure you could change that?"

"Maybe I could. I just don't know if I *want* to change that. I like my life. I've worked hard to build Kennedy Realty, and even harder on this project with Woody."

"I see." She studied the man across from her and though he wasn't sure he could be the kind of father his father had been, she was sure he could.

"And you, tell me why a baby matters so much to you?"

"Have you ever held a brand-new baby?"

He shook his head.

"Then I don't know if I can explain it. But there's something magical about babies. They make you believe that anything is possible, and when you look in that small trusting face, you realize that you're as close to perfection as you'll ever get here on earth."

"Magical, huh?"

She shrugged, suddenly embarrassed.

"And the demon-spawn? Are they magical?"

She laughed. "Even Woody's kids are magic. They're not demons, they just want to be noticed and to be loved. You have to admit, they have a novel way of getting things done."

"You call kidnapping my dog novel?" He smiled.

Hannah nodded. "And creative."

"You thought that was funny, didn't you?"

"Oh, Abel, no it was terrible, just terrible." She tried to sound sincere, but was afraid her giggle gave her away.

"You like them, don't you?"

"The kids? Sure I do. I like babies, but I think I like them even more as they grow up. You see, that magic only grows more powerful as they get older. And you have to admit, I handled them well. Didn't I?"

It wasn't just their deal that prompted her to ask.

Hannah wanted—no needed—to know what Abel thought of her. It was important, and she hated that it was. She didn't want to care about Abel's opinion of her. But she did.

"Tonight you did okay. But, as you pointed out," he said, "we only had a few hours before bedtime, so it's hard to tell. Tomorrow we have a full day. It will be different."

"Aren't you going to ask about my impressions of you?" she asked.

"You've already pointed out you know everything you need to know. I'm a living, breathing, semi-intelligent male who appears to be healthy and has a sense of humor." He paused and then added, "But there's one thing I don't think you've discovered yet."

"What's that?"

"I'm attracted to you."

Hannah gulped the remainder of her wine and took her glass to the counter to refill it. She was saved from responding when Marigold trotted into the room.

"Did we wake you up?" Abel asked as he picked up the dog and set her on one of the chairs.

Hannah couldn't help but notice how he doted on that rat-dog. He might think he wouldn't make a good father, but he would.

But she wasn't looking for him to be a father, she was merely looking for him to father a baby. There was a big difference—a difference she didn't dare forget.

"Aren't you going to say anything about my being attracted to you?" Abel asked softly from right behind her.

"I don't know what to say. The fact you don't think I'm a troll will certainly make having a baby together easier."

And the fact that he wasn't a troll either—not a troll by a long shot—was a good thing as well. But Hannah planned to keep that fact to herself.

Abel reached out, took her glass from her hands and set it on the counter behind her. "My attraction to you has nothing to do with having a baby."

"It doesn't?" Was that squeaky, shrillish voice hers?

"Actually, I'm attracted *despite* the fact you want my baby. That's saying something."

"What's it saying?" she asked.

"That maybe it's time I tried this..."

5

ABEL HADN'T BEEN able to stop thinking about this woman. He'd fantasized about a moment like this. He wasn't sure why.

"This will complicate things," she said.

"Maybe, but I've been going crazy wondering what it would be like. Just one kiss."

Just one, and maybe he'd be able to put this infatuation aside and get back to the business of convincing Hannah that she didn't want this baby, that she should sell the property.

Just one kiss and he'd be over whatever it was that was affecting him.

But the moment he touched her lips with his own, he realized once wasn't going to be enough. She tasted of pizza and wine. Who would have imagined it could be so intoxicating?

He wanted more. Much more.

He pulled her as close as he could, wanting to meld his body to hers.

He wanted—

Hannah drew away from him and it took every

ounce of self-control he possessed not to pull her back.

"We shouldn't do this," she stated, moving back, beyond his reach. "Like I said, it will complicate things."

"You're the one who's bargaining for this."

"I'm bargaining for a baby, not to..."

"Not to what, Hannah?" he asked softly. "I know that was only a kiss, but it left me wanting more, and I think if you're honest, it didn't leave you totally unaffected either."

"I have to go."

Abel didn't call out, didn't try to stop her. If their kiss had affected her half as much as it affected him, he could understand her need for distance. He wasn't exactly inexperienced, but he had never felt anything like what he'd felt when his lips touched hers. These feelings weren't part of his plan to convince Hannah to sell him the property, to give up on her crazy idea to have his baby.

Not to, she'd said. *Not to what?* That was the question that consumed Abel now. What did this growing attraction to Hannah Harrington mean to him, and to her absurd plan?

He'd been lying on Woody's lumpy couch trying to figure out just that question when she'd come down the stairs. But he hadn't come close to figuring out an answer.

And after that kiss he felt even further away from an answer than when he started.

Abel automatically started cleaning the kitchen. It was easier to put away the pizza than to put away the question of his growing attraction for this woman. A woman who wanted his baby, but apparently nothing else from him.

ATTRACTION. IT WAS a simple biological process.

The species needed to go on, and so nature made sure there was plenty of hormonal attraction flying around. A simple biological function, that was all. Hormones.

This had been Hannah's mantra all morning and it was still her mantra as the afternoon progressed. Hormones. Nothing else.

She breathed deeply, trying to let the scent of the beach soothe her. Despite a sleepless night, the beach along Lake Erie rejuvenated her, but she wasn't exactly soothed.

Hannah toed the rough sand as she wished she was alone on the beach. Maybe if she sat under the late afternoon sun long enough and stared at the waves she could figure out what was going on with her wild emotions that skittered first in one direction, then in another.

Instead of a solitary study of waves, she kept stealing glances at Abel. And looking at his bare chest wasn't conducive to figuring anything out. It just left her itching to touch him again. But she wasn't going to do that. So she was just left staring, and trying to think while he played a game of frisbee with the kids. He'd spent the day swimming with them, building sand castles and digging zebra mussels out of the lake for them to examine.

For someone who didn't like kids, he seemed comfortable with them today.

Comfortable was not a word Hannah would use to describe her feelings. Breakfast had been awkward for her, though the kids didn't seem to notice. They were too excited at the idea of spending the day at the beach. And Abel didn't seem to notice. No, he seemed to be going out of his way *not* to notice.

Was he as affected by their kiss as she was? After all, he was the one who had said he was attracted to her in a non-baby way. She hadn't admitted a thing.

Silence was her greatest defense.

Whenever she replayed that conversation—and she couldn't seem to stop replaying it—she couldn't help but feel a spurt of excitement at the thought of Abel being attracted to her. But fear followed right on its heels.

Driving to the peninsula had been a relief. The kids wanted to bring their bikes, so they'd loaded them into Abel's truck. But though he could fit the bikes, he couldn't fit everyone in the truck. So he'd driven the bikes and she'd driven the kids.

Hannah had been more than happy to drive her own vehicle even if she'd had to listen to the kids fight the whole way. She'd finally turned on the radio and drowned out the verbal clashes with loud music.

And now, sitting on the beach while he played frisbee with Lynda and Brandon would have been a relief as well, if the darned man would keep his clothes on.

The two older boys shouted loudly as they flew past her blanket.

"Robbie and Shane, would you settle it down? Someone's going to get hurt." Hannah wasn't sure they'd heard her over their loud whoops.

Abel was still tossing the frisbee to Brandon and Lynda, and the two older boys apparently decided it was time to do something else—and their something included driving all their neighboring sunbathers nuts, kicking up sand as they chased each other across the beach.

"Boys!"

Robbie turned. "What?"

"Settle it down."

He turned back, ready to continue his romp…right back into Shane. In a domino effect, Shane listed forward. If he'd fallen into the sand, everything would have been fine. But he fell into the lifeguard's chair. Hard.

Hannah raced across the sand, no longer concerned about neighboring blankets getting sand all over them, totally focused on the boy. "Are you okay?"

Shane looked up, blood gushing from his chin. He didn't cry. Ten-year-old boys were obviously too cool to cry in front of twelve-year-old brothers, but Hannah could see the unshed tears in his eyes.

"Robbie, go get me a towel. Here, let me look." It was a deep wound, but thankfully just below the chin. Any scar wouldn't show at all. "Looks like you get a trip to the hospital, bucko."

She could see the panic in his eyes. "Don't worry. I work there. They're cool down in the ER."

"What are they going to do?" Shane asked, his voice as wobbly as he looked.

Robbie arrived with the towel. Hannah put it against the gaping wound. "Here, keep pushing against it. The pressure will help it stop bleeding. You need a couple stitches, but," she added before he could panic again, "they'll give you something so it doesn't hurt."

"Will you stay with me?"

She wrapped him in her arms. She longed to simply scoop him up, but instead, she just held him tight. "You just try to get rid of me."

She turned to Robbie, who was standing behind her staring at his brother as if he was going to be sick. "Robbie, he's okay. Really. It was just an accident. Go get Abel."

She led Shane back to their blanket. "Come on. Let's go put your shoes on and I'll grab my stuff."

"You're sure we just can't put a bandage on it?" Shane asked.

"Sorry, sweetie, but you really did a number on it."

"What happened?" Abel panted, breathless from his sprint to the blanket.

"Shane had a small accident and needs a couple stitches. I'm going to take him to the ER."

"Okay, just let me pack up the rest of the crew—"

"There's no reason for all of us to go. I'll take Shane in, and when we're done we'll meet you all back at the house. We'll probably be at least an hour or so." She tried to hide her relief at having some time away from Abel. She needed that distance to try and sort things out.

Immediately she felt a small surge of guilt. When she'd been hoping for distance, this wasn't what she had in mind.

"If you take Shane to the hospital that means you're leaving me with," he jerked his head at the other three children, lined up along the blanket, staring at their brother.

"Yes."

"But the deal was you were spending the weekend with the four kids to see if *you* can handle it.

Me, I already know I can't handle it, and frankly I have no interest in handling it."

"I think you might surprise yourself in what you can manage." Abel didn't seem to realize how good he was with the kids, but Hannah did.

He folded his arms across his chest. "But the point here is I don't want to surprise myself, I want to surprise you at what you *can't* handle. I can take Shane in for stitches."

"No," Shane shrieked. "I want Hannah."

Hannah stroked the little boy's arm. "Don't worry. I promised I'd stay with you. And I keep my promises." She eyed Abel as she said the words.

"And as for our deal," she continued, "it will just have to wait because right now I'm going to have to show you I can cope with an emergency. Shane and I are going to the ER, and we'll see you at home later."

"But—"

"Come on, Shane." She led the boy, the towel still pressed to his chin, toward her car, forcing herself not to glance back at Abel and the kids.

Men. Did Abel think she planned to have Shane fall into a lifeguard tower? Did he think that taking the boy to the ER was high on her list of things to do this weekend?

She was still muttering to herself about men a half hour later when Rick wandered into the ER. "So what's up?"

"This is my buddy, Shane. The ER docs are busy and he needs a couple stitches."

"You can do stitches," Rick pointed out.

"Nah. Buddies don't stitch buddies. I'm feeling sort of queasy and Shane here has offered to hold my hand."

Rick caught her meaning and nodded his agreement. "I see." He focused his attention on the boy. "It's nice of you to take care of Hannah."

"Girls don't like blood," Shane whispered.

"Well, then let's see if we can get you cleaned up. Let me have a look." He peeled back the sterile gauze pad that had replaced the beach towel. "Bet I can close it in four."

"Is it going to hurt?" Shane asked.

Rick shook his head. "I'm going to put some stuff on it so it doesn't."

Hannah hadn't been lying when she said she was queasy. There was no way she could have stitched Shane's cut. She had occasionally worked in the ER back in her nursing days. And as a nurse midwife she'd stitched a torn perineum before, but watching Rick stitch Shane's chin had her fighting back a wave of nausea.

"So I guess this means you're moving ahead on the plan?" Rick asked.

"I told you I was."

"Are you okay?" Rick asked.

Hannah wasn't sure if he was asking about the

weekend or about the fact that she wasn't taking Shane's stitches professionally at all.

"Shane's got a tight grip," she said. From the look Rick shot her she knew he hadn't been talking about the stitches. But she refused to talk about anything else. So she asked Shane, "So what do you do, lift weights? I can't believe how strong you are."

"And brave," Rick added. "Not one peep." He clipped the thread. "There you go, champ. All done."

"That's it?" Shane asked, sounding surprised that his ordeal was over.

"Yes."

"That didn't hurt...much."

"It's because Rick's the best." Hannah's beeper buzzed at her waist. She pulled it off her waistband and read the display. "Looks like I have to make a call. Rick, do you think you could show my buddy where the ice cream's kept?"

"I haven't had supper yet," Shane admitted.

"That's okay," Rick reassured him as he led him down the hall toward the cafeteria. "Boys who are so brave get to have whatever they want."

Want.

Oh, Hannah knew all about want.

Now all she had to do was figure out just what she was going to do about it.

TWO HOURS AFTER they'd left everyone on the beach Hannah and a very tired Shane opened the door to a quiet house.

"Where are they?" Shane grumbled. He'd been chomping at the bit, anxious to show his siblings his stitches.

They walked into the living room and found a dozing Abel, cradling Lynda and Brandon on the couch, a book covering their collective laps.

Something twisted in Hannah. Though he might deny his ability with children, Abel looked totally at home holding them. A quick mental image of Abel cradling a baby flashed through Hannah's mind.

She shut it away.

She might want Abel's baby, but she didn't plan for him to remain in the picture past conception. He'd never hold her baby. Never be a true father to the child.

The something twisting within her hurt at the thought.

"Why don't you go find Robbie?" she whispered to Shane.

"But I want to show them," Shane whined.

The noise was enough to wake up Abel. "Hey, you're back. Let's see what they did to you."

Shane moved across the room and proudly lifted his chin so Abel had the full affect. "And I didn't cry at all, did I Hannah?"

"He sure didn't."

"Hannah was sick though, so I held her hand."

"You're a brave boy." Abel slid out from between the two children. "Let me just carry these two off to bed and you can tell me all about it.''

"You don't think they'll be up later because it's so early?''

"My theory is let sleeping dogs lie.''

"You take Lynda, I'll take Brandon,'' Hannah offered.

"I'm going to find Robbie and show him,'' Shane said, already charging toward their room.

Hannah and Abel carried the two sleeping children to their rooms and had just met back in the hall when Robbie asked, "Can we play a video game?''

"Sure,'' Hannah said. "But it's off by nine.''

The boys ran up the stairs leaving Abel and Hannah alone.

"So, how was the hospital?'' he asked, patting the couch next to him.

Gratefully, Hannah took the seat. "I stitched a lot of women, no problem. But watching Rick put those couple stitches in Shane's chin made me sick. He looked so vulnerable lying there.''

"Being a parent is tough work. Kids get hurt, they get sick. Think about all you'd have to deal with on your own.''

"You're right. I know you think I haven't thought this through, but I do realize that kids get sick, that they get hurt. That they deal with bullies at school and are pressured by their peers to do any number of things that make my hair gray just thinking about it. There's any number of ways a child can break your heart. But..." she paused a moment, trying to put her thoughts into words.

"But there are those moments that more than make up for all the pain. Like when Shane was lying there, getting those stitches, squeezing my hand. He gave me this look that said holding my hand—something that simple—was making it easier. That's when you know you've made a difference." Whether he knew it or not, this weekend with Abel had changed her. When she first met him, he'd been a way to reach her goal. Now he was more.

Just how much more, she had to decide.

"That's just it. There are other ways to satisfy this urge of yours."

"And I do that now. Helping a couple bring a baby into the world safely, well, it's that kind of feeling. But I want more. I want my own baby. I'd be a good mother. I know I would."

"But don't you think your baby needs a father?"

She was sure she could be a good mother to a baby. But watching Abel with the kids today made her wonder if she could be a good father, too. That's what she was proposing. She'd be her baby's mother and father. Could she do it all, and do it right?

THE NEXT MORNING Hannah rolled over in the big bed. She'd finally dozed off, she realized. She'd spent the bulk of the night tossing and turning. And it wasn't the kids. She'd made it through yesterday, stitches and all, and she'd make it through the weekend. The kids seemed to like her, and all Abel's dire predictions had proven false.

No, it was Abel who was on her mind last night, keeping her awake.

She was going to ignore her attraction to Abel and simply concentrate on the fact she was going be a mother. She'd have her own precious baby to shower with love.

Shower. The thought made Hannah realize her feet felt damp.

Her eyes snapped open and she found Marigold busily licking her toes.

"Get," she yelled.

She wiggled her de-dogged feet, and realized in addition to feeling slobbery wet, they felt sticky. A sinking sense of dread crept over her.

The kids.

She'd thought she tamed the demon-spawn, but she hadn't. They'd snuck in and put something on her feet.

Gingerly, she climbed out of bed and as she rose she caught a glimpse of herself in the mirror. They hadn't just attacked her toes.

Her reflection was scary. Her short hair was spiked. Hesitantly, she reached up and touched it. It was sticky—very sticky. She smelled her fingers.

Holy Hayley Mills, they'd used honey?

Her face was covered in what she assumed was supposed to look like makeup, but it looked more like markers. Hannah resisted a groan. She hoped like heck they were washable markers. She hoped Woody wouldn't bring permanent markers into a house full of demon-spawn.

Staring at her grotesque reflection Hannah realized she was going to have to do something about the kids. She couldn't let this attack go unchallenged. That was probably the reason they had been able to chase off all their sitters—the sitters didn't believe in retaliation. But Hannah did. The only question was, how best to seek her revenge?

She was still pondering her retaliation as she walked into the bathroom, Marigold on her heels.

"Oh, no you don't. I shower on my own." She shut the door in the rat-dog's face, and locked it, not because she was afraid of Marigold, but because she'd learned the hard way that it was best not to trust Woody's kids.

HALF AN HOUR later, Hannah was in the kitchen humming merrily as she cooked breakfast.

"What on earth happened to your hair?"

She turned around and smiled sweetly at Abel. "It's the newest fashion. Do you like?"

Hannah had found out an important fact about honey...it takes more than one shampoo and rinse to get it out of hair. Actually, it took more than three shampoos if the remaining stickiness was any indication.

"What did you do to your face?"

"Aw, come on, Abel. You can't tell makeup when you see it?"

Though she didn't think the kids had used permanent markers, she couldn't get all the color off her face.

The lovely red circles on her cheeks had turned a light shade of pink and the sky-blue eye shadow was a softer color, but both were still visible.

"I take it they didn't visit you last night?" she asked.

She studied Abel's perfect form. No. His dark hair looked perfect, as always, and she couldn't spot any other visible evidence of a midnight visit.

"I don't think I had any nightly visitors," he said.

"And the kids weren't the only ones. I woke up with Marigold licking the honey off my toes."

"Sorry. Guess she likes that as much as she likes spaghetti. Maybe she's Italian?"

Hannah didn't say a word about her doubts about the dog's Italian-ness and her growing conviction about its rattiness.

Abel was still staring at her. "They really did a number on you." He paused a moment and added, "I thought they liked you?"

"I think they're afraid I'll stay, and conversely,

they're afraid I'll leave. So it's better to make sure I do leave, only on their terms." She shook her head. "I sound like some pop-psychiatrist, I know."

Hannah glanced at Abel and knew just how the kids felt. Her feelings for Abel were growing and had very little to do with having a baby…and the fact that they didn't have to do with a baby made her want to pick up and run as far away from him as she could get.

Why?

She should consider herself the luckiest woman alive to have a man like Abel Kennedy desiring her.

But she was afraid. She'd never admit it out loud, but there it was.

She was afraid it would be all too easy to care for this man who only wanted her property. Oh, she was pretty sure he liked her too, but he'd made it clear that he wasn't in the market for a relationship, or a baby. And Hannah was most definitely in the market.

She needed to simply concentrate on her goals.

And at the top of the list right now was getting even with the demon-spawn.

"Well, I'll take care of them." Abel's taking care wouldn't be nearly half as much fun as hers. What she saw in his eyes didn't bode well for any of the children.

"Oh, no you won't," she said, though why she was protecting the monsters was unclear. The best reason she could come up with was that her revenge was better than anything Abel would do to them.

"You're going to pretend that there's nothing at all wrong with my face or hair—pretend that this is my normal appearance. And you're going to sit down and just play along with whatever I say."

"What do you have in mind?" he asked, obviously interested.

"The purpose of this weekend was for me to prove that I could handle kids. Well, you were right. If I can handle Woody's bunch, I can handle anything. So when this day's over, you're going to have to admit I deserve to be a mother."

Abel didn't say anything. He especially didn't say that he'd already decided that Hannah would be a fantastic mother. It was just that he wasn't sure he'd be a fantastic father.

Okay, so maybe this weekend had convinced him that kids weren't as bad as he thought. He wouldn't admit it to Hannah, but he enjoyed the beach, at least until Shane's fall. And he even enjoyed reading to Brandon and Lynda last night.

He'd even got three out of the four fed, cleaned and ready for bed. He was good at this stuff. That surprised him. He'd never imagined being good with kids, much less enjoying them so much. Well, enjoying them most of the time.

Maybe kids weren't as difficult to handle as he thought, but he still didn't have time for a family.

He had work, and more work. Of course Woody somehow balanced a family and a demanding job.

But whether or not he was willing to have kids was a moot point. Hannah wasn't asking him to be a father in the truest sense of the word, a fact that had been eating at him, nibbling away, always at the back of his mind.

It wasn't that he was ready to settle down.

No. Not at all.

A wife and family weren't in his plans. And he still had doubts about his fathering capabilities. But despite all his indecision and doubts, as he watched Hannah bustle around the stove, the idea didn't sound nearly as scary or absurd as it had a week ago.

Abel heard their thunderous steps before he saw them. "Morning!" the army of nighttime terrorists chorused.

Abel didn't say a word. He just sat back and watched, waiting with anticipation for Hannah to do her stuff.

She turned from the stove, with her oddly styled, stiff-looking hair and her terrible *makeup*, and smiled sweetly. She'd never looked better to him, he realized with a shock.

"Good morning," she said cheerfully.

Obviously her happy response was the last thing the kids expected because they exchanged nervous glances.

"And how did you all sleep?" she asked. "Because I slept wonderfully. The afternoon on the beach was just the thing to exhaust me. I mean, I slept so soundly that I never even stirred. I don't think there was much that could have woken me." She paused and added, "Did you all sleep that good?"

"Yeah." "Sure," came a chorus of mutters.

"Well, I'm thrilled. And to celebrate the last day of our baby-sitting, I made you a special breakfast. A very *special* breakfast."

She turned back to the stove and called over her shoulder. "You all just sit down and get comfortable. I hope you're hungry because I had to get up early to find all the ingredients for this omelette."

She came over to the table and set a pan containing a huge omelette down in the center of the table.

"It looks okay, doesn't it Shane?" Robbie asked. The way he was eyeing the omelette told Abel he wasn't sure just how okay it was.

"Yeah, it looks okay," Shane said, his bandaged chin wobbling as he nibbled his lips nervously. He stole guilty looks at Hannah, but she ignored them. Lynda and Brandon didn't say a word.

"Well, of course it looks okay. That's why I got up so early. You know the saying, *the early bird gets the worm.* Well, I wanted to be sure I had enough…time, yeah, time to get everything this very special omelette needed."

Seemingly oblivious to the kids' nervous looks, Hannah started dishing up slices of omelette to everyone.

"Oh, and Abel, we should really remember to get Woody my favorite book to read to the kids as a sort of thank you for the marvelous weekend. I know how much they enjoy stories and this one's special. I think they'll enjoy it, *especially* after today."

She put a huge piece of the omelette on Abel's plate. He eyed the egg concoction. There were small grayish flecks in it, hunks of cheese and what looked like parsley. It smelled wonderful, but Abel didn't take a bite. Like the kids, he wasn't sure what Hannah was up to, but he was not about to be the first one to find out.

Hannah placed the last piece on her plate, sat down and took a bite. Abel was studying her as closely as the kids were.

"Where was I?" she mumbled as she sat down. "Oh, my favorite book. Did you ever read the story, *How to Eat Fried Worms,* by Thomas Rockwell? It's a modern classic for kids," she said to the group.

"Yep, Rockwell knew all about the early bird getting the worm, only this time it was a boy who had a bet, so he had to *eat* worms. Lots of worms. Why, did you know that in addition to frying them, you can grind them up and put them in just about anything? Why if you grind them fine enough, no one would ever know."

She took another huge bite, and then looked around the table as if she was just noticing something. "Why look at all of you, just sitting there listening to me. *Dig* in. I worked hard to *dig up* all the very *special* ingredients for the omelette."

Robbie toyed with his omelette, prying at the gray flecks with his fork before pushing the plate back and saying, "Ah, I don't think we're hungry, right guys?"

"Yeah," Shane said.

"Well, I'm hungry," Lynda said.

"No, you're not," her two older brothers said. "You either, Brandon." They tried to pull the four-year-old out of his chair.

"No!" he cried.

"Fine. You just sit here and eat it then. You'll be sorry," Robbie hollered as the three oldest children ran from the kitchen.

"Well, if you're not going to eat breakfast, that's okay. I can make you all something *special* for lunch, too," Hannah called after them. "And if you're already done with breakfast, go upstairs and make sure your beds are made and your rooms are cleaned."

The three made their escape and Brandon took a bite.

"You didn't really, did you?" Abel asked quietly, a look of distaste on his face as he watched Brandon merrily munch on his omelette.

"Of course not," Hannah said. "Mushrooms, that's all. But you know what they say, sometimes the best offense is doing nothing. I'd say that it worked perfectly this time."

"You're a tricky, devious woman."

"Yeah, I know." She plopped another huge bite in her mouth. "Ain't it great?"

THE HOUSE WAS spotless and the three oldest children were hungry when Woody came home. Hannah had washed Woody's honey-covered sheets and taken another shower. She still looked a bit odd, but definitely better than she had when Marigold had been licking her feet.

"Hello!" Woody called as he threw open the door. All four kids came racing down the stairs and hugged him.

"So how was it?" he asked Abel and Hannah.

Abel didn't say a word, but Hannah said, "Oh, it was wonderful. We did have one small accident at the beach on Saturday. Shane has a couple stitches in his chin, but I don't think you'll even see a scar when they come out."

"What happened?" Woody asked, all four kids still crowded around him.

"He fell into a lifeguard's tower and—"

"And I went to the hospital with Hannah and I had ice cream, and Hannah fed us worms, but only Brandon ate them, and—"

"Wait a minute. Let's go back to the worms." He looked up at Hannah. "You fed my kids worms?"

She widened her eyes and strove to look innocent. "Why, I don't know what gave them that idea. I served a mushroom omelette with toast and *honey* this morning. Lots of warm, gooey *honey*. Come to think of it, the three older kids didn't eat a bite of it. Now, I wonder why that was? Kids, what would make you think I'd put worms in our omelette?"

The three older ones looked embarrassed and didn't say a word. But Brandon started crowing, "I ate worms. A worm omelette. It was good. Can you make worm omelettes, Daddy?"

Woody studied the entire group, then turned questioning eyes to Abel who merely shrugged. "I'd like to know exactly what went on here, but I think I'm better off not knowing."

"Sometimes the best offense is doing nothing," Abel said.

Hannah caught his eye and sent a smile aimed just at him. Abel winked at her and she knew he understood.

And that he understood was the scariest part of the whole weekend.

6

"YOU DID GOOD," Abel said. Why he felt the need to praise Hannah, or why when her face lit up at the compliment his heart skipped a beat, he wasn't sure.

They were sitting on her couch, watching the television in amicable silence…at least it had been silent until his statement.

He'd justified asking himself over to her house after Woody's return by insisting that he wanted to see where she lived, where she planned on raising her child—maybe his child. She'd seemed hesitant to invite him up, but Abel was glad she finally had.

Studying her home gave him insight into her character. The living room was full of loud patterns and bold colors splashed throughout. Reds, hunter greens, bright yellow. And yet in a small curio cabinet she had a collection of small glass figures.

Bold, yet delicate. That was her decorating scheme, and it was a reflection of Hannah herself. She'd come to him with a bold, audacious proposal. She handled the demon-spawn with unimaginable skill. And yet, beneath her strength, he sensed a delicate heart that could easily be crushed.

Not that he had anything to do with her heart.

Hannah had been mindlessly stroking Marigold, stopped midstroke and those baby-blue eyes, that still had a slight magic marker sheen on their lids, stared at him when he offered up the compliment about her baby-sitting skills.

"Thanks," was all she said.

She started stroking the dog again, and Abel found himself wondering what it would be like to have that hand stroke him as well. It was a tiny hand. Small, delicate, yet capable. She delivered babies. She comforted injured little boys. She cuddled Woody's kids with the ease of someone who'd been cuddling kids all her life.

Abel wished she'd cuddle him just a little. Oh, hell, who was he kidding. He wanted her to cuddle him...preferably naked. A long, hot, sweaty bout of naked *cuddling*.

He reached out and took the hand that had been stroking Marigold and used it to pull her toward him. The disgruntled dog jumped from the couch with a small yip.

"Abel, what are you doing?" Hannah asked. He'd been acting strange all evening. And now? There was something unfamiliar in his dark eyes, something that should have frightened her, but instead sent a wave of desire coursing through her body.

"I want you to come here a moment," he said,

pulling her until she was practically sitting on his lap, she was sitting so close.

"What can you say with me sitting here that you couldn't say with me sitting on the other end of the couch?"

"Who says anything about saying?"

"Abel, that sentence didn't make a bit of sense. *Who says anything about saying?*" She was babbling and she knew it, but babbling was safer than whatever it was she saw in Abel's eyes. "No, who says anything about saying, that's a dumb sentence. Who says anything about talking—now that might work. Or—"

"Hannah," he interrupted.

"What?"

"Shut up and kiss me."

"That's a Mary Chapin Carpenter song. I've gone to Chautauqua to hear her sing. She's been up there the last few summers." She paused, cast him a frightened look and continued in a breathless rush, "And, no. I don't think we should be kissing. I mean, we should be kissing as soon as you have your clean bill of health. Actually, we'll need to do more than kissing then if we—I mean I—want a baby the old-fashioned way, but we haven't decided on old-fashioned yet. It might be safer to just...well, you know. There's where you simply make your donation and..." Hannah could feel heat stealing into her cheeks and suspected she was blushing.

She could admit to herself that she didn't want to take the clinical approach to making a baby with Abel. She was a healthy woman, with healthy sexual needs and those needs right now were centered on Abel Kennedy.

So why did the thought of…she searched for a word. Making love didn't qualify. Sex seemed too raw a term. *Business* might be an apt description, but what she wanted was more than that.

"Hannah?" Abel said, waving a hand in front of her face, breaking into her absurd line of thought. "Earth calling Hannah."

She shook her head, remembering that they weren't discussing *business,* but kissing. Even if they decided to make a baby the old-fashioned way, kissing Abel for recreation instead of procreation was a dangerous step in the wrong direction. "Sorry. Where were we?"

"The question is, where were you?" He draped an arm around her shoulder, as if he'd always draped it there. But he hadn't and he shouldn't and she shouldn't let him.

"So where were you just now?" Abel asked again.

Hannah wasn't about to admit she was procreating with him in her mind. Nor was she going to admit she liked the way his arm felt on her shoulder, how protected she felt wrapped in his embrace.

No, she wasn't admitting to any of it.

"What do you mean?" she asked as innocently as she could manage.

"You totally zoned out midconversation."

"Oh, sorry." She gulped and tried to steady her nerves. "I do that sometimes when I'm nervous or tired."

"What are you nervous about?" His eyes narrowed and he studied her as he pulled her even closer.

Just what was he looking for? And what would he think if he found it?

She squirmed just a little, trying to prove to him— and maybe to herself as well—that she didn't need to be held. No, that she didn't *want* to be held.

"I'm not nervous," she blatantly lied. "Why on earth would you think I was nervous? I'm just tired. You'll have to admit that it was a long weekend and I'm simply exhausted. I don't know why I invited you over after we left Woody's. I should have just sent you home. See? I was too tired to think straight. And I—"

"Hannah, you don't just zone out when you're nervous, you babble." He took her chin in his hand and gently guided her head until she was facing him.

"I don't babble!" she snapped, and pulled away.

"Oh, yeah you do. But lucky for you I have a solution."

She tried to back up to her own side of the couch. A cushion between them wasn't much of a barrier, but it was safer than practically sitting on Abel's lap. But he held tight. "What solution?"

"This." His lips touched hers.

Get away, her mind screamed. *Stay,* her heart countered.

Unsure which command to follow—her heart or her head—she simply gave in and stayed. It was just a kiss. She was a healthy woman, he was a healthy man, and they were just, just, just...

As the kiss deepened, Hannah forgot to figure out what they were *just* doing, and lost herself in the wonder of the feel of his lips against hers.

Her hands slipped under his shirt. The texture of his chest, the hard muscle, the soft sprinkling of hair. The taste of him was the taste of summer, of life at its fullest. Texture, taste...her senses were overloaded until she couldn't tell where Abel stopped and Hannah began, or where Hannah stopped and Abel began. And all she knew was that she didn't want to know and she didn't want this moment to end. And that she needed to get away.

A burst of self-awareness struck her—she didn't want to get away. She didn't want any separation between them.

And the fact that she didn't want any separation, but craved getting even closer was enough of a reason to stop.

Abruptly she pulled back. "I don't think we should be doing this," she panted.

"Why?" he said, reaching for her.

She moved farther away, needing a physical distance.

"Because you're a nice guy. Maybe that's something that should have been on my initial list, but it wasn't. So I'm glad you are. But your being nice means I'm susceptible to liking you. I don't want to like you too much. I just want you to—"

"Have sex with you, impregnate you, then go on my merry way."

Abel sounded…maybe it was disappointed? But he'd known the ground rules going into this. Just like Hannah did. And changing them now could be messy.

"Yes," she said softly. "I think it's time for you to leave."

"What if leaving isn't what I want?" he asked.

"You said if I survived this weekend you'd… well, do it."

"Maybe I changed my mind. Maybe I want more."

"I've already promised you the property. What else could you want?"

"I don't know, dammit." He pulled his arm from her shoulder and slid against the side of the couch, creating a small space between them.

Hannah realized with undeniable sadness that she was going to do her best to widen the space.

"Abel, like I said that first time we talked, a relationship built around having a baby could never last. I don't want to become emotionally dependent on you. I want to keep this business, because in the end that's all it is. Can you understand that?''

"Sure. You're afraid," he said, resignation in his voice.

"That's not what I said." Afraid? Hannah wasn't afraid of anything. If she was the type of person who was afraid, she wouldn't be in this absurd situation in the first place.

"I know what it's like to be afraid. It might not be the most manly thing to admit, but whatever this is between us scares me as well. I'm a flop at relationships—they're just too hard to juggle with work, and all. But I find I don't mind the thought of juggling if what I'm juggling is you."

"I'm sorry. I can't do it, Abel."

"Have you ever failed at anything?" he asked quietly.

"Pardon?"

"Have you ever set out to do something and failed?"

Unsure where he was going with the question, Hannah nonetheless shook her head. "No. I'm a firm believer in planning what I want and going after it. Nursing school, midwifery training, even working for Stephanson and Associates. Rick didn't want to hire me," she smiled at the memory. "I convinced him otherwise."

"I thought as much." He gave a discreet little nod, as if he'd just learned something about her that she didn't even know herself.

Hannah wasn't sure she wanted to know what he thought he knew, but she found herself asking, "Why?"

"You came to me with a list of father requirements. Despite how stupid the entire idea was, here I am. You're the type of woman who goes after what she wants and doesn't take no for an answer."

"There you see, I don't run from problems."

"That's not what I said. You go after what you want, things you can realistically control. School, jobs, even becoming a mother. But a relationship? You can't control that, so you run. That first day I thought you were nuts, but I also thought you were a brave woman. I was wrong. You're nuts and you're a coward."

"Since when do real estate agents practice psychoanalysis on the side? I'm not running, I'm just keeping things in perspective."

"You just keep telling yourself that." He stood. "I'll let myself out."

Hannah followed him to the door. "Abel?"

"I'll call you when my test results are in," he said tersely.

"You mean you're going to go through with it?"

"Yes." He walked out of her house and slammed the door.

She'd done it. She'd kept the distance between them, she'd gotten exactly what she wanted. A father for her baby, no strings attached.

So why did she feel so hollow?

FOR THE HUNDREDTH time since the night they'd fought, Hannah picked up the phone, wanting to call Abel. And for the hundredth time, she set it back on the receiver without making the call.

What was there to say?

Nothing.

So she didn't call. But that didn't mean she didn't think about him, dream about him, and worry about the things he said.

Was she really running?

Hannah didn't know. She'd spent Monday, Tuesday, Wednesday and all day today wondering what she was going to do about Abel Kennedy, and still she didn't have a clue.

She was sitting in her office, pretending to do paperwork, when in actuality she was simply trying to work out a plan. And for the first time in her life, Hannah didn't know where to begin.

Abel was haunting her dreams, both at night and during the day. She couldn't function and it was all his fault.

As if he knew she was thinking about him, her office door opened and there he was.

Without preliminaries, he shut the door behind him and said, "My tests came back."

Hannah dropped the pen she'd been fiddling with as she supposedly updated charts.

"And?" She knew the answer. Deep down inside, maybe she'd known that Abel Kennedy was destined to father her baby. But nothing more, she sternly warned herself.

He took the chair on the other side of her desk, drawing out the suspense. Settled, he said, "Clean bill of health."

"Oh." She picked up the pen and began to doodle on her notebook.

"So are you ready?" he asked.

Hannah suddenly found herself choking on absolutely nothing, and devoutly hoping she had misunderstood. "Ready for what?"

"Why, ready to make a baby," he said with a smile. "I did promise that if you survived the weekend with Woody's kids and all my tests came back okay we'd do it. So, here I am."

"You mean, you want to do *it* just like that?" Images that had assaulted Hannah for days, images of Abel next to her in her bed flooded her mind, and for a moment, those fantasies were all she could see.

"You made yourself clear Sunday night. This is business, pure and simple. It has nothing to do with romance, and everything to do with cold, clinical sex. It's not as if we need candles and champagne for me to serve as your stud.''

Her fantasies shattered at his cold words. ''That's not what I want.''

''You've decided to forgo the old-fashioned way and want me to just deposit my sperm somewhere?''

''That's not what I want either.''

''Well, what do you want?'' he asked gently. ''Every time I think I've figured it out, you seem to change your mind.''

When she had first approached Abel she'd known just what she wanted, but now everything was blurred. ''That's the problem, I don't know.''

She wanted a baby. Abel was the only man she wanted to father her baby. She *wanted* Abel. Wanting him should make having a baby with him easier. She should jump up, lock her office door and have her way with him right here.

Yet, wanting him only muddied the waters.

What Abel proposed—no, to be fair, what she'd proposed—didn't even begin to fulfill everything she wanted. But she didn't have the right to ask for more than just his *stud service,* and even if she did, she wasn't sure she could.

''It was all clear and straightforward at first, but now nothing feels the least bit clear,'' she admitted.

It was Abel's doing. When she'd first met him she'd known he was a good-looking man on the outside, but spending time with him had shown her he was even better looking on the inside, appealing in a way that no man had ever appealed to her.

She liked Abel. She cared about him. And she certainly wanted him on a physical level. That was the problem.

''I thought I could go through with this, but now I don't know,'' she said, hoping he didn't ask why, and conversely, hoping he would.

He didn't ask. He simply stood and threw a file on her desk. ''Well, let me know when you do. First you want me, now you don't know. Did a weekend with Woody's kids convince you that a baby grows up into something that might be more than you can handle on your own?''

''No.'' There might be a lot of things she was unsure about, but wanting a baby wasn't one of them.

''Then what?''

The question she longed for and loathed, was on the table, and Hannah still didn't have a clue how to answer it. ''I don't know. I'm confused.''

''Well, like I said, be sure to let me know when you've figured it out. I still need that property, and you're not going to sell until you have a baby, so I'd like to take care of business as soon as possible.'' He walked out of her office and slammed the door.

UNLIKE HANNAH, Abel knew exactly what he wanted, and it wasn't the property. It was a small feisty blonde. And he didn't want her for however long it took to create a baby. He wanted her a lot longer. Now all he had to do was convince her that *he* was what she wanted.

The thought that he was the one pushing to make this a relationship, not just a business deal, was bizarre. Having a relationship meant taking time and energy away from his business, something he'd never been willing to do before. But for Hannah he'd do more...much more. These feelings for her were deep enough to override everything else.

Abel wasn't going to blithely make love to her, take his property and walk away. He was going to keep chipping away at her until he made her realize there was something more going on between them. He was more than just a stud. He wanted more, and he suspected that, though she was scared of the idea, so did she.

Sunday, as he'd held her, he'd realized how much that wanting had grown. It was as if finding Hannah was finding a piece of himself that had been missing, a piece he'd never realized existed until she walked into his life and turned it upside down.

At first he'd simply played along with her, hoping to win the land. Now, land be dammed. He was playing for something more important. Abel knew that Hannah Harrington was as vital to his happiness as oxygen was to his breathing.

Why?

Because he loved her.

It wasn't just attraction. It wasn't about babies or property. It wasn't about deals. It was love.

Now all he had to do was convince her that she loved him, too.

7

"BREATHE," Hannah commanded.

"I don't want to breathe," Patty Martin growled.

Hannah resisted chuckling. Patty's antagonistic mood was a good sign. The labor was progressing rapidly. Soon Patty would forget everything she'd gone through as she held her new baby in her arms.

Thinking about Patty holding her baby sent a stab of envy coursing through Hannah.

A baby. No matter how confused things were becoming, she had to remember why she was going through all this. She wanted to hold a child of her own.

"Okay, so don't breathe," she said with a smile.

As the contraction ebbed, Patty looked contrite. "I guess that was a stupid thing to say," she panted.

"No, it was a labor-thing to say," Hannah soothed.

"I just wish Jim would get here."

"He's on his way." Patty's husband was at a business meeting in Pittsburgh when the first contractions hit. Now he was speeding back to Erie.

"But what if he doesn't make it in time? This is going fast—too fast," Patty said, voicing her fear.

"Then he'll just have to spend the next month or two making it up to you."

Patty's weak smile faded as she fell into the grip of another strong contraction. "Breathe with me, Patty," Hannah crooned. "In, out, in, out…" She kept up the chant through the contraction, as she gently massaged the laboring woman's back. "And there, a deep cleansing breath."

The door to the room burst open.

"Jim," Patty cried, opening her arms and welcoming her husband to what would be the most profound moment of their marriage. The birth of their first child.

Hannah backed away, giving the couple a moment of privacy, but she couldn't quite tear her eyes away from the scene as Jim embraced his wife and they whispered back and forth.

Who would rush to her side when she was in labor? She touched her flat stomach and felt a wave of sadness as she realized no one would.

Oh, she knew that Lucy, Irene or even Rick, despite his disapproval, would be with her if she asked. But Abel wouldn't be there. He wouldn't rush to her side and hold her hand. He wouldn't listen to her be cranky throughout the labor. He wouldn't soothe her fears. He wouldn't help with the midnight feedings.

He wouldn't worry about the baby's every little sniffle, every little cough.

Her baby wouldn't have a father.

Watching Jim and Patty, thinking about the baby that would be here soon and would be welcomed by two parents united in love, Hannah knew that she couldn't do it.

She pressed against her flat stomach and knew that it was destined to stay that way.

No, she couldn't go through with her plan. Rick and Abel had both been right—it was a crazy plan.

She realized what had held her back when Abel brought her his test results. She'd been fooling herself when she thought she could go through with just having sex. Especially just having cold, clinical sex with Abel.

She couldn't do it to herself, to her baby, or to him.

How had she thought she could simply make a baby with Abel and walk away, not giving him another thought? Even without a baby in the picture, walking away from Abel was going to be the hardest thing she'd ever done. But she'd have to walk away. Despite the fact there was chemistry between them, there was nothing there emotionally but a business contract. A relationship built around chemistry and business could never survive.

"Hannah!" Patty gasped.

Hannah put aside her thoughts of the baby-that-could-have-been but never-would-be, and rushed to her patient's side. An hour and a half later, she delivered a beautiful eight-pound, ten-ounce, twenty-one-inch baby boy.

She managed to smile as she presented him to his parents, but inside her heart was breaking. She'd never hold Abel's baby to her breast, and Abel would never sit next to her, staring in rapt awe at the child they'd created.

There would be no child.

Later, in the middle of a sleepless night, Hannah realized that she might be able to set aside her dreams of a baby, but her dreams of Abel Kennedy wouldn't be quite so easy to rid herself of.

Abel, who needed her property.

Abel, who stirred feelings in her that she never thought she'd experience—feelings she didn't want to put a name to. Because if she did, the name for her feeling might have to be love.

She loved Abel Kennedy.

Abel, who only saw a relationship with her as a means to an end. A means that her decision would end.

What was she going to do about Abel? About this feeling?

HANNAH HARRINGTON knew just what she was doing because she was bold. She was adventurous. She was moving fearlessly forward.

She was...naked.

Oh, she'd been naked before, but never in Abel's apartment.

Getting naked at Abel's had been more trouble than she could have imagined. It wasn't just taking off her clothes. From getting Abel's apartment manager to let her into his place with some cockamamie story about being his out-of-town sister, to practically buying out Kmart's supply of candles which she'd lit and placed all over the living room—getting naked had never been so tough. But the effort was worth it. At least she hoped it would be once Abel was here and naked with her.

Hannah wasn't sure when that would happen. Waiting was probably the hardest part of this entire scheme. She was nervous. She tried concentrating on her fearlessness but that didn't help. So to distract herself from the fact that she was naked, she decided to study Abel's apartment.

It wasn't what she'd expected. After seeing Woody's idea of a clean house, she'd been surprised by Abel's neatly decorated home. Panelled walls, leather furniture, shelves lined with an eclectic mix of books. It was an orderly, clearly male space. Hardly romantic. But now it had dozens of candles. Their flickering light softened the room, turning it into a magical place.

Hannah might not be willing to have a baby with a man she loved, and then walk away from him. But she could give herself one night—one magical night—with Abel before she left his life forever.

One night she'd made sure wouldn't result in a baby.

She'd give Abel his property, give him his dream and take with her one sweet memory instead of a baby.

The seducing him part had given her problems. She wasn't sure how to go about it. In desperation, she'd borrowed a book from the library. *How to Seduce Your Man.* Suggestions ran the gamut, from wild things with plastic wrap to edible unmentionables, from leather to feathers. And she'd refused to even read the chapter entitled, *Toys for You and Your Boy.*

No, none of the suggestions sounded overly seductive to Hannah, which was why she'd decided on something entirely different. And as she sat naked on Abel's leather sofa waiting, she was having second thoughts about her naked decision. A good layer of plastic wrap might be preferable to sitting with her bare butt on leather.

She had tried to be up-front and honest with Abel from the beginning, and though she wanted to seduce him into bed for purely carnal reasons, she worried that it was a bit dishonest.

After all, he thought she wanted to have sex with him to have a baby. However, this wasn't about babies. This wasn't about the land she owned. This was sensual, lascivious, wanton, untamed sex.

No. She might want to tell herself that it was just wild sex, but it was more. She'd make love to him this once when she'd seen to it there would be no chance of conceiving a baby. She'd get him out of her system, she'd tell him he'd fulfilled their bargain and give him his land.

She'd have this one night with Abel to remember for the rest of her life.

She shifted her position and her skin squeaked against the leather. Bbbb. It sounded like a kid blowing a raspberry. Actually, it sounded worse than that. It sounded like something no lady wanted to be sounding like—a bad attack of gas.

If things went the way she hoped, she'd have to see to it that they made love on some other piece of furniture, not on this couch. Hannah could just see herself in the middle of passionate ecstasy, screaming Abel's name as she reached the heights she was becoming more convinced that only Abel could ever take her to when...Bbbb, that sound would ring out.

No, that was too embarrassing.

She should add a chapter to the book. "Where Not to Make Love to Your Man." Leather sofas would head the list.

Maybe she should put her robe on now? Would it be more sexy to be found naked, or wrapped in that little bit of silk the salesclerk had assured her constituted a robe? Nope. Chapter Two had clearly stated, "Less is More."

But then there was Chapter Three—"Leather, Lace and How to Set the Pace with Clothes." Yep, maybe her sheer silk robe would be a better idea. She rose to grab it when a key rattled in the door.

It was him!

"Hey, Abel?" Woody Pembrooke called as he opened the door and walked into the apartment.

Hannah dove for her robe.

Woody spotted her middive. "Hannah?"

Quickly wrapping the thin scrap of silk around her, she looked up and tried to smile, as if being caught naked on a man's couch was an everyday occurrence. "Woody. What a surprise!"

"You're not kidding." He backed toward the door, obviously anxious to make his escape.

She sighed and clutched the robe a little tighter. "No, don't go. I think I need to leave."

This was a sign from the powers-that-be that she wasn't meant to seduce Abel. This plan was all wrong.

"No, no, just sit down," Woody said in a rush. "I'm sorry for barging in. You and Abel are obviously busy."

"No, we're not busy, I'm just busy." Woody looked confused, so Hannah tried to explain. "I mean, I wasn't even busy. I was waiting for Abel, but I'm having second thoughts, so I'm going to go

before I embarrass myself in front of him just the
way I've embarrassed myself in front of you.''

''You didn't...''

Hannah's eyebrows shot up and she thought she
detected a rosy blush beneath his beard.

He offered her a sheepish grin. ''Well, what I
mean is I'm sure you're embarrassed, but there's no
need. I've seen naked women before.''

''Oh, thanks. That helps.''

''I mean...'' The giant bear of a man was definitely blushing. And it was no longer just a rosy
pink, but a deep scarlet red.

''Really, Woody, your arrival has merely saved
me from making a fool of myself in front of Abel.
This was a mistake.''

''Not if you want a baby,'' he pointed out gently.

''But I don't...'' She paused, not wanting to admit
the truth—she just plain wanted Abel Kennedy.

''You don't want what?'' he pressed.

''This wasn't about a baby,'' she confessed softly.

''Oh.'' A second later, understanding dawning, he
said, ''Oh!''

''Yeah, *oh*. If it was about a baby, that would be
one thing. But since it's not about a baby, it's entirely another thing. And the more I think about it,
my being here under false pretenses, as it were, is
wrong.''

''If it's not about a baby, it's about...?'' He left

the question hanging. He moved closer to Hannah, studying her.

"Abel."

"How do you feel about Abel?" he asked.

"I don't know for sure," she said, even though she was pretty sure what her feelings were.

"But," she continued, "I do know whatever it is I feel is not what I intended when I made my list. I wanted something quick, and simple. I wanted a father for my baby, but there's nothing simple about Abel and the way I feel about him."

"You care about him," Woody stated, rather than asked.

She cared. Well, yes, of course she cared—more than cared—but he didn't. He just wanted the land. Oh, maybe he lusted after her a bit.

She thought about their kisses. Maybe more than a bit. But lust wasn't love. So she'd give herself this one night, and move on.

She had a career she loved. It was demanding and time consuming. She would have really had to work to give her baby a proper amount of time and attention. Serving her patients' and her baby's best interests would be next to impossible. Abandoning her baby plans was right.

Satisfying her longing for Abel wasn't. These feelings she had for him were just an aberration. Her subconscious's attempt to justify having sex just to have a baby.

That she was waiting in his apartment not to have a baby, but to satisfy that longing was cheating.

Woody must have decided she'd had enough time to think because he asked, "So what are you going to do?"

"I'm going to get out of here."

She could have had sex with Abel to have a baby, that would have been honest. But having sex with him to scratch an itch, well, that was as dishonest as it came and she wasn't going to have anything to do with it.

Decision made, she raced past Woody, anxious to get to the bathroom and forget about seducing Abel for totally carnal reasons.

In the end what she forgot was to watch where she put her feet. She tripped over the coffee table and descended right toward Woody.

"Gotcha," he said as he caught her on his lap.

"Thanks."

Hannah leaned and rubbed her shin. It was definitely going to bruise.

What else could go wrong?

As if on cue, just as she started to rise, the door opened, and Abel stood staring at the tableaux Woody, still holding Hannah on his lap, created. "What ...?"

Abel didn't finish the sentence. Hannah figured that wasn't a very good sign.

"I can explain," she said, standing. Realizing her

robe was gaping at the top, she clutched it to her, wishing she'd brought flannel instead of silk.

"So can I," Woody added in a rush.

"I'd like to hear an explanation, because it sort of looks to me as if you've made some new baby-making plans."

"I don't want to sleep with Woody." She didn't want to hurt the big guy's feelings, so she hastily added, "Sorry, Woody."

"No problem, Hannah. I don't want to sleep with you either." Woody started toward the door, obviously hoping to make his escape.

Well, let him escape. Hannah was going to be right on his heels as soon as she pounded some sense into Abel's thick skull.

She left Woody to his slinking and turned back to Abel. "You're nuts if you think I'd come to your house and seduce your partner."

"I'm nuts? *I'm nuts, she says,*" he said more to himself than either Woody or Hannah. "I'm not the one that came up with this absurd plan to have some stranger—who just happened to be a living, breathing male—father my baby."

"You forgot healthy and sense of humor. But I was wrong, you don't have a sense of humor or you'd see what a comedy of errors this whole situation is."

"I don't see anything funny about it." Abel folded his arms across his chest.

"You're right, it isn't funny. It's absurd. My plan was a mistake. One I plan to rectify right now."

She stormed into the bathroom and slammed the door.

"She's right," Woody said to Abel.

He whirled around and faced Woody. "Right about what?"

"You're nuts. She didn't come here to seduce me. I walked in on her sitting naked on your couch, waiting to seduce you."

An image of Hannah naked on his couch tried to squeeze past his anger, but Abel wouldn't allow it.

"She didn't want me when I offered." There, that was a good angry thought, and right now he wanted to hang on to his anger. His anger was all that protected him from other feelings...feelings he didn't know what to do with. He loved Hannah, but she just saw him as a sperm-bank.

"How did you offer?" Woody asked.

"I took her the test results and said we could go ahead and do it. And she just sat there with a horrified look on her face. What does she want from me?"

"Just like that?" Woody asked.

"What? What was wrong with that?"

Abel had just tried to give the woman what she wanted and she got all huffy. It was a prime example of why he avoided becoming involved with women...

they were irrational creatures. They asked for one thing when they really wanted another.

"A woman doesn't want to just *go ahead and do it*. She wants romance," Woody said.

"And you're such an expert?" Abel shot back. He could have kicked himself the minute the words were out of his mouth. "Sorry," he said.

"You're right, I'm no expert, but I do know that *let's go ahead and do it* won't do it. A woman wants more."

"This one doesn't." And the fact that she didn't ate at Abel like an ulcer in his stomach. It burned a little hotter each day.

He wanted to romance her. He'd like to wine and dine her, seduce her, and eventually confess that he loved her. If this was a traditional situation, that's just what he'd do. But this was anything but traditional.

"She just sees me as a sperm-mobile." And that was the crux of his dilemma—how did he get Hannah to see him as something more?

"I don't think you have a clue what Hannah sees in you. Look around this room. She went to a lot of trouble to romance you, and you still don't have a clue," Woody argued.

"Sure I do. She's told me straight out that she doesn't want a relationship. She just wants my baby. That was the deal."

A deal Abel regretted. His growing love for Hannah confused him and irritated him, as much as Hannah herself confused and irritated him.

And yet through all the confusion, through all the misery this situation was putting him through, there was the certainty that he loved her. That Hannah Harrington was the woman he was destined for.

"Things change," Woody said quietly.

A surge of hope flared in Abel's chest. "You're saying—"

"I'm not saying anything," Woody said quickly, cutting him off. "I'm going to forget today ever happened. I didn't come to your house, didn't see Hannah naked—"

"You saw Hannah naked?" For a moment he'd almost forgotten that pertinent fact.

Woody had seen Hannah naked and Abel hadn't. At least not yet. All Abel had seen of her body was what could be viewed through her sheer robe. It had been enough to make him wish Woody hadn't been present. It had been enough to make him want to toss her to the floor and...

"I didn't see or say anything. I wasn't ever here."

"Coward," Abel said, his anger gone. He felt bereft without it and wished he could figure out how to get it back.

"It's a wise man that gets when the getting's good." Woody started toward the door.

"But, what about—"

Woody turned around and simply said, "Figure it

out,'' just before he walked out the door and slammed it behind him.

Just as the front door slammed Hannah emerged from the bathroom, fully clothed and carrying a backpack.

''Do you want to explain just what was going on?'' Abel asked.

''No,'' was her monosyllabic, flat response. She too started for the front door, but Abel caught her by the shoulder and spun her around.

''You can't just leave.''

She squirmed. ''I can, too. I've changed my mind.''

''You wanted a baby, so you needed to have sex. You chase me, try to convince me to father your baby, and I finally stop running and you start. That's not logical.''

LOGIC?

The man wanted logic?

She could barely breathe under the weight of her longing for him. Barely think when he was near.

''I don't have to be logical,'' she said. Good thing because nothing about this entire situation was logical. And that was her fault. She'd tried to blackmail a man—a good man with vision—into doing something that went against his moral grain.

''I'm glad you realize it, because you definitely

are not logical.'' He took the backpack from her shoulder and tossed it to the ground.

"You just said that. You're repeating yourself." She didn't feel angry anymore. As a matter of fact, even her embarrassment had faded. All that was left was her need to be near this man.

The need she felt for Abel had nothing to do with babies, nothing to do with some property she owned, nothing to do with anything but Abel himself.

"I'm repeating myself because you're driving me crazy," he murmured.

And the fact that her need for Abel was growing so rapidly was the reason she had to go. She'd thought she could have a nice casual little tryst with him—scratch her itch and be done with it—but she realized that she couldn't. There was nothing casual about the way Abel made her feel.

"You can't change your mind," he said.

"I'm a woman and it's our prerogative to change our minds as frequently as we want. And I want to now." She picked up her bag. "Your weekend with Woody's kids worked. I don't want a baby anymore."

"Liar." He took another step.

"Oh, go away, Abel."

He reached out and caught her wrist. "It's my house."

She tried to pull from his grasp, but he held tight. "So let me go and I'll go away."

"No." He took her backpack for the second time.

"What are you doing?"

"Taking your bag." He tossed the backpack onto the couch. "And now that your hands are empty I'm going to fill them with something else."

"What?" The question was little more than a whisper, but try as she might, Hannah couldn't afford any more breath than that. Abel seemed to take up too much space in the room, too much oxygen. That was the only explanation for her sudden attack of breathlessness and weak knees.

"What?" She tried again.

"Me." He moved toward her, stopping right in front of her, yet not touching her. "I want you."

"You want the land," she said, needing to keep things in perspective. Despite her growing feelings for him, she needed to remember Abel's motivation was the property, not anything deeper.

"That too, but right now, I'm not thinking about land."

"What are you thinking about?" Her voice quivered. She heard it and hated it. It meant he was getting to her, and Hannah couldn't afford to let Abel Kennedy get to her.

"What I'm thinking about is a crazy blonde who turned my life upside down. She changed my perspective, and I've found I sort of like the view." He looked down at her and smiled. I like it a lot."

Before Hannah could say anything else, he kissed her.

8

ABEL HAD KISSED women before. He'd kissed a
number of women. Hell, he'd kissed Hannah before,
but he wasn't prepared for the sensation that twisted
in his gut as his lips met hers. He tried for control,
but was soon hungrily feasting on her lips. She
didn't seem to mind. In fact, she pressed against him,
molding her body to his. "Abel," she sighed. Just
his name. But it only made that twisty feeling intensify.

This woman, it seemed to cry. *This woman.*

This woman was meant for him. He'd give her
anything, do anything to convince her to stay, because if she went through with her plan and left
him…Abel wasn't sure what he'd do. He didn't
want to explore the possibilities because the mere
thought was agonizing.

Hannah was here now, and that's all he was going
to focus on. Just Hannah.

He reached up and ran his fingers through her
short hair. It was soft. So soft. Slowly, he traced her
jawline, down her neck and finally he tugged her
shirt out of her jeans and reached beneath it, cupping

her breast. Desire and need vibrated throughout his body.

This woman.

He broke their kiss, and breathless from the experience, said, "I need you to tell me that you want this. I won't have you saying I seduced you. I won't allow you to regret it later." His body throbbed, urging him to forget the talk and just satisfy his desire—the need for connection with *this woman* that had nothing at all to do with sex. "Say yes."

"Yes," she whispered, almost too soft for him to hear.

"Louder," he demanded, his hands still exploring her body, his senses reveling in the feel, the scent, the taste of her. "Do you want me?"

"I'm here aren't I?"

"Such romantic words, sweetheart." Gently he traced the line of her jaw again. So strong, yet beneath that strength there was vulnerability.

Hannah quivered again at that one small touch.

The force of her desire for Abel was overwhelming. And though part of the desire was physical, it went so much deeper than that. Hannah wanted to be held by him, wanted to hold him in return. She wanted to learn every little facet of who he was, and she wanted to share every little piece of herself with him.

She wanted so much, and would have to simply settle for such a small part of what she desired.

She reached out and placed her hand on his chest. She could feel his heart pounding. She laid her head against him and listened for a moment, letting the beat of it imprint itself on her body.

She'd cling to this night, to the memory of it, for the rest of her life. She wanted to remember his smell. The feel of his body, hot and hard against hers, his heart beating in her ear.

"Hannah, before we...Well, I want to know, could you..." He paused a moment, as if he was looking for the right word. "Is there a chance you could get pregnant tonight?"

"No," she whispered. "Tonight isn't about a baby."

She might not tell him everything tonight was, at least for her, but she'd be at least this honest. "It's about you, and me, and how much I want you."

"But—" he started.

She could sense his confusion. He wanted her to clarify what she said. She knew that, and yet, she'd been as honest as she could be. She'd told him this wasn't about the baby. She refused to tell him what exactly it was about—that for her, at least, it was about love.

Abel started to steer her toward the couch, but Hannah pulled back.

"Not there," she said. "Your room."

Without a word, he took her hand and guided her into his room. She'd been in here too, lighting candles. She'd even replaced his cotton sheets with satin ones. The mood was set, but Hannah realized as Abel backed her up against the bed, the mood was set long before she'd added her romantic touches to his room.

The mood had been set in her office, at that first meeting. When she'd met him deep down she'd instinctually known it could be like this—primal and passionate—with Abel.

Only with Abel.

Shadows flickered against the walls, but they were the only thing moving. Abel and Hannah stood at the edge of his large bed, locked in the moment.

"You're sure?" he softly asked again.

"Sure that I want you more than I've ever wanted anything before."

"Then you'll have me."

Abel began to unbutton her blouse as he studied the woman who'd fallen into his life like a sweet tornado, whirling everything together until he didn't know if he was coming or going. But right now, it didn't matter.

All that mattered was she was here with him and soon they would be joined as intimately as a man and woman could be joined.

He wanted her, and she wanted him. That was all she was going to concentrate on.

He pulled her blouse off and let it slip to the floor. "You're beautiful," he murmured as he grazed his hand over the smooth white silk bra he left in place. Hannah shivered against his touch.

"Tell me what you want," Abel said, his voice as soft as the caresses he stroked along Hannah's back. "Don't worry about right or wrong, just tell me what you want."

"You." Hannah was confused about so many things, but this one thing she was certain about. "I want you."

She didn't wait for Abel to take the lead. Instead she tilted her head up and touched his lips with her own. The feel of him was intoxicating, addictive even. She explored his mouth, but it wasn't enough. Needing more, she unbuttoned his shirt and stroked his bare skin. The light sprinkling of hair caused her palms to tingle, and the sensation quickly spread to the rest of her body.

Gently Abel lowered her onto the bed. The satin felt cool against her bare back, distinctly contrasting with the warmth of Abel pressed against her chest. She deepened the kiss, and he began to fumble with the button on her jeans.

He pulled away from her embrace, and stood as he tugged on the pant's waist. "I need to see you," he murmured. The jeans stuck on her hips. He gave another tug and…wham!

Satin was slippery, Hannah realized as she landed on the floor.

"Hannah," he said. "I'm so sorry. Are you okay?"

She nodded and started to giggle. The giggle grew until it was out-and-out laughter. "Satin sheets might be romantic, but I think cotton is safer."

Laughing himself, Abel offered her a hand and pulled her to her feet. "I think you may be right."

"I like your laugh," she said, pressed against his body. "That first day, in my office, I liked everything, but it was your laugh that really convinced me…"

"Convinced you, what?" he prompted.

"Convinced me that you were perfect." She ran her fingers lightly across his chest. Perfect. She hadn't known then how right she was.

"The perfect father candidate for your baby?"

That's not what she'd meant. What she'd felt for him, even then, was more than just a potential father for her baby. But Hannah let his interpretation stand, and simply nodded.

If he thought that, leaving him would be easier. She didn't want him to realize how deep her feelings ran. She didn't want him to feel responsible for those feelings.

She didn't want his pity.

Maybe their mishap should have killed the mood, but instead, Hannah found their laughter had only intensified her desire. Loving and laughter should go together she realized.

She smiled. "Shall we move back up to the bed, or stay where we are?"

"Honey, I'd make love to you anywhere. You deserve even more than a bed and satin sheets." He paused a moment and then added, with a grin, "But maybe we should finish undressing first. Satin is slippery." She started sliding her jeans from her body, but Abel stilled her hands and with agonizing slowness, drew the denim to the floor exposing her body inch by inch.

"You make me happy. Sometimes when I'm with you the happiness just takes my breath away," he murmured as he lifted her and placed her safely in the middle of the bed.

Hannah watched him. His eyes never left her as he slipped off his pants, then crawled onto the bed next to her.

He ran his finger slowly down the length of her body, then stopped and simply looked at her a moment, looked at every inch of her.

"I lied when I said you were beautiful, you're more. You dazzle me."

"You dazzle me as well."

He chuckled, a low rumble in his chest that she could feel vibrate through her own. "Men aren't dazzling."

"Most men aren't, but you are." She pulled him to her. She was done with talk. She'd said everything she could say. There was more, but those things she'd keep to herself.

And though she might not be willing to put all the things she felt into words, she wanted to show him. She needed to tell Abel how much she felt for him, if only in a physical way.

Greedily, needing to show him now, she began her assault. She explored his body, wanting to memorize every line and curve against the day that he wouldn't be there, when all she'd have left are her memories.

The thought spurred her on. If this was all she was going to have, then she was going to make the most of it.

She traced the length of his body, hungrily tasting and teasing and stroking. A feeling of power hit her as Abel groaned at her intimate embrace. There were so many things she couldn't control, couldn't do, but this one thing she could. She could give him pleasure.

Deliberately, Abel interrupted her and began his own journey of discovery. As his mouth touched her taut nipple, Hannah quivered with desire. More than desire, it was a pressure that needed to be abated. She needed him. She could feel that need blaze and intensify. It washed through her, a desperate yearning that had to be satisfied. She pressed her body to his, opening to his intimate touch.

"Now," she whispered and he obliged.

Their merging was wild. Hannah wasn't prepared for the force of her reaction. She wanted all Abel could give, and then she wanted more. She matched his every move, pulling him deeper within her, wanting more than just sex, but a merging. She wanted to be a part of this man. She wanted to brand the feel of him onto her very soul. Rise, fall, rise, fall. They found their rhythm. A primal beat as old as time, and yet because it was the two of them, it was something new and wonderful.

"Abel," she gasped as her climax took her to the edge of sanity and back. She sensed his release deep within her and felt empowered.

As he settled next to her, facing her, his arm loped over her, Hannah reached out and stroked his face. She loved this man. Regardless of his feelings, her own were stronger than ever.

Hannah loved Abel. And because of that love, she wanted nothing more than to make him happy. To give him everything he wanted.

She pressed against him, wishing they could stay like this forever. Wishing he wanted more from her than some land. But since that's what he wanted, she would see to it that he got it. She'd already seen a lawyer, already signed over the property that meant so much to him.

Again, she touched his face wishing she could tell him how much she loved him, but knowing she wouldn't. She'd give him his dream, and that would be enough.

It would have to be.

She waited, storing every sensation, every memory. She tried to memorize everything about him. Watching his every movement as he drifted off to sleep. And when he slept, she tiptoed from the bed and dressed. She pulled an envelope from her backpack and glanced at Abel's sleeping form. The realization hit her again—each time she acknowledged it, there was a stabbing pain in her heart. She loved him and he would never know. She'd burdened him enough by bribing him into fathering her child. She wouldn't burden him with her unwanted love.

She set the envelope on his nightstand and crept from the room.

Hannah loved Abel.

And because she loved him, using him to father her baby was out of the question.

Hannah couldn't sleep with Abel again—couldn't even see him again—because she loved him.

ABEL AWOKE IN the early morning light and found himself alone in bed. Hannah was gone. He didn't need to call out and see if she'd just gone to another room. He knew.

Hannah had gotten what she wanted and had left.

No. She hadn't gotten what she wanted.

He thought about last night. When he asked her

last night if she could get pregnant, she'd been clear about there being no chance at all. Why had she come to him if she couldn't get pregnant?

He turned on the lamp on the nightstand and spotted the envelope. Fingers trembling he opened it.

A Post-it note that simply said, *thank you,* was stuck to three deeds. Deeds to the property he and Woody needed. Deeds that had been signed over to him.

He held in his hand the reason he'd gotten into this situation. And realized the reason he'd stayed in the situation had just slipped through his fingers.

Kennedy Realty and the new subdivision had both been the center of his life for years. And that was sad. No business should be the sole reason for someone to exist. He'd told Hannah he didn't know if he could make something other than business his priority. He didn't know if he could be the kind of father his dad was.

And though he still might not be sure of his fathering skills, he knew that Kennedy Realty and his project with Woody had long since stopped being his priority. Hannah was.

Why had she left him the property? She'd said she couldn't get pregnant last night, that it wasn't about a baby.

"Tonight isn't about a baby. It's about you, and

me, and how much I want you.'' That's what she
said.

Why would Hannah make love to him if it wasn't
to have a baby? Better yet, why would she leave
him the deeds to the property—her bargaining
chip—if she was reasonably sure she wasn't pregnant?

Questions hammered at Abel, but their answers
remained elusive.

Only one question really now mattered, How he
was going to get Hannah back?

"I HAVE AN APPOINTMENT,'' Abel announced that
afternoon, ignoring the curious looks everyone, including the receptionist, was giving him.

"What's your wife's name?'' she asked.

The woman stared at him, and Abel simply
smiled. This wasn't the woman who'd showed him
into Hannah's office that first day. She was older,
and she appeared even more interested in his visit
than the first woman.

"No wife. No woman in my life at all at the moment.'' Though he was hoping to change that soon.
"*I* have an appointment. A. Kennedy.''

"Um, Mr. Kennedy,'' she whispered. "You do
realize that you scheduled an appointment with a
midwife? Ms. Harrington deals strictly with…well,
female health-care needs.''

"I assure you that I do indeed understand the situation." Unfortunately, he was the only one who did seem to understand.

"But..." The poor befuddled woman obviously couldn't come up with a thing to say, so she said nothing. "Here. Go fill this out and...well, I'll tell Hannah you're here."

"Thank you."

He glanced around the stomach-bulging, crowded office looking for a seat. The only vacancy was a middle cushion on the couch. "Pardon me, ladies. Do you mind if I sit down?"

"Of course not." A dark-haired woman scooted over, leaving Abel room to sit—albeit minimal room. He sank between the two women, clipboard with form on his lap and started to fill out the patient history section.

Name. Address. These two were easy enough to fill out, but the next question gave him pause.

Insurance. Abel sighed. There was no insurance this crazy plan would work. But if it didn't, he'd come up with something else.

He hadn't been looking for a relationship, and even if he was, he wouldn't have been looking for someone like Hannah. She was irrational, and had the craziest ideas. When he first met her he would have said that she could never come up with a crazier idea than having a stranger father her baby.

Now, he'd have to say her craziest idea was thinking she could live without him in her life, because Abel was utterly certain he couldn't live without her.

Previous conditions? He checked *heart.* Yep, he had a terrible heart condition and Hannah was the only health-care provider in the world who could cure it.

Once upon a time he thought he could dictate to his heart. Let it know when it was a convenient time to fall in love and start a family. This certainly wasn't convenient—he glanced around the room— overflowing with overflowing women. Not convenient at all. But his heart had its own timetable, it seemed.

A redhead next to him leaned as close as her enormous stomach would allow and whispered, "Do you mind us asking what you're doing here?"

He slipped his pencil behind his ear. Filling the stupid form out was just something to do, something to keep his mind off bigger things he had to do.

Welcoming a distraction, he said, "I have a medical problem that only Hannah Harrington, RN, CNM can fix."

"What's that?" the dark-haired woman asked.

"A broken heart." It felt as if everything was oozing out of the crack Hannah had left in there. He needed quick medical intervention before he simply lost everything.

"Oh." The redhead gave a little sigh. "Hannah's broke your heart and you're here to get her back?"

"Something like that. Though I'm not actually getting her back. If I ever do manage to get her, I won't be losing her and having to get her back."

Warming to his captive audience he continued, "You see, she just wanted me to father her baby, but I want more. Now I just have to convince her."

"How are you going to do that?"

"That's just it, I don't know. She walked out of my apartment early this morning and even left me the property."

"What property?" the redhead asked.

"The property I need. Property that she owned. I just have to explain to her that I need her more than any land."

He had come up with a plan for those lots—a plan that would only work if he could convince Hannah she needed him for more than his baby-making capabilities.

"Why do you suppose she gave you the property?" the redhead pressed.

"Because I had sex with her." Abel Kennedy, superstud, he thought morosely. "I was paid, just like a gigolo."

"That's one answer," the dark-haired woman said over him to the redhead, who simply grinned her answer—an answer Abel didn't understand.

"What's the other answer?" he demanded.

"She gave it to you because she loves you," the redhead said, a swoon in her voice that had nothing to do with being pregnant and everything to do with some romantic vision of love.

Abel was a closet romantic as well, something he'd never suspected until he met Hannah. Thinking about her made him think about flowers, and candies...and even diamond engagement rings. Yep, he was a romantic, all right.

"No, Hannah doesn't love me, at least not yet," he said. "I'm hoping with time I can convince her though." He wasn't just hoping, he was determined. He didn't give a flying fig about his business, didn't care about anything but her.

"Have you told her how you feel?" the dark-haired woman asked, gently rubbing her protruding stomach.

Would Hannah look like this, pregnant with his child? His body tightened at the thought. If he couldn't convince her to let him into her life, would he ever know? How was he going to tell her how he felt?

"Have you told her?" the dark-haired woman asked again, softer this time.

"No. She'd never see me again if she knew I was breaking our deal and falling in love with her. I just want her to let me into her life and gradually I'll show her. If I go too fast she might run."

"You might be surprised."

Abel was about to snort, but the door into the waiting room burst open and Hannah stood, arms on hips ready to fight. She was the most beautiful thing he'd ever seen.

She walked directly toward the couch. "What do you think you're doing?" Everyone in the room knew exactly who she was talking to.

9

ABEL WANTED TO jump up, scoop her into his arms, and carry her someplace he could have her all to himself. Instead, he forced a smile. "Filling out my information for your files."

"Abel, this isn't funny. This is my place of business. You can't just barge in here—"

"I didn't barge. I made an appointment." He tried to stand, but with a pregnant woman on either side, and no couch space left to lean on, he struggled. Both women ended up giving him a little shove, as if they knew exactly how he felt.

"I doubt you need a pregnancy test," his sweet little Hannah practically growled. If she knew how cute she looked, she'd growl even more and if he tried to tell her she might just do more than growl— his life could be in jeopardy.

"You're right," he said with a smile. "I don't need a pregnancy test. But I almost wish you did. Are you positive you don't, positive that you couldn't get pregnant last night?"

She blushed then, his Amazon warrior woman. "Let's take this to my office."

He followed her down the hall to the cry of "Go get her," from his couchmates. He turned and gave them both a thumb's-up sign, then trudged down the hall, ready for the biggest fight in his life.

As soon as they were ensconced in her office, she asked again, "Just what do you think you're doing?"

"Last I know I asked a question." Slowly, as if talking to someone hard of hearing, enunciating each word carefully, he said, "Are you sure last night couldn't result in a pregnancy?"

"Positive."

Part of Abel was relieved that she wasn't pregnant, that she still needed him. She couldn't get pregnant on her own, after all. And while she needed him, she'd have to see him and he had time to convince her that there was something more than land and babies going on here.

Part of him was crushed. He wanted to see Hannah swollen with his child. He wanted to have them both wrapped in his arms.

And part of him wanted to know why she made love to him if she knew she couldn't get pregnant. That was the biggest part.

"Abel, I told you last night that I couldn't get pregnant." There was a finality in her tone.

"Oh, you got your..." he paused and felt heat rush to his face.

"No. I didn't get my period," she said, saving

him from finding a word. "I know I'm not pregnant because I used protection. I used a diaphragm."

Everything he was prepared to hear, everything he planned to argue for...none of the scenarios he'd run over and over again in his head had included the idea of contraception.

"You what?" he asked, sure he'd heard her wrong.

"A diaphragm. A contraceptive device."

"I know what a diaphragm is, but what I want to know is why you used one. You wanted to get pregnant. I was to father your baby, then bow out of the picture, property in hand. Using a diaphragm doesn't make sense. So why did you use one?"

Hannah steeled her heart, and silenced all the things she was dying to say. "Listen, why I used it doesn't matter, that I'm not pregnant does. You fulfilled your part of the bargain, you had sex with me. It didn't work—"

"It didn't work because you made sure it wouldn't," he argued.

"Doesn't matter. You upheld our agreement and you've got your property. There's nothing more to say."

"You think so?"

"I know so," she said, but with all her heart she wished there was more to say. She wanted to tell him how she felt, but it wasn't part of their bargain. She wanted to reach out and touch him. She just wanted Abel. ''You have your property, so there's nothing left to say.''

''Well, I have more to say—a lot more. How about I start by saying I can't stop thinking about you?''

''That's only because you thought you still owed me a baby. You don't owe me anything. I changed my mind. You have your land and I can't have a baby with you. We're even.''

''Why?''

''Because I can't have your baby.''

''I fit all your requirements,'' he pointed out.

''Not any more. I revised my list.'' And Abel was missing one vital ingredient.

''So now what do you want?'' he said wearily.

She wanted to soothe him, wanted to hold him and apologize for everything she'd put him through. She wanted to, but couldn't.

''I want something you can't give me.''

''What?'' he pressed.

''You!'' she practically shouted. Then stopped short, realizing what she'd said.

''I want you,'' she repeated, softer now. ''I know it's stupid, but there it is. It's your fault, you know.''

''My fault?''

''Yeah. It's all your fault. I had it all planned. I just wanted to get pregnant. I had a list even. I didn't want to make love. Just a business agreement. And you ruined it.''

"And how on earth did I ruin that?" Abel asked softly.

"You made me fall in love with you." She rushed on before he could interrupt. "Oh, I know you didn't mean to do it, but it's still your fault. The way you said you didn't like kids, and yet watching you with Woody's brood, I realized that you did. You were great with them. You might not think you can be as good a dad as your father was, but I think someday, with the right person, you'll be even better. And there was Marigold."

"My dog?" he asked.

"That ugly little rat-dog. At first I laughed, seeing how you were with her. But then it hit me—you don't see her as a rat-dog. You think she's beautiful."

"Marigold is beautiful, smart and spunky."

"You're right, she is, but only because you love her. Your love turned that pseudo-rat into something precious. I'm jealous of her, you know."

Even as she said the words, Hannah realized how ridiculous it sounded. But the feeling was there and she was raw with the intensity of it.

"You don't have to be." He moved toward her, but Hannah didn't move away. She stood her ground. She was done running from her feelings— feelings that kept growing whether she was with Abel or hiding from him.

She loved him.

He didn't love her back, and that was okay. But she'd simply had to tell him, to release some of the pressure, or simply explode.

"I know. It's stupid, but there it is." She laughed, but there was no humor in the sound, but a bitterness that came from wanting what no list, no amount of planning could give her. "I just wanted you for sex, but instead I fell in love with you and now I can't have sex with you."

"Have I ever mentioned I think you're beautiful?" He was now directly in front of her, standing at the side of her desk.

"Maybe when we were having sex—"

"Making love," he interrupted and corrected her.

"But you were just saying that because you thought you had to."

She'd always wished she was tall and gorgeous. But now her greatest wish was that Abel could love her. Instead, she was short, a little too round, with blond spiky hair, and Abel didn't love her.

"Here." He set an envelope on her desk.

Hannah picked it up and immediately recognized it. "What's this?"

"The deeds to your lots."

"I can see that. What I mean is, why? We had a deal. And I honor my deals. They're yours." She thrust them at him.

Abel took the envelope and set it back on the desk. "I don't want them."

"Sure you do. You need them to finish your sub-division, so city council will let you close the area to through traffic and make it a real subdivision within the city."

If she couldn't have Abel's love, couldn't have his baby, she would at least have the knowledge that she'd given him something no one else could give him...she'd given him his dreams.

Those three parcels of land would allow him to build his subdivision. Abel and Woody would build it and she was sure it would be a success. And some-day when it was done, she'd drive through it and admire what the man she loved accomplished on his own.

Without her by his side. A side she so longed to be next to.

"The property doesn't matter now," he said.

"Of course it does. It's the most important thing in your life." She thrust the envelope at him again, but he didn't take it.

He simply shook his head. "No. Building that subdivision *was* my dream. It *was* the most impor-tant thing in my life. I wanted to make a difference. But now..."

"Now?"

"Now I realize that though building something that will change the city for the better is a good and noble dream, there's something bigger and better I want to accomplish. There's this certain woman who manages to fit the biggest heart I've ever seen in that small body. She's more important than the project I've spent two years working on. She's more important than my beautiful rat-dog. She's more important than breathing. As a matter of fact, without her in my life breathing seems rather pointless.''

The black hole that had consumed her heart, sucking in every good and wonderful thought she had and leaving just a void, suddenly eased a bit.

"You're just saying that," she whispered, not quite willing to trust what she'd heard.

"No. I know it doesn't sound like me. Let's face it, waxing poetic isn't my normal style, but I don't feel normal when I'm around you. You're one of the most incredible women I've ever met—inside and out." He wrapped his arms around her and led her to the sofa. He sat, pulling her onto his lap. "And I've missed you."

He kissed her then, pulling her against him, needing to rid all the barriers, both physical and mental, that stood between them. He tugged her shirt out of her waistband and his hand crept beneath it. He revelled in the feel of her.

"Abel, this is my office!"

That brought him back to his senses.

"Tonight then." He paused a moment, then asked, "Do you have your diaphragm in?"

"You don't wear them full-time. Only when

you're going to…'' She paused, again unsure what term to use.

"Make love. That's what we're going to do tonight, make love." He smiled. "I want you to throw the thing out."

She tried to tuck in her blouse, but her hands were trembling. "I've decided I don't want to have a baby on my own anymore."

"Good."

"Wait. Didn't you hear me? I don't want a baby."

"I heard you and that's not what you said. You don't want to have a baby *on your own*, and you're not going to." He paused and then added, "Because you're going to have it with me."

"What?"

"I said it once already. Weren't you listening? We didn't have sex. We made love. And making love with you wasn't some business agreement. It has nothing to do with land or babies, or even inner-city subdivisions. It was something more."

She'd heard him the first time, but she wasn't able to process his words. She backed up, needing to put distance between them.

He matched her every step, but she was getting dizzy, not just from the chase, but from the conversation. She didn't know what he wanted, didn't know what he meant. "What is it then? Stop talking in riddles."

"This is love."

She stopped cold, forgetting that she'd been trying to keep her distance. "You can't love me. You haven't known me long enough."

He stopped as well and smiled at her in that all-knowing, superconfident way of his that set her teeth on edge.

"Oh, I've known you long enough," he assured her softly. "And I've picked up a few of your habits as well."

"Such as?" she asked.

"I have a list." He reached in his back pocket and pulled out a rather mutilated piece of paper.

"What kind of list?" Hannah asked, eyeing the tattered sheet.

"A list of what I need in the woman I love." He thrust it across the desk.

"And what items are on your list?"

He didn't say a word, just held the paper out, waiting. Reluctantly, she took it. Her mind froze as she stared at what he'd written.

"As you can see, there's just one thing on my list. The woman I love has got to be you."

"Oh." *Hannah.* That's all that was written on the paper. Just Hannah.

He loved her?

"What time are you done at work?" he asked abruptly.

"Pardon?" *Hannah.* She stared at the paper, wondering if she stopped looking at it if the name would disappear.

"What time are you done here?"

"Sixish tonight."

"Wait here. I'll pick you up." It wasn't a request but an order.

She bristled. "Abel, we're not done talking about this." She clutched the piece of paper.

"You're right about that. But we'll finish tonight when you don't have an office full of pregnant women waiting for you."

She'd forgotten her patients. See what this man did to her? He was messing with her life, messing with her goals, messing with her mind. And mainly, he was messing with her heart.

"Tonight then."

He was almost out the door when he turned and said, "Hannah, I love you." He shut the door and Hannah leaned against the desk, hoping it would steady her, but wondering if she'd ever be steady again.

Abel Kennedy loved her.

"I love you, too," she said to the empty room, then laughed for the sheer joy of just saying the words.

"ABEL, IT'S ME." Hannah glanced at her patient. "I'm not at home." Duh. Of course he knew she wasn't at home.

"I don't have your cell phone number, so I'm just leaving a message here." Another duh statement. If he was listening to this he knew she was leaving him a message. Hannah sighed and continued, "I'm at the hospital delivering a baby. I don't know when I'll be home. I'll call you."

She put the phone back on the cradle and stared blankly into space. He loved her? The wonder of that statement had been playing over and over again in her head all afternoon. Abel Kennedy loved her?

She loved him, too.

It was a feeling that kept growing bigger and bigger.

She'd never been so excited, so scared, so...just *so* everything all at once in her life. She was mixed up and befuddled, but she was in love and it was wonderful.

"Hannah!" Kristin, a nurse on ob-gyn, called from Tammy's room. "She's almost there."

Hannah forced thoughts of Abel from her mind. She had a baby to deliver.

10

"YOU'RE AT TEN centimeters now, Tammy. This is where the fun begins," Hannah said.

"You mean we haven't been having fun until now?" Tammy panted.

"Well, there's fun and then there's fun." Hannah looked with concern at her patient. "Are you sure there's no one you want me to call?"

"If you're referring to the baby's father, no. This baby has no father. Just me."

"Lucky baby," Kristin said. "And I'm happy to volunteer my hand if you need to hold on to someone."

A contraction hit, and Tammy grimaced as she bit out a faint, "Thanks."

"It's time to push now," Hannah said.

"Push," Kristin said. "One, two, three, four—"

"Hannah?" It was Abel, calling her name from behind the curtain that was drawn around the bed.

"Abel, what are you doing here?" she hollered through the curtain. "This is a birthing room. You can't be in here."

"—five, six, seven, eight, nine, ten," Kristin finished.

Tammy flopped back against the bed.

"You're avoiding me. I scared you today by saying I loved you." He finally peeked beyond the curtain. "Oh. I'm so sorry," he cried and ducked back behind the curtain's shelter.

"I'm a little busy right now," Hannah gritted out from between her clenched teeth.

"He can come in," Tammy said midpant. "It's not like half your hospital staff hasn't been in here."

The fact that tonight was extremely busy on the ob-gyn floor was why Hannah had pulled the curtain, hoping to give them all a little privacy.

"I'll wait out in the waiting room," Abel said.

"Take a deep cleansing breath," Hannah said. "Here comes another one." She couldn't wonder what Abel was doing here. She had a patient to worry about.

"I said, come in." Tammy practically shouted. "It's not like everyone hasn't seen what I've got. You can let me squeeze your hand, since the baby's father is MIA. I'll squeeze and pretend, just for a moment, that he was a better man than he was."

"Oh, come on. Tammy could use the support," Hannah seconded.

"I'm Tammy, and this is my nurse, Kristin. It seems you know Hannah. So why don't you tell us who you are, and why you think she's avoiding you."

A contraction gripped the woman, Kristin moved over to the other side and Abel crept back around the curtain and took her hand.

The woman's grip was like a vise, but he bore it with stoicism. He shouldn't have come here.

"One, two, three, four, five, six, seven, eight, nine, ten," Kristin chanted.

"Tell me what you're here for," Tammy ordered Abel, as she fell back against the pillow.

Before he could answer, Hannah said, "I left you a message. I told you I had a patient."

Abel ignored Hannah's scolding and answered Tammy instead, "I came to talk to Hannah about something important. I thought she was avoiding me. I said something this afternoon I thought might have scared her."

"You said that before." Another contraction hit and Tammy moaned as she pushed.

"Hold her leg," Hannah barked.

Abel grabbed her leg and Kristin got the other one as she started chanting. "One, two, three, four, five…"

"Okay, ease off a bit, Tammy. We've got a head full of dark hair. This is going easier than I expected."

"Easy?" Tammy groaned. "This is easy?"

"Is it a boy or a girl?" Abel asked.

Tammy panted.

"It's a little hard to tell from this end," Hannah said.

"Oh." Abel held this stranger and for a moment imagined what it would be like when he and Hannah had their baby. *When*, not if.

"Okay, push again," Hannah said.

"Six, seven, eight, nine, ten," Kristin finished.

Tammy slumped against the pillow, panting. "What did you say this afternoon?" she asked Abel between pants.

"I told Hannah I loved her this afternoon, which was a big hurdle, but we still have two more things to take care of."

"What things?" Tammy pressed.

"You don't want to hear about that now," Hannah protested. "You've got more important things to worry about."

"Since it's obvious that the love bug isn't biting me and I'm flying solo, I'd say this was a totally appropriate time to be reminded that love still exists." Tammy smiled encouragingly at Abel.

"Well, I planned a romantic dinner where I would pop the question."

"You're going to ask Hannah to marry you?" Tammy asked.

"And—"

"Oh," Tammy groaned.

"Come on, Tammy. Push."

"One," Kristin started.

Tammy gripped Abel's hand and sat up, straining forward as she pushed.

"Two, three—"

"Here come the shoulders. Ease up now. Pant. Don't push the rest of this contraction."

Panting, Tammy flopped back on her pillow.

"What else?" she asked, her voice a breathless whisper.

"What?" Abel asked. He hadn't expected this much pain, this much exertion was involved with having a baby. There was no way in hell he was going to let Hannah go through this. They could remain childless—they'd have each other, after all. Or they'd adopt.

Whatever they did he wasn't letting Hannah suffer like this.

"You said you had two things to clear up," Tammy said. "Asking her to marry you and, what else?"

"Oh, I planned on asking her to have my baby." But he was reconsidering that part.

"You can't beat that deal," Tammy panted at Hannah.

Hannah glanced up over the sheet that covered Tammy's legs and smiled at him. "You're right, I can't."

"So what are you going to do?"

Head back beneath the sheet, Hannah said, "I'm going to tell you to push with the next contraction."

"I think she meant about me," Abel said.

"I don't have a clue what to do with you."

"Oh." That wasn't quite the response he'd wanted, but she hadn't said no. He'd hold on to that thought.

"Here comes another one," Tammy said.

"Push," Hannah said.

Tammy made a guttural groan as she pushed.

"One, two, three, four—" Kristin started.

"That's it, here we go," Hannah cried from beneath the drape. "It's a girl!"

A reassuring squall filled the room. "She's beautiful!" Hannah said. She handed the baby to the nurse who busied herself cleaning the baby up as Hannah silently went back to work beneath the drape on the mother.

The nurse handed Tammy her baby. Watching her face light up, Abel suddenly understood why women put themselves through the pain. He still didn't like the thought of Hannah suffering, but he looked at the baby nestled in her mother's arms, and he understood why Hannah had wanted a child of her own—of *their* own.

She wasn't going through this on her own. He'd be here, holding her, supporting her. Whether she wanted him or not.

"Thank you for staying with me," Tammy said.

"It was my pleasure and if you ever need anything, you just come see me. I feel like I have a vested interest in this little girl."

"Thanks," Tammy said, without looking up from her daughter. "She's so beautiful."

"Just like her mom," Abel said.

Suddenly he felt like an outsider. Unnecessary and superfluous. "Why don't I let you two finish here and I'll wait for you outside, Hannah."

"Fine," came her short response.

"Abel?" Tammy said.

"Hmm?"

"Would you like to hold the baby before you leave?" She looked at him and he just couldn't say no.

He held the baby close. Dark hair framed a perfectly angelic face. "She's absolutely perfect. Someone once told me that when you hold a new baby like this it's magic. They were right."

"Magic," Tammy whispered. "That about says it all."

Abel reluctantly handed the baby back to Tammy and hurried from the room. He'd been a pretty good substitute coach for her. He'd do even better when it was Hannah's turn, when she was having their baby.

The thought sustained him as he waited.

"So?" Hannah said as she walked into the lounge forty-five minutes later. He'd sat where he had a good view of the hall, just in case she tried to dodge him again.

Admittedly, his proposal hadn't been the most romantic, but he hoped—

"Abel?"

"Hannah." He jumped to his feet. "How are they?"

"Mom and baby are doing fine. You were a real help in there," her tone softened. "She says she's glad the father left, that he wasn't cut out to be a father, but it's been tough on her."

"That's my point exactly. You shouldn't have this baby on your own. With your hours, think how tough it would be. You need someone to help you. Someone to share the parenting."

"And you're volunteering?"

"Yes. But not just for that. I wanted to see you tonight and make things clear. You see, there's one more thing you need even more than a father for your baby."

"What's that?" she asked.

"You need me."

Hannah studied the man she loved. "You're right," she said.

She did need him. How she'd lived her whole life to this point without him was a mystery. He was a living, breathing, healthy, intelligent male with a sense of humor. But he was more than any of that.

He was the man she loved.

Hannah Harrington loved Abel Kennedy.

"I'm right about what?" he asked, as if he was afraid there was some punch line coming.

"I need you," she said. She needed to make him understand. "That's why I wore the diaphragm when we made love."

"Pardon?"

Hannah sighed. How to explain to Abel what she barely understood herself. "I wasn't supposed to need you. I was just supposed to need you to father my baby. And when I discovered I wanted you more than I wanted a baby, more than I wanted almost anything else, I decided that I couldn't go through with it."

"So you left me the property?"

She nodded. "You deserved it. But more than that, I love you. I wanted you to have your dream, even if I didn't have mine. I couldn't have mine because it had changed. When I went into this, all I could think about was having a baby, but after I got to know you, all I could think about was how much I needed you in my life."

"You've got me." He pulled her into his arms.

"What you said in the delivery room. You meant it?" she asked. Needing to hear him say the words.

"Yes. I love you." He paused a moment and asked, "Does this mean you'll do it? You'll marry me?"

She nodded, afraid to try and say anything, not even sure if she could with so many emotions clogging her throat.

"And my baby? Could I interest you in one, or maybe two?"

"I thought you didn't want kids," she reminded him. She already knew he did. He might have thought he didn't, but after what they'd gone through together she knew he would be a great father—the best.

"Actually, if you're my baby's mother the idea is downright appealing." He paused a moment. "So, want to get started?"

"On the wedding?" she asked.

"Well, that too, but I was thinking more along the lines of starting on that baby. Your biological clock and all." He made a ticking sound.

Hannah slugged him playfully. "You're saying the only reason you want me in bed is because of my biological clock?"

He nipped at her neck. "Well, there's that and then there's the fact I love you, and I'm ready, willing and able to serve."

"Oh, I like the sound of that. After all, when I started this I wanted a man who was ready, willing and able, and now, I find that what I really wanted was simply Abel."

"You've got him." He kissed her then. Hannah had thought their other kisses were special, but she'd been wrong. This one was more, so much more because he loved her. "I'm ready, willing and I'm Abel, so we can start anytime you say."

"Let's go home." Hannah walked out of the hospital and toward her new life. One she was ready and willing to accept as long as there was Abel at her side.

Epilogue

"MY WIFE," Abel said. The way he looked at her turned Hannah's insides to mush.

They were lying in a small cabin on their cruise ship. It barely had room for anything but the bed, but the bed was all they really needed.

They'd talked about big weddings, but they both wanted something more personal, more intimate. They'd have a big reception maybe later, but they didn't want to *wait* to plan a wedding. The need to be together was too great.

So with Rick covering for Hannah, and Abel hiring a friend to cover for him at the real estate office, they'd settled on getting married on a cruise ship a month after Abel's offbeat proposal.

"I have something for you," Hannah said, handing him a small box from her nightstand. "A wedding present, of sorts."

"Hmm, funny how that works. I have something for you as well." He leaned over and reached for a long flat package he'd tucked between the bed and the nightstand and handed it to her. "You first. Open it," he prompted.

Hannah tore through the plain brown packaging and found a pile of papers. On top were the deeds. "Abel, these are for you. You and Woody needed them in order for city council to close the through traffic."

"I found a way for you to keep your property, and to take care of the subdivision. Keep looking."

Another set of deeds were beneath them.

"Those papers are for some property about eight blocks from the subdivision. For your health center. Keep going."

Finally at the bottom of the pile were blueprints. "Remember before we left on the cruise we talked about what we wanted in our house?"

She nodded. Her hands trembled as she studied the plans.

"Well, if this meets your approval, ours will be the first house Woody starts in the subdivision. We're building on your property."

"Oh, Abel." She stared at the blueprints. Everything she'd talked about was there, from a first-floor laundry room to a huge office area for both of them to share. She checked that one special, and soon to be necessary, room was present.

"Um, you mentioned a present for me?" Abel asked, eyeing the box that sat next to her.

She laughed. He sounded just like a little kid on Christmas morning. "Well, I hope you like it, because I can't return it."

He tore through the festive paper, tore off the lid and simply stared at the contents.

"Does this mean what I think it means?"

She smiled as she looked at the book in his hands. "*Belinda Mae's New Baby*. I thought we should probably start our own collection of children's books. After all, I've heard you should start reading to babies even before they're born." She touched the blueprints. "Looks like we're going to need that nursery in about eight months. Do you think Woody can have it done by then?"

"I think that can be arranged. I can't think of a better present." He reached out and reverently touched her still flat stomach. That one small touch said more than any words ever could.

"And Abel, you remember what we did last night?"

He grinned. "Barely."

"Do you think we could try for a repeat performance?"

"You know, I'm always ready, willing and able to oblige."

"That's what I'm counting on," she said with a heart overflowing. "That's what I'm counting on."

Raising Cain

Holly Jacobs

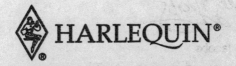

HARLEQUIN®

TORONTO • NEW YORK • LONDON
AMSTERDAM • PARIS • SYDNEY • HAMBURG
STOCKHOLM • ATHENS • TOKYO • MILAN • MADRID
PRAGUE • WARSAW • BUDAPEST • AUCKLAND

Dear Reader,

Each book is my favorite while I'm working on it. But as I finished writing Abel and Hannah's story, I realized I just couldn't let go. I knew that Woody Pembrooke needed his own special woman. I hope you'll agree that Lucy is just that woman. Plus, finding Woody his happily-ever-after meant that I had the chance to revisit the demon-spawn! And once again, I'll add a disclaimer that they have nothing to do with being modeled after my kids.

Writing this book also meant exploring the relationship between two women who weren't related by blood, but were sisters in every sense of the word. I grew up with brothers, but in school I made a friend. Someone who became so much more than a buddy. She is, in every way that matters, my sister. Hannah and Lucy have that type of relationship, one that is forged with memories, laughter and love—one I hope I've done justice to. One I hope that some of you recognize. Because as Woody and Lucy discover, family isn't just about blood, it's about the heart.

Enjoy!

Holly Jacobs

Holly Jacobs

Books by Holly Jacobs

HARLEQUIN DUETS
43B—I WAXED MY LEGS FOR *THIS?*

For Lori "Lucy" Lewis.
Who is more than a friend. She's the sister of my heart.

1

WELCOME HOME, Lucy Caldwell.

Well, not exactly home.

She sat in the mini-van and stared at the strange house. It was beautiful. Rough wood siding, stained a dark chestnut brown. Stonework emphasizing its unexpected angles which, instead of being jarring, lent the house an air of sophistication.

Yes, the house was beautiful, but it wasn't her home. It was just a way stop.

"Mom, are you going to just stand there all day?"

Shaken from her reverie, she looked over at her son and smiled. "No, of course not. I was just thinking. Come on, let's get out."

Cain climbed across the van and got out on her side.

"You know, you have a door on your side as well," she said for the millionth time.

Cain shifted from foot to foot, jostling a brown curl lose that spilled onto his forehead. "I gotta go."

Lucy brushed her son's unruly curl—the bane of his eight-year-old existence—back into place. "I know. We've got to go in and meet—"

"No. I gotta *go!*"

She noticed that particular eight-year-old-boy wiggle and knew precisely where Cain had to *go,* and what a small window of opportunity she had to get him there.

"Well, then, let's knock on the door and you can *go* inside." Lucy left her bags in the van, took Cain by the hand and marched resolutely up the front walk.

This was going to be the start of a great summer, she assured herself. She'd thought this move out, planned for every possibility.

She rang the bell and waited.

She rang again.

And again.

"Mom, I really gotta go." The rise in Cain's voice told her that window of opportunity was shrinking by the second.

Okay, maybe she hadn't planned for a bathroom emergency, and for no one being at the house to let them in.

"Cain, we just left Aunt Hannah's. Why didn't you go there?"

"'Cause I didn't have to go then."

The mystery of a little boy's bladder was going to have to be solved by someone wiser than Lucy. She gave his hand a quick squeeze, then opened the screen door and rapped on the door itself, praying maybe the bell was broken and someone would answer now.

"Mom!"

She pounded on the door.

"Cain, what do you expect me to do?"

No one was coming and, judging by the speed of Cain's jiggle, there wasn't enough time to toss him back in the car and return to Hannah's.

"There. See that big bush? Go behind it and...well, you know."

"You want me to do it outside? Cool!"

He raced behind the bush.

Lucy let the screen door bang shut. Great.

When she'd originally decided to come here, it had sounded like a life-altering, brilliant idea. Now, her kid was peeing in a bush, her life was reduced to what could fit in a Lumina Van, it was almost eight o'clock at night, and no one was home at Woody Pembrooke's house.

Though it was life-altering, maybe it hadn't been such a brilliant idea after all.

"Mom!" Cain shouted. "I did it. I peed on the bush. There was this dead leaf on the ground and I hit it the whole time. I never missed."

"Too bad you couldn't hit the toilet bowl that accurately," she teased. "Come on. We're going back to Aunt Hannah's."

"But I thought we were moving in."

"Since no one's home, it doesn't look as if we're moving anywhere but back into the car, and back to Aunt Hannah's house," she said, taking his hand

and turning toward the van. "We can't just stand out here all night."

"But, Mom, this is our new house and—"

Cain stopped midsentence and simply stared at the truck pulling in the driveway behind Lucy's van. Lucy couldn't help but follow suit.

"Oh, my God," was her semiaudible prayer as she stared at it in horror.

The noise coming from the truck was the first assault on her senses. It wasn't the truck itself that was loud. It was the people in it making all the noise. If someone had been playing music at the same decibel as the truck's passengers were screaming, they'd blow a speaker.

There was an army of children in that truck. Loud, wild children, if the gyrating hands and feet were any indication. But it was the man climbing out of the cab that totally floored her.

"He's a giant," Cain whispered. "Just like Jack and the Beanstalk."

Giant was an appropriate description. Topping six feet, by how much she wouldn't even venture to guess, he was built like a lumberjack—big and muscular. A lumberjack who looked like a bear, what with the scruffy beard on his face and wild dark hair on his head. But not a tame teddy bear. No he was a great big grizzly bear.

A sense of foreboding hit her. Like a grizzly, this man could be dangerous.

"Ms. Caldwell?" he asked, his deep, gravelly

voice only helping to reinforce the bearish resemblance. If bears talked, they'd sound like this man.

"Just Lucy, Mr. Pembrooke," she corrected him, hoping her voice didn't betray her nervousness. "When I left my old corporate life behind I left those sort of pretensions as well. I'm simply Lucy."

No Lucille Caldwell, vice president of marketing at Sky International here. Just plain, old Lucy, keeper of demon-spawn.

She eyed the four children who tumbled out of the truck and peeked at her from behind their father.

"I never had those pretensions you left behind. Woody is fine."

"Woody then." She was still trying to study the children. The two tallest boys were as dark as their father.

The next one down the line was fairer, sandy brown hair streaked blond under the summer sun. Hannah had said at first she thought this was another boy, but despite the short, hacked hair, Lucy would never have made that mistake. This little girl was going to be a beauty when she grew into her features. And the baby of the group had lighter hair than his brothers and dark eyes that were watching her warily.

She realized Woody was speaking. "I'm sorry we weren't here to meet you. I told Hannah we would be, but then Robbie had a bit of a problem."

"Oh?"

"Yeah. He seemed to think he was Evel Knievel. Only instead of a motorcycle he was riding a bike."

The second tallest boy was sporting a bandaged arm and Lucy had a sneaking sense of what had happened. "And instead of jumping trucks?"

"He decide to jump siblings. Unfortunately, Shane's arm was over his head as he lay under the ramp. And even more unfortunate, Robbie missed the ramp."

"I would have been fine if stupid had his arm folded on his chest like I told him. But no, does he listen?" the tallest boy, Robbie, said.

"I think you better stop right there, young man." The look Woody shot the boy should have been enough to silence him. It would be enough to silence Lucy.

But instead of keeping quiet, Robbie said, "And you make it sound worse than it was."

To Lucy he explained, "I made them all wear helmets. I had mine on too."

"Um." She wasn't sure what to say. "Good for you?"

"See, she understands." Robbie looked pleased.

Woody sighed. "Why don't we go inside, introduce the kids, and then get you two settled before we call it a night."

Woody's four children ran into the house, whose door obviously wasn't locked.

"Hey kid," Robbie cried to Cain, "come on."

Cain followed them slowly, glancing back at Lucy, as if to confirm she was indeed following him.

She gave him what she hoped was a reassuring smile, and wished someone was here to reassure her. She glanced at Woody Pembrooke's towering form walking next to her and felt she could use all the reassurance she could get.

"I left it open for you," he said.

Woody's form might be intimidating, but his voice was a deep, quiet rumble that seemed to reverberate in the center of her chest, like the vibrations of a plane passing overhead. It probably could be an intimidating voice if he wanted it to be, but at the moment it was pleasant.

Very pleasant.

Lucy couldn't help but wonder just what he'd look like without the beard. She suspected he'd look mighty good, what with his pronounced bone structure and come-hither eyes. Not that it mattered to her. She hadn't been in the market for a man in a long, long time. And she didn't plan to be in the market for some time to come. She had a son and a new business to think about. She didn't have time to waste on men.

But there was no harm in appreciating this man's masculine charms.

"You could have let yourself in," he added.

Pulling her thoughts away from rumbling voices and chiseled features, she said, "Oh, I never would have even thought to try. We were heading back to Hannah's.''

"Lucy, for the summer, or for as long as you're living here," there was an underlying sound of doubt in his voice, as if he didn't believe that *as long* would be very long at all, and certainly not an entire summer, "this is your house too. You're to come and go at will. While I'm at work, I expect you to watch the kids, but when I'm home, you're free to do whatever it is you normally do.''

Normally she'd come home from work, visit with Cain over a quiet evening meal, and then they would maybe play a game, or read a story before his bedtime.

The noise coming from inside told her that she wouldn't be getting a lot of quiet time in this house.

"Dad, Dad, guess what Cain did?" Robbie said as he turned to his father.

"What did Cain do?" Woody asked, his attention focused on the boy, as if, despite his annoyance with his son, whatever Robbie was about to say was the most important thing in the world.

"He peed on your hydrangea bush."

The tone in Robbie's voice suggested that peeing on Woody's hydrangea bush was a major transgression and that Robbie was waiting to see just what was going to happen.

Woody didn't say a word, just turned and looked questioningly at Lucy.

She could feel heat spill into her cheeks. "I'm so

sorry, but as I said, I didn't know the door was open and he had to go to the bathroom—''

"I really had to go," Cain said, trying to help. He wedged himself against Lucy, whether for comfort or support, she wasn't sure. She patted his shoulder, hoping to reassure him. He'd never had a man in his life, and she prayed Woody Pembrooke would go gently.

"And there was no way he was going to make it back to Hannah's so I let him…well, you know. I'm so sorry."

There was a glint of humor in Woody's bright green eyes. "No problem," with a cough that could have been an attempt to disguise a chortle of laughter. "Robbie's just anxious to get someone else in trouble so I'll forget how annoyed I am with him."

He turned to his oldest son. "It didn't work."

"I can see how it's going to be. The new kid can do anything. He's going to run the house and probably pee on everything. But me? One little jump—"

"Over your brothers and sister."

"—and you're all over me."

"And speaking of all over you, why don't you say good-night to our guests and head upstairs," Woody said.

"Good night," was Robbie's sullen response as he pounded up the stairs.

"Well, now you've met my oldest pride-and-joy. And you'll have no trouble telling who Shane is."

The white bandaged arm gave a brief wave.

"And this is Lynda."

The girl's curt nod was the only indication she'd heard her father. Her hair was much lighter than the boys' and had summer-streaked blond highlights.

"And last, but not least, Brandon."

The little boy looked more like his sister than his brothers. He ducked behind his father's very-duckable-form and called out a muffled, "Hi."

"And this is Cain," Lucy said. Cain inched a little closer. "He's excited to have new friends to play with."

She glanced at her son. Excited might not be the most apt description. Petrified might be better. But having kids to play with was one of the reasons she'd taken this summer job with Woody Pembrooke.

When her friend Hannah had suggested it, Lucy had jumped at the opportunity. Hannah's husband Abel worked with Woody. And she insisted that Lucy would love it here.

"I'm sure you'd like to get settled. Like Hannah told you, we have a small, furnished apartment over the garage. A few of our other sitters have lived there. It's not big. There's not a lot of privacy with two of you in it, I'm afraid."

"I'm sure it will be fine," she said. "It won't be for that long."

"Let me help you unpack the van."

"No, truly. We traveled light. There's not that

much. Cain and I've got it. You have the kids to get settled in here."

"Suit yourself," Woody said with a shrug.

"Thanks. I will."

WOODROW PEMBROOKE watched the woman, Lucy, make at least ten trips up and down the stairs on the outside of the garage that led to the small, efficient apartment.

He'd moved a single bed into the apartment for the boy, and roughed up a small screen to give them each a bit of privacy, but added to the double bed that was already there, it was going to be a tight fit for them. He should have worked out a more acceptable solution. But he hadn't had time. Hannah had called him just three days ago and asked if he was still looking for help.

He was.

Another nanny, baby-sitter, housekeeper—whatever you wanted to call her—had just quit two weeks ago and he couldn't find anyone else. He'd been filling the void with neighborhood teens, but he was running through teenaged sitters almost as rapidly as he'd run through adult nannies.

Woody didn't know this Lucy Caldwell, but he was desperate. Plus, Hannah vouched for her, and that was enough for him. Hannah loved his kids, despite the fact her husband called them demon-spawn. If she said spending a summer with Lucy would be good for them, then that was okay with Woody.

He smiled. His kids were rambunctious, but they were good kids. They'd been through a tough time since their mother had up and walked out on him...on them. That was enough to mess anyone up, especially a kid. And no matter how big they were getting, they were still just kids.

Robbie would turn thirteen in August. Woody was almost the father of a teenager. How had that happened? You'd think by the time a parent had a teen he'd know what he was doing, but Woody still felt unsure.

He worried about them. And this musical-chair-nanny stuff wasn't helping. Of course, the kids were the ones driving the sitters away.

But this new one—he watched her pulling a huge suitcase up the stairs—she was obviously stubborn. Maybe she was stubborn enough to last a while, at least until he could find someone else? With all the kids finally in school all day next year, finding someone permanent should be easier.

It couldn't be harder.

Lucy Caldwell.

He rolled her name around silently on his tongue. She was tall. That was one of the first things he'd noticed. Okay, so maybe he was man enough to notice her small but ample attributes first—but then he'd noticed how tall she was. Her height looked good on her. She didn't hunch over or slouch, like so many tall women did. Of course he still had her by about six inches.

Middrag up the stairs, she gave her head a toss, trying to clear her long, brown hair out of her face before she started tugging the suitcase again. There was a lot of power packed into that slim body.

Yes, maybe Lucy Caldwell would last a little longer than the rest.

As he watched her disappear into the small apartment over the garage, Woody found himself hoping so.

Lucy sank, exhausted, onto the bed.

When Sky International was bought out and merged with Edison Corporation, she'd had a brilliant idea. She'd take their severance package and do something new, something she'd always dreamed of doing.

She'd start her own business.

But before doing that, she'd spend the summer with her son. No work. No school. Just an entire summer of being together day in and day out.

Of course, as generous as the severance package was, and despite the fact she had savings, she couldn't take off the entire summer without pay and still have enough to get a business off the ground.

She still needed some income.

Hannah Harrington Kennedy, Lucy's foster sister and best friend, had suggested this job as nanny to her husband, Abel's, best friend's children.

It seemed serendipitous.

Cain would have other children in his life, and Lucy would get to spend the summer with him, still make money, and lay down the groundwork for her new business.

Why, Woody Pembrooke had even offered her an apartment.

She wanted to take her years of business experience and use them to start a consulting firm. She'd work with small businesses, giving them big business resources and advice. She had the whole summer to plan and prepare.

After all, how hard could taking care of Woody's four kids be? She'd handled Cain on her own all these years, and he was pretty independent. She was sure Woody's kids were as well.

"This is cool," said Cain. "We live in a garage."

"Over a garage," she corrected.

The apartment was tiny, but it was clean. And she'd be spending most of her days in the house, watching Woody's kids and being with Cain, so its smallness didn't matter.

"I can't wait to tell all my friends. Me and my mom live in a garage with the cars. Do you think Mr. Pembrooke would let me move my bed down next to the truck? I'd like to sleep next to a truck."

"Mr. Pembrooke might, but your mother won't. You're stuck up here with me, bucko." Cain saw this move as an adventure every bit as much as she did. But adventure or not, Cain was not sleeping next to a truck.

"Ah, Mom."

"Ah, Cain," she said, mimicking his whine.

She should tell him to go get a shower. But last year showers had suddenly become nightly battles, and she didn't have the energy to deal with it tonight. "Why don't you go put on your pajamas? It's almost bedtime."

"I thought since we shared a room, we'd share a bedtime."

The small apartment had one bedroom that barely held a twin and a double bed. She noted that Mr. Pembrooke, Woody, had been thoughtful enough to squeeze a small privacy screen between her side of the room and Cain's. Other than the bedroom there was a small kitchen/living/dining room. The only other area was the tiny bathroom. She could probably sit on the toilet and wash her hands at the same time, it was that compact.

It reminded her of the tree house she and Hannah had built when they were twelve. She smiled at the memory, then realized that Cain was still standing there, looking at her.

"Pajamas. Bedtime is still bedtime."

"Ah, Mom. First you won't let me sleep with the truck, now I have to go to bed at the same stupid time. I'm eight. I should stay up later."

"Sorry, Charlie."

"Yeah, sure." He stomped into the small bathroom and slammed the door.

"Just be glad I'm not making you take a shower tonight," she called.

"Hey, yeah!" His voice brightened. "Thanks, Mom."

There, problem solved.

Too bad she couldn't solve all life's problems by simply skipping a shower.

Stinking and happy wouldn't be such a bad way to go through life.

2

SOMETHING STUNK.

Lucy woke up with a start and started to gag.

"Mom, you farted." Cain sat up in bed and started to laugh as he pointed at her. "You say I get bad farts, but boy, Mom, that's the worst I've ever smelled. And I sat next to Bobby last year and thought his were the worst."

"I didn't," Lucy denied. "That's not me."

"I didn't do it neither." Cain pulled his blanket up over his nose. "But it's really gross."

"So what is that smell?"

Lucy buried her nose in the crook of her arm, hoping to block some of the scent, as she wandered through the small apartment looking for the source of the odor.

It was definitely strongest in the bedroom. And it seemed to be coming from the floor in the west corner. But there was nothing there.

"Why don't you get dressed while I go check the garage. Maybe there's something in there that smells."

"I'm getting dressed then I'm going outside. This really stinks."

"Okay."

She put on her robe and went downstairs into the garage. She turned in a circle, and tried to orient the garage to the apartment upstairs. There. That shelf. The closer she got to the shelf, the stronger the smell.

She scanned the shelves, but couldn't see anything that would cause such a pungent odor. There was only one place left to look.

There was a stepladder against the wall and she slid it over to the shelf, climbed up and peeked on the top shelf to see just what was rotten in Denmark.

"Oh, yuck."

Rotten was the appropriate word. There was a tray filled with about a dozen broken eggs—broken, rotten eggs.

Trying not to inhale too deeply, and yet not wanting to breath the sulfur smell through her mouth, Lucy carried the tray out of the garage, across the small space of yard that separated it from the house, and to the backdoor. She banged the door with her foot.

Woody answered, wearing sweats and a T-shirt.

"You're early. I don't leave for work until after nine."

"I wondered if you'd be so kind as to return these to your children."

Woody's nose wrinkled. "What is that?"

"*That* is the present left on top of one of your shelves in the garage, directly below a hole drilled into my floor…the floor of my bedroom. *That* is what I woke up to this morning."

"I'll kill them." He turned and bellowed, "Kids!"

He turned back to Lucy. "I'm so sorry. I know this doesn't look good. I know Abel's told you stories about my kids—Abel loves to tell stories—and I know you believe every one of them now. But I hope you'll at least give me time to find someone else before you pack up and leave."

As much as Lucy wanted to turn around, pack her bags, retrieve her son and leave this man and his demon-spawn children, Lucy Caldwell didn't quit. She didn't walk out on a job. And she certainly wasn't about to let four children drive her away.

"I'm not leaving," she said.

"You're not?" Before he could ask why, Robbie, Shane, Lynda and Brandon trooped into the kitchen, looking like soldiers on their way to a firing squad.

"You called, Woody?" Lynda asked.

"Don't call me Woody, call me Dad. And yes, I called. Would you like to explain this?" He nodded at the reeking tray of eggs.

"Breakfast?" Robbie asked.

Woody didn't say a word. He simply stared at the children.

"It was Shane's idea," Brandon said. "We baked the eggs on top of the garage for—"

"Two weeks," Lynda supplied.

"Two weeks?" Woody said weakly.

"Yeah. We knew that McGillicuty was on her way out," Robbie said. "And we knew the new sitter would stink, so we got ready."

"You're all grounded from playing video games for a week," Woody said.

"Whatever," Robbie said. The rest of the group simply took their punishment silently.

"And you owe Ms. Caldwell an apology."

"Sorry," four voices, sounding decidedly unsorry, said in unison.

"Fine. I'll accept your apology. But I think I'd better warn the four of you. I'm not like your other sitters. I'm here for the summer. I'm not leaving…at least not because you chase me out. I don't chase easily."

Lucy had always tried to chase after her dreams, and even four demon-spawn weren't going to make her turn away from this one. She was going to spend the summer here and she was going to enjoy every minute of it, even if it killed her.

"I'll let this one incident go unchallenged, but I warn you, next time, I shall seek revenge."

All four children simply stared at her a moment, and then, in unison, they started to laugh.

"Go get dressed," Woody said to the children. To Lucy he said, "Again, I'm sorry."

"Don't be. Just know that I meant what I said. If

your kids attack again, they're not getting away with it.''

"You wouldn't hurt them, would you?" He studied her. "I mean, I wouldn't let anyone hurt my kids.''

Woody's concern for his children, though they were demons, touched her and she smiled. "No. I won't hurt them, but I will convince them that it's safer to behave.''

He relaxed. "You know, I think you just might last longer than the rest have.''

"I'll last the entire summer. You just watch and see if I don't.''

"DAD'S GONE AT LAST," Robbie said an hour later.

There was a glimmer of something in Robbie's eyes as he made the proclamation. Whatever that *something* was made Lucy distinctly nervous. As she watched Woody's truck back out of the driveway it felt as if she'd lost her only ally.

"I guess he is," she said.

"So how many kids have you baby-sat before?" the boy asked, but all the children, even Cain, waited with their eyes glued to her, for her answer.

"None."

But she had handled a major corporation, she reminded herself. She'd delegated. She'd negotiated. And she'd handled Cain on her own for the last eight years. She could certainly handle the Pembrooke children.

"None?" Robbie asked. "You mean you never baby-sat anyone before? Not even when you were a kid?"

"No, I never baby-sat kids. I did baby-sit babies though. Hannah and I had a lot of babies around, but the only kid I've ever dealt with is Cain."

Irene, her foster mother, had taken care of babies while they waited to be cleared for adoption. So Lucy and Hannah had learned everything there was to know about babies. Just not so much about kids.

But as Cain had grown they'd entered the uncharted territory of childhood together. So far Lucy thought she'd done a good job. But nothing Cain had ever done could possibly have prepared her for the four children lined up in front of her.

"We'll go easy on you," Robbie promised.

"Yeah, easy on you," Shane echoed as the younger two nodded their agreement.

Easy.

The word did little to comfort her.

Lucy had handled a corporation, she reminded herself again. Handling four children and Cain couldn't be any more difficult. After all, this is what she wanted. Cain would be part of a family. He'd be surrounded by pseudo-siblings. And she'd be there to enjoy every minute of it.

And like the saying went, this was the first day of the rest of her summer. And she was going to get through it gloriously.

"Okay, what should we do today?" she asked the five children assembled before her.

None of them answered. Cain looked uncertain, and the other four just smiled a smile that didn't bode well for the rest of her first day as a babysitter.

"HOW DID YOUR first day go?" Woody asked at five-thirty that afternoon.

Lucy didn't answer. She couldn't. Talking would require energy and she didn't have any energy left.

She was sitting at the kitchen table, staring at the mug of coffee she had hoped would revive her. She didn't even have the energy to lift it to her lips.

"Lucy?" he asked.

"I'm fine," she said, more to remind herself than reassure Woody.

"And the kids? Are they fine, too?"

"They're all alive. Although it was a near thing." She rubbed her temple, but the soothing motion did nothing to ease the pounding in her head.

"What happened?" Woody tossed a battered briefcase on the table and slid into the chair across from her.

"I thought it was all under control. That was my first and biggest mistake," Lucy said. "I mean, Hannah had told me about pick-up parties, and I thought it sounded like a good idea. So I decided to head to the bargaining table. I offered the kids lunch anywhere they wanted if they would pick up the house with me. Nothing personal, Woody, but the house was a bit of a mess. More than a bit, actually.''

''It's hard to handle things when I'm between help. And it seems I've spent most of the last few years between help.''

''Well, they accepted the deal, and we cleaned. I thought baby-sitting was going to be easier than I imagined. See, the house looks better.''

Woody glanced around the kitchen. He lifted the lid to the cookie jar.

''Yep, we even cleaned out the cookie jar.''

Abel had clued her in on the kids' favorite place to hide unwanted food. The molding mass at the bottom had been gross, but it was gone now.

''So, the day went well?'' he asked.

He'd thought Lucy was tough yesterday when she lugged all her suitcases into the apartment, never slowing until the task was complete. He'd been even more impressed this morning when she'd laid down the law after the stinking-egg debacle. He'd had high hopes that this sitter would outlast the rest.

A sense of relief flooded his body. He'd been right to hire her even though Hannah had told him Lucy was more at home behind a desk than at home with kids. She looked exhausted, but she'd survived the first day.

''Oh, it seemed to be going well. I mean, right up until lunch. They asked for Playtime Pizza,'' she said, her voice devoid of emotion.

''Oh.'' Woody's heart sank. Playtime Pizza was

controlled chaos on its own, but when his kids were thrown into the mix, the control part vanished and all that was left was chaos. "How bad was it?"

"I've gone to Playtime Pizza with Cain before. I even know the song. But I've never attempted it with five kids." She massaged her temple again. "They asked us to leave."

"Why?"

"The kids took over the ball pit. They were bombing the other children who wanted to play."

She lifted her coffee mug halfway to her mouth, then let it sink back to the table, as if it was too much of an effort to raise it the rest of the way.

"So they asked you to leave?" Well, throwing soft plastic balls wasn't so bad. He'd feared it was something worse.

"Oh, not then. They just banned the children from the ball pit. It was when Pete Za, that costumed mascot of theirs, came out—that's when they asked us to leave." Lucy gave a delicate little shudder.

Woody's heart sank as he forced himself to ask, "What did they do?"

"They de-pizza'd him. They snuck up as he was leading the dance and unzipped the costume. And it turns out that the Pete Za costume is quite heavy and hot, so Pete just wears boxer shorts under it and, well, let's just say seeing an older man in his Happy Face boxers is a scary sight. I never heard such a mixture of laughter and screaming before. It was right after that the manager suggested we best be going. Uh, the children are banned for life.''

Another sitter was about to quit. Now Woody was the one who wanted to massage his temples. What was he going to do? He couldn't keep juggling the kids and work. The subdivision he was working on with Abel was going fast and furious, and it demanded so much personal attention. He needed to know the kids were cared for when he wasn't home.

''I'm so sorry,'' he apologized as he wondered what he could offer Lucy to convince her to stay on, at least until he found a replacement. ''I'll talk to them. It doesn't sound as if it was the best first day. But tomorrow will be better.''

''Oh, no. That was the good part. At least I got to sit down and drink a couple cups of coffee while they terrorized the restaurant. It was after we came home that things were bad.''

''It got worse than stripping a giant pizza slice?'' Woody began mentally running through friends and family he might be able to beg or bribe into helping him out.

The problem was, he'd begged and bribed all of them in the past, so it was getting harder, and more expensive as time went on.

''Well, when Lynda plugged up the upstairs toilet and it overflowed into the kitchen, I thought it was as bad as it could get. But you see, they used that as a diversion. While I was de-stopping it, they asked if they could play camping outside. So I said yeah, thinking if they were outside, I could clean up in here. They took some old blankets and were making tents over the clothesline. I checked. It appeared to be a harmless pastime, and I foolishly thought I'd finally conquered the demon-spawn.''

She made no apologies this time for using Abel's pet phrase for the kids, and Woody didn't protest.

Lucy looked exhausted and utterly drained.

Again, she raised her coffee mug, and this time it made it to her lips and she took a healthy swig before she continued, ''But while I was cleaning up the water from the bathroom floor and downstairs in the kitchen—there's a water spot on the ceiling, by the way—they decided they needed a campfire. So they got a brick from the garage, you know the kind with the two holes in it?''

''A cinder block?'' Woody asked. When she nodded, he prodded her, ''And?''

''And they started a fire in it. Well, not a blazing sort of fire, but more a smoldering mass of wet leaves. Lots of smoke, no flames. When I finished cleaning up the water, I went out back to check on them and they had Cain tied up to the clothesline pole and smoke pouring out the brick in front of him. Only Robbie didn't want me to see the smoke, so he sat on it.''

''He sat on it?''

''Yep. Luckily, since there weren't any flames, he didn't get hurt. And there I was, toilet water splashed all over me, Cain tied up to a pole, Robbie sitting on a smoking brick, and the other three were just staring at me.''

Woody kicked back his chair and stood. ''Where are they now?''

''In their rooms, sitting on their beds and waiting for you. I stuck Cain in your room. I hope you don't mind.''

Woody stared at Lucy. ''You sent them to their rooms and they listened?''

She blushed, her fair skin turned a rosy pink. ''Ah, sort of.''

''What did you do?''

''I told them I'd called the fire inspector and he was coming to investigate the fire. I told him that there were stiff charges for arson. Then I told them that I'd lie for them—cover so they weren't charged with arson—but only if I didn't hear or see them for the next hour until you came home. I sent them to their rooms and they're hiding out there. And I know I lied, and I know I shouldn't scare kids, but they're not really children at all. Abel was right. They're demons.''

Woody sank back in his chair. Lucy had them contained, at least for the time being. He could use these few quiet moments to decide what to do now.

He looked at the dark smudges under her eyes and suddenly wanted to reach out and touch her. He wanted to wipe those smudges away and see her smile.

But he didn't. He simply asked, "So you're turning in your resignation?"

Her coffee mug thumped onto the table. "What makes you think I'm resigning?"

"I mean after today..." He left the sentence hanging.

A day like today had wiped out more than one of his other sitters—women who were used to kids, who knew all about them. If those women couldn't handle his children, why had he ever thought Lucy, an ex-corporate executive, could?

"I'm not quitting. I told you that before. I'm here for the summer. After today I'm more determined than ever to stick this out. When I leave it will be because you've fired me, or summer is over and I'm ready to leave. It will not be because your children have scared me off. I don't scare easily. As a matter fact, I don't scare at all."

Woody simply stared at her with admiration. He admitted his children were a handful. But they were good kids. It's just none of the other sitters had stuck around long enough to discover that for themselves.

"You're staying?" he asked, unsure he'd heard her right. He'd thought she was tough last night, he was more convinced of her toughness this morning with the eggs, but this woman was stronger than he'd given her credit for.

Lucy nodded. "Yes, I'm staying."

THIS CORPORATE MERGER had given Lucy a chance to live out her dream. She was going to spend her summer with Cain, move back to Erie where she had a family and a best friend wrapped up in Hannah.

Lucy wanted to be here when her foster sister gave birth. She wanted to hold this niece or nephew, and be available to help. She wanted to plan her new business. And she was going to do all that and more, doggone it. Four demon-spawned children weren't going to scare her away.

Okay, maybe terrorizing the kids into behaving wasn't the best plan, but she'd do better tomorrow. She was a good mother and she'd learn to be a good baby-sitter.

That is, she'd do better tomorrow if Woody didn't fire her. He hadn't said another word. He was simply staring at her.

Lucy twirled the mug around on the table. "Mr. Pembrooke, I said your kids weren't going to scare me away, but after today's events, if you'd be more comfortable having someone else look after them, I understand."

She had enough money from her severance package to still take the summer off. She'd just have to scale back on her ideas for her business.

Though working for Woody Pembrooke had been more than just a way to save money while she spent her summer with her son. It had meant giving Cain a taste of what a real family was. What it meant to have siblings.

Growing up with Hannah in Irene Cahill's care

had been the best time of Lucy's life. They might not have been related by blood, but they'd been a family. Irene always said families weren't made with blood. They were made with the heart.

Lucy had hoped that the Pembrookes could give Cain that same experience. Family. Siblings. She'd tried to give her son everything, but this one thing hadn't been in her power to grant, until now.

"Really, I would understand," she said with a sigh.

"Lady, I wouldn't let you leave if you wanted to. You survived the first day. That's more than a few sitters have done. You not only survived, you triumphed. I think I love you."

He grinned then beneath his big bush beard.

"You've got a very nice smile, at least what I can see of it under all that hair."

She realized what she'd said, and wondered where it came from. What did she care if Woody Pembrooke hid beneath a mountain of hair?

"I'm so sorry," she said hastily. "That was totally uncalled for."

"You don't like the beard?" he asked.

"It doesn't matter if I like it. It's your face, your hair. And they're your kids," she felt it was wise to remind him. "What are you going to do about their pyromaniac tendencies?"

"Nothing," he said with a grin.

"What do you mean, nothing?" She'd been

counting on Woody to take care of the little fire incident.

Nothing?

He was going to desert her and leave her without an ally against the demon-spawn?

"Sounds like you have things under control. Maybe that's where I went wrong with the rest of the sitters. Maybe if I let you and the kids establish your own…"

"War?" she supplied.

"Relationship," he corrected. "Maybe things will be easier for you."

"So you're saying I'm on my own?" she asked.

"Yeah."

She looked thoughtfully into her mug. What did she know about kids? About demon-spawn?

Nothing. That's what she knew. But she had survived the first day. The kids were all in their bedrooms, a little singed, but none-the-worse for wear. Maybe Woody was right to allow her to come to terms with his kids.

"You'll support my decisions?" she asked.

"Yeah."

"Well, okay then." She took a long drink of her coffee. She was going to need all the fortification she could get if she was going to be waging this battle on her own.

"What's that smell?" Woody asked.

"Oh, since I had an hour of peace and quiet, I started dinner."

"You cooked?" His delight was obvious.

He really had a nice smile, Lucy thought. She wondered why he buried it beneath all that fuzz, but cut the thought off. What Woody Pembrooke covered himself with was his business, not hers.

"It's nothing fancy," she said. "I found some chicken in the freezer and made some soup. If you'd like, I could go shopping for you. You could use a real stock-up. Like Old Mother Hubbard your cupboards are looking a little bare."

"How would you like a raise?" he asked suddenly, a gentle teasing in his voice.

Despite her bone-deep weariness, Lucy grinned. "It's only been a day."

"But you not only terrorized the kids and you cooked, but you've offered to shop. That deserves a raise. A big one." Woody laughed then. The sound was more appealing than his speaking voice. Deep, rich and infective, Lucy couldn't help but laugh right along with him.

"Let's just see if I live through tomorrow," she said.

"Lady, I have no doubt you'll live."

THAT NIGHT, after Lucy had taken Cain and crossed the driveway to her apartment over the garage, Woody tucked in Brandon.

"So what did you think of Lucy?" he asked his youngest son.

The little boy yawned and grinned. "She's nice.

She didn't even scream when Robbie showed her the snake.''

"Snake?" Woody had heard about the de-pizzaing and the fire, but he hadn't heard about the snake.

"Yeah. It was only a little red-belly racer. He put it in a box and showed it to her and she never even screamed. Mrs. Wagner screamed real loud when we showed her one. Lucy just picked it up and put it out in the yard. She's not afraid like most girls."

"Lynda's a girl and she's not afraid of snakes."

"Lynda's not a girl, she's a sister. And all the other baby-sitters were afraid of snakes."

"Well, that makes Lucy special."

Special. Lucy Caldwell was that.

It took a special lady to handle his kids, and she'd done more than handle it today…she'd even picked up a snake. His admiration grew, which he hadn't thought possible.

"Now go to sleep, and no snakes for Lucy tomorrow." Woody kissed his youngest son and turned off the light as he left the room.

"No rotten eggs, or fires either," he added for good measure just before he shut the door.

Snake, huh? She hadn't told him about the snake.

He ran his hand over his beard. Lucy said she thought he had a nice smile hidden behind his beard. It had been a long time since he'd been clean-shaven.

Growing a beard meant he didn't have to shave

in the morning, and not shaving meant one less chore. Trying to get the kids and himself up and off every morning meant he needed to take all the short-cuts he could.

And yet, it would be nice to be clean-shaven now that the weather was warmer. His beard was thick and hot during the summer. But comfort would be the only reason he'd shave.

It wasn't that he was thinking about shaving just because Lucy had suggested it. He wasn't trying to impress his newest sitter. He was done trying to impress women. He learned his lesson when Ashley, his ex-wife, had left. And after all the sitters he'd gone through in the last few years, he knew that women didn't tend to stick around when there were four rambunctious kids to deal with.

No, he wouldn't be trying to impress Lucy by shaving.

But she'd impressed him. She'd handled every-thing the kids had dished out. She hadn't run screaming from snakes, or de-panted pizzas, or over-flowing toilets, or fires. No, she'd just dealt with it and then got on with whatever needed done. She'd got through the first day without threatening to quit.

He really did like and admire this woman.

Woody went to tuck in Lynda and then he was having a long talk with his oldest sons. Maybe he could head off the worst of their plans for tomorrow.

3

"I'M GOING TO BE at the site all day. If you need me, don't even try the office, just call my cell phone," Woody said the next morning.

Lucy looked up from loading the dishes into the dishwasher. "You shaved."

Woody rubbed his bare chin. "Do you like it?"

She studied the face he'd kept hidden behind his bushy beard. Her first thought was *yummy*.

Woody's face was all hard angles and weathered skin. Without the beard the impression of a grizzly bear, or lumberjack even, faded. What was left was a chiseled face that a camera would love.

Woody Pembrooke was hot.

Just looking at him was enough to send her temperature rising.

Darn.

The last thing Lucy needed now was a surge of hormones.

"So? What do you think?" he asked.

"It looks okay," she said, striving to sound blasé. "I mean, it's going to take some getting used to, but you won't scare any babies."

No, he might make their mamas drool, but he wouldn't scare the babies.

He stared at her a moment. Lucy wondered what he was looking for. Whatever it was, he simply nodded, and grinned again. "Maybe scaring children wouldn't be such a bad thing. I tried to put the fear of God into mine, so maybe you'll have a better day than yesterday."

"I don't think they fear anything. Not you, not me, not even divine retribution."

"You didn't tell me about the snake yesterday."

Hannah shrugged, and turned back to loading the dishwasher. Concentrating on cleaning was easier than staring at Woody Pembrooke's too-good-looking-for-comfort face.

"With everything else that happened, that was a small thing. Hannah and I used to catch snakes, toads, salamanders, whatever we could get our hands on, all the time. Actually those are the kind of things I want to do with the kids this summer. Reptiles I can deal with. It's exposed boxer shorts and fires that make me nervous."

He stepped closer. She didn't have to be looking at him to realize he was within touching range. She zealously scrubbed dried-on cereal out of a bowl and ignored his proximity.

"Well, I tried to head off most of the trouble," he said.

She swore she could feel his breath on her neck.

"Thanks," she managed to say.

"So what are you all going to do today?"

She turned around and there he was, right next to her. "Uh," what was the question? All she could see was Woody's very nice-looking chin.

No, she wasn't thinking about hairless, sexy chins, she was thinking about kids.

Demon-spawn.

"Oh, the kids. Well, I'm going to play it by ear and see what happens. Hannah said she might come over."

Woody smiled at the mention of Hannah's name. "She's got the kids wrapped around her little finger, so maybe it will be a better day."

"Maybe." But Lucy didn't feel very confident. If Woody's de-haired chin was any indication, today could be even worse than yesterday.

At least yesterday she was just dealing with demon-spawn. Looking at Woody's exposed chin meant she had to deal with the demon of lust, as well. And lusting after Woody Pembrooke was not on her list of things to do this summer.

"Where are the kids now?" he asked.

Kids.

She had to start thinking about the kids and stop thinking about how hot their father was.

"I'm not sure," she said. "Robbie let us in and then Cain ran upstairs with him to the boys' room. That's the last I saw of him, or them. I figured you were still here so they weren't going to try anything."

"Why don't I just go check on them when I say goodbye," he said with a smile.

Nuts. Without the beard, she had an unimpeded view of his stunningly spectacular smile.

"Thanks," she managed, hoping he didn't notice how he was affecting her.

"Anytime. And don't forget, call me if you need me. I'm heading out after I say goodbye to the kids."

Need him?

No way. Lucy didn't need any man.

She was an independent, stands-on-her-own-two-feet kind of woman.

She breathed a sigh of relief as he left the kitchen. She wasn't about to call him. If she talked to him on the phone she'd end up thinking about his attractive chin and there was no way she wanted to think about that.

She finished tidying up the kitchen and poured herself a fortifying cup of coffee when she heard his truck pull out of the driveway.

There. He was gone. Now she could get on with the rest of her day and not have to worry about his de-haired face interrupting her thoughts.

The kids were still quiet. Maybe Woody had scared them into behaving better.

Minutes later, as if on cue, a black Saturn pulled in the driveway. Hannah Harrington Kennedy got out and waddled into the kitchen without knocking.

"You're looking..." Lucy let the sentence die off,

searching for the right word to describe her friend. She'd just seen her the day before yesterday, but Hannah looked even bigger, if that was possible.

"Is fat the word you're looking for?" Hannah asked as she sank into the chair with a gusty sigh.

"No. Pregnant. But that wasn't what I was going to say either. You're glowing."

There was an aura of happiness that surrounded Hannah. Lucy's friend had wanted a baby for so long—just a baby. But now she was getting a baby and had a husband to boot. Husbands and babies looked good on Lucy's dearest friend.

"That's not glowing," Hannah said, wiping at her brow with her sleeve. "That's sweat. This baby is like a furnace. I swear I experience the world ten degrees hotter than anyone else."

"It won't be long now," Lucy tried to commiserate. She remembered those last days of her pregnancy with Cain. Anticipation warred with bone-deep exhaustion and a healthy dose of terror. "Can I get you something to drink?"

"How about some juice?"

As Lucy got up and got the glass, Hannah said, "What is that note on the cupboard?"

"It's just a Post-it note. It says, Put your dirty dishes in the dishwasher."

"You're leaving the kids memos?" Hannah laughed. "I think we got you out of that corporate office just in time."

"Well, you should have seen the sink this morning. It was overflowing, and the dishwasher was empty. Like it would have hurt any of them to stick their dishes in the dishwasher instead of the sink?''

"Only you, Luce."

Lucy set a glass of juice in front of Hannah and slid into her seat. "Well, just because they're demons, doesn't mean they can't be clean demons."

Hannah rubbed her back.

"How are you feeling? We didn't really get to talk at your house the other day."

"This baby can't come soon enough. And as much as I feel like a walking, sweating blimp, that's not the problem. It's Abel. He's driving me insane. He's hovering. Calling me every hour asking me if it's time yet. And he won't let me lift a finger and do anything. At least when I was working, I had that, but now that the new midwife has started at the office, I don't even have work for a distraction. That's why I'm here. Distract me."

Hannah was a nurse midwife at Stephanson and Associates Obstetrics. Up until now she'd been the only associate, but with her pregnancy they'd hired a new midwife to pick up the slack until Hannah was ready to return to the office, and then to add to the patient base once she was back.

Lucy smiled. Hannah wanted distracted? "I can call the kids down. They'll distract you all right."

"Abel says it's best to let sleeping dogs lie, so we'll wait for them to discover I'm here on their own. Speaking of distracting kids, how was yesterday?''

Lucy shuddered at the memory. "So, what part do you want to hear first? There's the naked pizza slice, the butt on the smoking brick part, or the snake part.''

"Uh, I think I've got the idea, so you better stop. Nightmares aren't good for the baby.''

Lucy took a sip of her coffee. "Despite what I told Woody, I don't know if I'm cut out for this, Hannah.''

"It's just for the summer. It's not as if you signed on for life. You handled an international corporation, surely you can handle four kids.''

"Five if you count Cain,'' Lucy corrected her. She wanted credit for every single child she was responsible for.

Five?

What on earth had she been thinking? Hannah was the one who had always dreamed of being a mother. Lucy was more than content with just Cain.

One child. That was so much easier than five.

"And I'm not sure we can count Woody's bunch as kids,'' she added. "Abel was right, they're demon-spawn.''

Hannah laughed. "They're just energetic. You've got to find some way to channel that energy.''

"Any suggestions?'' She'd take any help she could get.

"I brought you this.'' Hannah opened up her

purse, pulled out a slightly tattered book and handed it to Lucy.

Lucy fingered the well-loved book. "*The Trouble With Harry*. I remember the first time Irene read us this."

"She started it your first night with us."

"Remember when we tried to build our own tree house?"

"It collapsed."

Lucy laughed. "We were planning to spend the night out there, too. Thank goodness it collapsed before we had a chance to."

"I thought you might want to read it to the kids. Remember how Julia couldn't stand Harry at first? They ended up being best friends. And I thought, as you read it, you might remember that sometimes if you look close enough, you'll find something wonderful you never expected to find. That's what happened to Julia when she got to know Harry. She found a friend."

Something wonderful?

When she'd taken the job, Lucy had hoped that's just what she'd find here at the Pembrookes'.

Now?

She just hoped she survived.

AFTER HANNAH LEFT and lunch was finished, Lucy pulled out the book. "I thought we'd start a tradition. After lunch everyday, I'll read you a chapter of a book."

If the kids were sitting and listening to a book, they couldn't get into any trouble, could they? It was a brilliant plan. And if it worked, Lucy would owe Hannah big time.

She picked the book up off the counter and led the kids into the living room. "When Hannah came over today, she brought one of our favorite books. Irene used to read it to us."

"It's old," Lynda said.

"Not old, ancient," Robbie corrected. "I mean, if it was around when you were a kid, then it's too old to read it to us. And, I'm too old to be read to anyway. I'm almost thirteen. I can read books by myself any time I want."

Shane waved his bandaged arm around, trying to get Lucy's attention.

"What Shane?"

"I'm too old too, and if you read that book when you were little, then it's way too old to be any good."

"Hey, I'm not that old. This is not optional, it's mandatory. So, everyone find a seat," Hannah said as she sat on the middle of the couch.

Lynda and Brandon sat next to her, while the three bigger boys sat on the floor around her.

"Uh, Mom?" Cain said. There was that devilish gleam in his eye that said he had something up his sleeve.

"Yes?" Lucy asked, waiting.

"You turned twenty-eight on your last birthday. Twenty-eight is old. Real old."

"Twenty-eight," the other four said in hushed and awed tones.

"Twenty-eight isn't ancient," Lucy protested.

Five sets of eyes looked at her with dubious disbelief.

"It's not old," she said with more force.

"Well, my dad is even older than your mom," Shane said. "He turned thirty-three his last birthday."

"Wow, how did you get all the candles on the cake?" Cain asked.

"We didn't. He said after you turn thirty you just use one candle," Lynda said, and added with a giggle, "all we had was pink."

Cain nodded, as if he saw the wisdom in this practice and grinned at the pink candle part. Every boy knew pink candles were only for girls.

Sensing his thought, and not liking to stereotype anything, even colors, Lucy said, "And boys can like pink."

Again, five sets of eyes looked at her with disbelief. "Well, they can."

Before they could argue, she hastily added, "Now, let's get to the story. The very good, not that old, story."

"Fine, we'll try it, but we're not going to like it," Robbie warned.

"The Trouble With Harry, by H. J. Fuhrmann,"

Lucy read. "*Julia Estella Trenton groaned. Every year the teachers put the students in alphabetical order for the first few weeks of school. They said it was easier to learn the kids names that way. And every year Julia Estella Trenton had to sit next to Harry Troutman. It wasn't fair, it just wasn't fair, she thought as she angrily marched to the desk the teacher had pointed to. She knew what was coming next and it just wasn't fair. 'Harriet Troutman?' Mrs. Ahearn called.*"

"Girls? This story is about girls?" Shane asked, his distress evident in his tone.

"What's wrong with girls?" Lynda demanded.

"Girls are sissies. They play with paper dolls and have tea parties. They don't do anything fun," Robbie said, and the rest of the boys agreed quite vocally.

"But," Lucy interrupted, "Harry isn't a sissy girl, not by a long stretch of the imagination. And she's got a brother."

"I don't want to read some book about a girl," Robbie insisted.

"Yeah," Shane said.

Cain and Brandon sat silently, neither looking pleased at the prospect.

"Well, I'm a girl, and I'm not a sissy," Lynda said. "Girls can do anything boys can do. Right, Lucy?"

"They can't be a father," Robbie said before Lucy could answer.

"It's not so much mother or father, people are parents, and boys or girls can both do that," she said, proud that she'd come up with an answer.

"Yeah? Well, girls can't play professional sports," Robbie said, in a mocking tone.

Professional sports? How had they jumped from parenting to professional sports? And why on earth had she listened to Hannah? Lucy sensed that their quiet reading time was about to erupt into a brawl.

"There's the WMBA," she offered. "It's professional, and a sport, and played by women."

"How about football?" Shane asked. "Girls don't play professional football."

"Girls are too smart to play football. Who wants people hitting you?" Lynda said.

"It's 'cause they're afraid," said Shane.

Lucy pressed her fingers into her temple, hoping to stop the pounding that had begun beating a cadence in her brain.

"Not afraid. Smart," Lynda said. "Right, Lucy?"

Lucy had no idea how to argue the merits of women playing football and decided to leave that particular discussion up to Woody. She picked up the book again.

"Let's get back to the story. We'll try a chapter and if you don't like it, we'll find something different for tomorrow."

The boys continued grumbling, Robbie continued to protest, and Lynda looked pleased as Lucy jumped back into Julia and Harry's story.

Woody had spent the entire morning worrying about Lucy as he imagined all the things his kids had done to other sitters, and might try on her.

Lucy Caldwell had spunk, he'd give her that. But it took more than spunk to handle his kids. And since he didn't want to lose Lucy, he figured he'd just go home at lunch and check on things.

The fact that he didn't want to lose Lucy had nothing to do with her personally as a woman. He had decided to give up on women.

After all, who would be interested in a man with four kids? No one.

So, it wasn't personal interest that prompted his need to keep Lucy around, because he was totally immune to her cute little behind, and that little dimple in her cheek when she frowned.

Yep, he was immune. Totally immune.

It was just that he didn't want to go through the hassle of hiring another sitter. Once school started, things would be easier. He was lucky to have Lucy for the summer and he intended to keep her.

He opened the kitchen door and heard...nothing. Lucy's van was in the drive, so he was sure they hadn't gone anywhere. Maybe she'd sent them all to their rooms again?

He crept through the kitchen. He heard Lucy and followed the sound of her voice to the living room. He paused just beyond the doorway, and listened. After the first few sentences, he realized she wasn't talking to the kids, she was reading to them.

"'Harriet?' Mrs. Ahearn said.

'My name's Harry,' Harry told the teacher.

'Your name is Harriet,' Mrs. Ahearn insisted.

Julia groaned. Arguing with Harry didn't work. She just twisted things until she won.

'Ma'am, my name's Harry and Harry will be the only name I answer to,' Harry said politely.

Mrs. Ahearn just looked at Harry and her face turned colors. Julia watched with fascination as it went from slightly pink to fire-truck red.''

"Uh-oh," Shane said. "Harry's going to get it."

"What does it matter to the teacher if she's called Harriet or Harry?" Lynda asked. "When I was little, I changed my name to Mark for a whole month."

"Why did you change your name to Mark?" Lucy asked.

"Because I wanted to build houses like my daddy and so I wanted to be a boy. But then one day Daddy took me out to the house he was building and told me that I could be a girl and build houses. He let me meet Marge. She works with Daddy and is a girl."

"Your daddy is a very smart man," Lucy said. "Girls can do anything boys can do."

"See, I told you. Girls can do anything boys can," she said to the boys. "That teacher should let Harry be Harry."

"Well, let's see what happens." Lucy started to read again before someone brought up professional football.

"'Harriet,' Mrs. Ahearn gasped and then said nothing else, as if she couldn't think of a thing to say. It wouldn't matter anyway, since Harry was staring out the window.

'Harriet?' Harry still didn't look. Mrs. Ahearn sighed. 'Harry?'

'Yes ma'am?' Harry asked all innocent like.

'Will you please read your essay?'"

All five children cheered. Woody was tempted to cheer as well. But he didn't make a sound because he didn't want them to know he was here. He peeked around the corner. Lucy was sitting on the couch, Lynda on one side, Brandon on the other, and the three bigger boys scattered on the floor at her feet.

He watched as Lucy's arm slipped casually over Brandon's shoulder. The sight warmed him. Brandon missed having a woman around the house. Woody cuddled his son as much as possible, but the five-year-old needed more. He could hardly remember having a mother in the house.

Lucy was still reading and Woody felt himself every bit as drawn into the story as the kids were.

"'This summer me and Andrew built a tree house. We studied some architects…' Harry looked up from her paper. 'They're the guys who make designs for buildings,' she told the class. Harry liked to use big new words, but she was good about explaining them. 'And we learned about blueprints…' She looked up again and explained, 'They're the drawings archi-

tects make showing how they plan to build a building.'''

"And my daddy is the guy who builds the buildings," Brandon said.

"You're right, he does. And Hannah says he builds great buildings. He built her house and I think it's the best house I've ever seen, except for maybe this one," Lucy said.

"He built this one, too," Robbie said.

"Well, he's a very talented man."

Even though Lucy didn't know he'd overheard, Woody felt warmed by her compliment. She liked the houses he had built.

Hannah and Abel's house was the first house completed in the new subdivision in the heart of Erie's downtown. It was his and Abel's showcase. But more than that—it was a home.

Woody had never seen a couple as happy as Abel and Hannah. A long time ago, Woody had dreamed about that kind of relationship, but he'd learned to put those dreams away.

And no matter how attracted he was to Lucy, he wasn't going to pursue the feelings. She'd be gone soon. But while she was here, he would simply enjoy the view and not long for things that could never be.

Again, he studied the woman reading to his children.

"Returning to her essay Harry said, 'And we drew our own. We spent two weeks studying and planning, then we spent the rest of the summer building. We have three rooms, one for each of us and

*one we share. After the second week, when we had
the floors and the walls up, we moved in.'*

'Moved in?' Mrs. Ahearn interrupted.''

By the end of the chapter, Woody was as enchanted as the children with the girl who moved into
a tree house for the summer, whose family had
French night and ate escargot, and the girl who knew
how to politely stand up for herself. But more than
that, he was even more enchanted by this new sitter.

Thankfully Lucy had made it perfectly clear that
she was only staying until the end of the summer.
She was leaving. It was important to remember that.

And, after all, Woody was done with relationships, at least until his kids were grown and out of
the house. No woman wanted an instant family, and
his kids had never found a woman they liked, except
for Hannah, and Woody didn't think Abel would let
her go.

Although he was done thinking about relationships with women, he could still find a woman captivating.

As Lucy told the kids they'd have to wait until
tomorrow for the next chapter, Woody stepped quietly into the room.

"Woody. Is something wrong?" she asked. "It's
not Hannah and the baby, is it?"

"No. No. As far as I know she's still waiting. And
with the way Abel's acting, I'm sure I'd know if
something changed. Just thought I'd sneak home for

lunch and make sure things were going better." He eyed all the children. "And they are going better, right?"

"Yeah," came a chorus of voices.

"Daddy, guess what?" Brandon asked as he tugged on his father's pant leg.

"What?" Woody asked, scooping his youngest son into his arms.

"Harry—"

"In the book," Shane interrupted.

Brandon nodded so hard Woody wondered that his head didn't fall off. "Yeah, in the book, she built a tree house."

"A cool tree house that she lived in with her brother," Lynda added.

"Just for the summer," Shane said.

Robbie took a step closer. "And we were wondering—"

"Yeah, wondering," Shane interrupted.

"I mean, you build houses, right?" Robbie asked.

"Right?" Shane said.

Before Woody could respond, Robbie was continuing, "And maybe sometimes you've got leftovers."

"We've always got leftover peas," Brandon said to Lucy. "We hate peas."

"And we hide them in the cookie jar," Lynda stage-whispered. When Woody caught her eye, she hastily amended, "We used to hide them there, but that was a long time ago."

"You know I'm going to go check the cookie jar, don't you?" Woody asked. His four children exchanged looks that left him certain *a long time ago* was a relative term. "So now we know I'm a builder, and yes, sometimes there are scraps left over when I build a house."

He knew what they wanted and resisted giving them an answer outright. If they had to actually ask, they'd owe him and maybe he could collect by having them behave and make Lucy's life easier. And maybe if her life was easier, she'd stay.

Woody really wanted her to stay.

"Well, Dad," Robbie said, stepping into his role as spokesman for the group. "You know how you always say we should find something productive to do. Maybe we could make blueprints like Harry in the book did, and after you said okay, we could use some of your leftovers and build a tree house. I know I'm too old for kid stuff like this, but since it will help you out, I'll supervise."

"We don't have any trees big enough in the back," Woody pointed out. "The oak is too small to support a tree house."

"But, maybe you could build a clubhouse," Lucy hastily added. She stood behind the boys and put her hand on Cain and Robbie's shoulders. "It would be educational, Woody. And it would keep them occupied. I'm sure Robbie can handle supervising."

The thought of occupying the children seemed to please her as much as it pleased him. But, not ready to make it too easy, Woody rubbed his chin. He missed having a beard to touch, and simply stroked the stubble that had already formed on his chin.

"You know building materials, even scraps, are expensive," he said.

"We could pay you from out of our allowances," Robbie said.

"I don't want your money, but maybe you could think of something we could trade. I'd help you come up with your blueprints, and provide the material, and you'd—"

"Pick up our rooms?" Shane asked.

"No. That goes without saying. They're your rooms and you're responsible for cleaning them, not me and not Lucy. I won't pay you for something like that."

Shane started, "We could—"

Robbie interrupted as if he was afraid Shane would give too much away. "What did you have in mind, Dad?"

"Lucy, can you think of anything the kids could trade us with for my help?"

"I'm sure it's up to you, Woody."

"Maybe, if you're good for Lucy—I mean, no more fires or snakes, or anything—maybe I could see my way clear to sharing some scraps."

"How 'bout frogs?" Shane asked.

"I don't mind frogs, Woody," Lucy said. "Hannah and I used to spend our summers catching frogs."

"And snakes," Brandon added for her.

Woody messed his youngest son's hair. "But whether or not Lucy chooses to catch them on her own is one thing. Whether you hide them on her hoping to scare her is another. So no snakes or frogs."

"We'll be good, really," Robbie said.

"Then you've got yourself a deal," Woody said.

The kids all cheered and Lucy shot him a smile that warmed him.

"Can you bring some home tonight, Daddy?" Brandon asked. "When will you be home? How 'bout nails? We'd need lots of nails, wouldn't we, Cain?"

Lucy's small, quiet son, nodded. "Lots of nails, and hammers. Though we'll be very careful with the hammers, Mr. Pembrooke."

"Mr. Pembrooke is an awful lot of name. Why don't we settle for Woody?"

"Mom would say it was rude. I should call grown-ups Mr. or Mrs. or sir or ma'am."

"Lucy?" Woody asked.

"I guess if Mr. Pembrooke prefers that you call him Woody, then it would be rude not to," she said.

"So, Woody it is," he said. "And I'll see what I can find on the site that might work."

"Don't forget the nails, Daddy," Brandon said. "Lots of nails."

"I won't." He shot Lucy an appreciative smile.

He'd had a lot of sitters in the last few years, but not one had ever sparked such excitement in his kids.

Nor, in their father, for that matter.

4

LUCY SAT ON THE apartment stairs the following week, and gazed at the stars. This was probably her favorite time of day. Cain was safely tucked in bed, all her work was done, and she had a few quiet minutes to herself to sit back and just think, to just be.

Right now she was doing more thinking than being. And that wouldn't be bad except she was thinking about Woody Pembrooke.

The last week had gone well. The kids were caught up with their clubhouse plans. They'd finished over half of *The Trouble With Harry,* and each chapter gave the kids new ideas. They'd started working on the foundation today. Digging a hole in the ground had kept them all busy. Too busy for trouble.

Woody had called around four o'clock and said he'd be late getting home, would she mind feeding the kids and staying on? He'd had some snafu at the site. But working late wasn't the problem that was on her mind.

No, what was plaguing her was the rush of pleasure she felt when he finally opened the door at almost seven. And it wasn't as if she were pleased to see him because the kids had been misbehaving.

What she didn't want was to think about the pleasure she'd experienced when Woody Pembrooke and his ultranice-looking face walked in the door. By seven at night it was no longer quite as clean-shaven as it was in the mornings. As a matter of fact, it was decidedly seven-o'clock shadowed. But stubble looked good on him.

Very good.

And that was the problem. His very good-looking face kept inserting itself into her just-sitting-on-the-porch-and-being, and made her think about it— about Woody himself. Well, she was done thinking about Woody.

Enough was enough.

Lucy was going to put him completely out of her mind. She'd think about her business. She had to make some calls and start looking for a place to build Caldwell Consulting. She had to start making some contacts. Maybe Woody knew of some business organizations she could connect with. After all, he owned his own business.

Darn. There she was again, thinking about Woody.

She wasn't going to ask him for any help. She was going to build her company by herself.

"Pardon me, is this step taken?"

Drat. She wasn't just thinking about him, she was

looking at him standing in front of her, moonlight casting just enough light so she could see him. And seeing him in the flesh, after seeing him in her daydreams wasn't a good idea.

"Lucy?"

There was no way out of letting him sit down. It was his step, after all. And it would be wrong to tell him he couldn't sit on his own step. So she nodded. "Help yourself."

Rather than taking one of any number of empty stairs, he took the one right next to her. The staircase was wide enough so that he didn't touch her, but he was close.

Too close.

And he smelled good. Woodsy with a hint of spice.

Why couldn't he smell sweaty and stinky? That's how a man who spent his day building houses should smell.

"Things seem to be going good this week," he finally said, breaking the silence with that low, rumbly voice of his. "Oh, there was that microwave incident—"

Lucy groaned, remembering the hour it took her to scrub the kids' potion off the interior of the microwave. It wouldn't have been so bad if they hadn't included egg. Exploded egg was tough to pry off sides of the microwave.

If she had to smell one more stinking egg, she might have to give up that food entirely.

"—and of course, Cain's haircut."

Lynda had been exploring the fine art of hairstyling, and had decided to help Cain deal with his hated curls by cutting them off. The result was worse than any curls could ever be.

Woody had given her son a crew cut when he got home, which looked far better than Lynda's stylistic endeavors.

"But everyone's survived, so I guess you could say it's going well."

"Not only survived, they're thriving," Woody said. "And you're still here. I think we're working on a record. After that first day, I thought for sure the record we were going to set was one for how fast a sitter could leave."

Lucy ignored the fact that his voice vibrated in the center of her chest and stirred butterflies in her stomach.

"Well, the first day was such a challenge that even microwave explosions and haircuts seem easy. Almost anything short of a nuclear explosion would be better than that first day," she managed to reply, surprised at how normal her voice sounded.

She didn't feel normal. She felt…well, she wasn't sure what she felt, but it wasn't normal. And she didn't like it.

The kids. Think about the kids and not this nice-smelling, handsomely stubble-faced man. "The kids really are hung up on this clubhouse idea."

"Keeping them occupied is good. None of the other sitters tried something like that."

"None of the other sitters were naive enough to give them tools. You do realize that once this foundation is set, they're going to start on the clubhouse, and in order to do that we're going to have to arm them. Hammers. Saws. Sharp, pointy nails. But I draw the line at power tools. If they can strip a pizza without any help at all, do you realize what they could do with a cordless drill?"

"No power tools," Woody promised with a chuckle.

"Okay."

They sat in companionable silence.

Cozy silence.

Intimate silence.

Intimate silence wouldn't do at all. Intimacy was the last thing she wanted with Woody Pembrooke, even if it was the silent type.

Lucy needed to fill the quiet evening with something. She almost wished the kids had misbehaved, then she'd have something else to say. But they'd been good. And not a single, solitary thing came to mind.

What did men like to talk about?

His job. She'd ask Woody about his job.

Almost giddy with relief to have something to say, she asked, "What happened at the site today?"

Woody frowned in annoyance. "I wasn't happy with the plumber in this new house. They used plastic pipes, which is okay according to code, but I specifically told him to use copper. When I finish a house, I want the owners to know they're getting quality, not just good enough. I preach *The Pembrooke Tradition of Quality* to my crew, and I expect it from subcontractors as well."

"So what did you do?" she asked.

"I told him to rip out what he'd done and redo it with the copper pipe, like we agreed."

The Pembrooke Tradition of Quality.

Good enough wasn't good enough for Woody. She liked that. And liking that wasn't a good thing. After all, she already liked his face, and even though it had been a week since he shaved off his beard, she couldn't stop thinking about it. If anything, every day she spent a little more time thinking about his face.

But that was superficial and not overly distressing. She'd found men attractive before, and she was perfectly able to resist a physical attraction. But finding out he had integrity, that was worse. It wouldn't do to like anything deeper about the man. Deep was hard to resist.

Deep was dangerous.

"Pembrooke's guarantees quality, not just good enough."

"A company's reputation is important. It's good that you value yours."

Good for him. Good for his clients.

Not so good for Lucy's peace of mind. The man

was gorgeous and had integrity. And he loved his kids to distraction and was the best father she'd ever seen. Add to that, he was sitting next to her, smelling good and messing with her hormones.

Lucy had to be the most unlucky woman around.

"Speaking of companies," he said. "I know you plan to start your own consulting business, but you haven't really gone into detail. Tell me about it."

Something to talk about. Something she could sound semi-intelligent conversing about. Something that couldn't possibly increase her interest in Woody Pembrooke.

Lucy grabbed the opportunity to fill the quiet with noise and maybe forget that this nice-voiced, sexy-faced, good-smelling, kid-loving man with integrity was sitting next to her.

"I worked as the vice president in marketing for three years with Sky International. When they were bought out, I took the severance package and am finally in the financial position to do what I've always wanted to do, to work for myself. Caldwell Consulting."

"Good, strong name. It says it all."

Lucy smiled, more because until he spoke she'd forgotten his nice voice. Before she could remember anything else, she continued. "Thanks. It's not the most creative name, but it's mine. Just like the company will be. I want to take what I've learned and work with small businesses. So many times they have a great product and know their business, but don't have a clue how to market it appropriately. That's where I'd come in. I'd—'' she cut herself off. She'd wanted to forget her sexy employer, not talk his ear off. "I'm sorry."

"Sorry for what?" Woody asked.

"You came out here for some peace and quiet, and here I am running at the mouth. I guess after spending a day with five kids, I'm simply starved for adult conversation."

Any adult would do, she told herself, though she sensed that it wasn't quite a true statement.

"I wouldn't have asked if I hadn't wanted to hear what you had to say," Woody said softly. "Four of those five kids are mine, so I owe you all the adult conversation you want. And I may be able to help you with your business. I know a lot of people in town, and those I don't know, Abel probably does. Between the two of us, we should be able to put the word out about your plans."

"Really, I didn't say anything in order to garner your support. I wasn't digging for help."

Drat. Couldn't this man leave well enough alone. Sexy. Nice-smelling. Integrity. And now helpful and concerned.

Drat and double drat.

"I didn't think you were digging for help. And I wouldn't have offered if I didn't want to. Do you have any prospects for an office?"

She wanted to leave.

Well, she didn't *want* to leave, which meant it was

time to leave, but instead of getting up and bolting into the apartment, she found herself answering, "That's what I was sitting here thinking about. It's been a long time since I lived in Erie, so I'm really going to have to consider where I want to locate. I'll start looking next week."

"Talk to Abel. That's right up his alley."

Lucy sat a little straighter. "I don't like asking for favors."

"If you don't talk to him he'll be insulted. You might know about marketing, but he knows real estate, specifically he knows Erie's real estate. He'll save you a lot of leg work, and make sure you get the best deal."

Lucy shook her head. "But —"

"No buts about it," Woody said, that endearing smile that had been hidden away once, now lit up his face in the pale moonlight.

"Are you always this overbearing, Mr. Pembrooke?" Lucy asked more sharply than she intended. She was touched by his concern, and that was even worse than thinking the man had integrity and a sexy chin.

"Are you always this reluctant to accept a friendly hand?" he countered.

Taking the question seriously, she nodded. "Yes. I like to stand on my own two feet. If you start leaning on other people, eventually you're going to take a fall."

He shrugged. "That's a sad way to look at life,

but suit yourself. The offer was sincere. And I know Abel would want to help as well."

He stood and started down the stairs, then abruptly turned around. "And Lucy, I'd like to point out that if I were truly an overbearing clod, I would have kissed you just now."

"What?"

He couldn't have said what she thought he'd just said.

Instead of answering her *what*, he continued, "Did you know that when you're surprised or annoyed by something, you get this tiny dimple on your cheek? It's not there when you smile, just when you're serious. And you get these little crinkles at the corner of your eyes."

"Not only are you overbearing, and trying to arrange my business for me, but now you're saying I have wrinkles."

Rather than becoming defensive, Woody simply laughed. "See, there you go, that cute little dimple and the crinkles are back, and they make me want to kiss you."

There. He'd said it again. Woody Pembrooke was talking about kissing her.

"Kiss me?" she asked.

"I said I wanted to, I didn't say I was going to, but if you insist—" He leaned toward her.

She pushed against his chest. "I don't want you to kiss me."

Woody stood back up. "Well, that makes the two

of us even, because I don't want to want to kiss you.''

"I—"

"So, I'm going to leave before I do something we'll both regret." He started into the house. "Sweet dreams, Lucy."

SWEET DREAMS?

Lucy hustled her son out the door and toward the Pembrookes' and wished to pete she'd had sweet dreams. But she hadn't. No, not one.

However, she had dreamed last night after Woody's disturbing exit.

Oh, she'd dreamed all right. But they weren't sweet dreams at all. They were kissing dreams, and all of them focused on Woody Pembrooke. Lots and lots of kissing.

Lucy didn't like it at all.

She didn't like it one bit.

"It's raining, Mom," Cain said as he peered out the apartment door.

"You won't melt in a little water. Just make a quick dash for it."

Cain bolted down the stairs and across the yard to Woody's kitchen door. Lucy followed suit and was hot on his trail.

"I was just going to call you," Woody said, the phone in his hand.

"I'm sorry." She glanced at her watch. "Was I late?"

She shut the door as Woody hung up the phone.

"No," he said. "Abel called. Hannah's in labor."

A surge of excitement flooded Lucy's system. Hannah was going to have her baby. Lucy was going to be an aunt.

"I've got to go. Hannah might be a midwife, but this is her first baby, and she's bound to be nervous, not that she doesn't have Abel, but a woman needs her family around her."

She opened the backdoor, and then shut it again abruptly. "Oh, the kids. I'm so sorry. I don't know what I was thinking. I'll…I'll simply call Hannah and go over tonight after you're done at work."

"Don't worry about the kids, I'll take care of them. It's raining anyway. This will give me an excuse to stay inside where it's dry."

"Really, I couldn't." She'd taken this job. She was here to watch Woody's kids, not to have him watch hers.

"I'm the boss, and you can. Just go."

"You're sure? You'd watch Cain, too?"

"Lucy, one more kid can't be that much harder. You've been managing four more, after all." He stepped past her and opened the door. "Go."

There it was again, that woodsy, outdoor scent that Woody radiated. It made Lucy want to inhale as deeply as possible. It made her want to move closer, and see if the smell intensified, and if Woody felt as warm and as welcoming as he smelled. It made her want to tell him about her dreams. "I—"

"Hannah needs you, maybe more than you know. Did she mention how Abel's been handling the pregnancy?"

Lucy nodded since she couldn't seem to get her voice to work right. And even if she did, she was afraid that she'd simply blurt out *I was kissing you all night in my dreams.* That wouldn't do. So nodding seemed like the safest route.

Woody searched the coatrack and found a rain jacket. "Put this on, it's pouring. And go help out Hannah. Actually, from his phone call, I think Abel's handling the labor even worse than the pregnancy."

Lucy took the coat and slid it on. It was huge, so she rolled up the sleeves and looked at the big man standing just an arm's reach away. The urge to span that distance and simply touch him came over her, but she resisted, and smiled.

"Thanks for the coat. And if Abel's worse now, Hannah's got to be going crazy. I didn't know it could get any worse."

"Hey, you don't know Abel. It could get a lot worse. He's totally in love with Hannah. That kind of love can make the sanest man totally nuts. Listen, I've been where he is four times, and it's horrible to feel so…useless, I guess." He did up the zipper on her coat.

The warmth that flooded her body had nothing to do with the jacket, and everything to do with the man. Lucy hadn't felt this coddled since...well, not since she was a girl living with Irene.

Before she could say anything else, he held the door open and said, "Just go."

"If you're sure."

"I'm sure, positive even. They're at Hamot Hospital."

Lucy went. She sprinted up the stairs to her apartment, grabbed her purse and could barely contain her trembling as she tried to get the van out of the garage. As she backed out she saw Woody still standing in the kitchen doorway. He smiled and gave a little wave.

She waved back. She was warmed by his smile and at his understanding. He knew how much it meant to her to be with Hannah. He—

No, as nice as he was, she wasn't going to think about him. She was going to think about Hannah and this new baby, this new member of her family.

Absolutely putting Woody and his killer smile out of her mind, Lucy didn't even notice the scenery as she made it to the hospital in record time ignoring all thoughts of Woody Pembrooke.

5

LUCY FOUND HANNAH and Abel walking down the hall on the obstetrics floor.

"Hannah!" she cried.

But before Hannah could say a word, Abel said, "Lucy, thank goodness you're here. Maybe you can talk some sense into her."

There was no doubt in Lucy's mind who her was. Hannah smiled indulgently as her husband continued.

"She should be in bed, but instead she's walking up and down this hall. I've been up and down it so many times I can tell you which mother is in what room. She's wearing a path in the floor, and wearing herself out. She's—"

"Abel, I'm perfectly fine." Hannah said to Lucy, "He's been uptight, but I've never seen him like this."

"You've never had a baby before," Abel said. "And I guarantee, I am like this every time my wife has a baby."

"Then we might be destined to be the parents of

an only child," Hannah assured him with a hint of laughter in her voice.

"You know that when the moment's right, I could talk you into having another. Actually, when the moment's right, I can talk you into just about anything. Remember that night we went parking at—"

"That's enough." Hannah gave Abel a mock slug on the shoulder. "Lucy's here, and she still thinks I'm sweet and innocent."

Lucy laughed as she hugged her friend. "Hannah, I never thought you were sweet and innocent."

"Some friend you are," Hannah grumbled even as she sent Lucy a quick wink. Their squabbling had sidetracked Abel from his worry.

They'd reached the end of the hallway and turned to walk back down the corridor.

"What did you do with the demon-spawn?" Abel asked.

"They're at home with Woody," Lucy said. She fingered the coat he'd given her. Woody Pembrooke was a nice man, darn it all.

"Did I ever tell you about our baby-sitting weekend with them?" Hannah said. The look she shot said this was another blatant attempt to keep Abel sidetracked.

"I believe I heard something about kidnapped dogs and honeyed hair," Lucy said.

"Oh, you don't know the half of it," Abel grumbled. "They totally ruined my dog. Every time they come over she goes nuts until Lynda picks her up.

Marigold's a traitor. I think they fed her cookies. That's the only way she'd go over to the dark side. Marigold would do just about anything for cookies.''

''Tell Abel about your first day and maybe he'll stop harping about how hard our weekend was,'' Hannah said. She paused and took a deep breath as a contraction hit. Hannah closed her eyes and Abel turned pale.

Trying to distract him, Lucy said, ''Well, other than some rotten eggs, stripping a pizza and starting a fire—''

''Don't forget the toilet,'' Hannah said through clenched teeth.

''And a stopped-up toilet, it hasn't been bad. Actually, it's been almost good since then. I mean, if you don't count the microwave explosion, or Cain's haircut, which was worse than your honeyed hair, Hannah, you wimp.''

Abel winked at Lucy. His expression said he knew what Hannah was up to, but would do anything for his wife, even be sidetracked. ''Good? That's when you need to be afraid…very afraid. It means they're thinking up some new nefarious scheme.''

''I think they're so focused on the clubhouse that they've forgotten about schemes. They're digging a foundation now, and that's keeping them occupied. At least for a while.''

Hannah took a deep cleansing breath.

The tension melted from Abel's face as she did.

''It won't last,'' he promised. ''They'll get you,

just you remember, I told you. I told Hannah she was nuts sending you over there for the summer, but she didn't listen.''

Hannah started shuffling down the hall again and Abel and Lucy tagged along. "By the way, you've mentioned the kids, but not their father. How are you and Woody getting along? What do you think?''

What did she think?

Lucy thought Woody was sexy, but there was no way she was going to say that out loud. So she settled for a noncommittal, "He seems nice enough. I mean, he took the kids, Cain too, so I could be with you. And he gave me his raincoat to put on.''

Hannah simply stared at Lucy, and Lucy had a feeling her best friend could see right through her evasion, but Hannah didn't call her on it.

In an attempt to change the subject, she said, "Did you call Irene?''

"She's on her way," Abel said. "I called her before we left the house.''

"Actually, he called her at five o'clock in the morning. He was going to call you too, but I told him you weren't coming from Florida, just from across town, and he should hold off.''

"You could have called," Lucy said.

"I know," Hannah reached out and took her hand and gave it a squeeze. "Don't you think I know that?''

Lucy knew that Hannah knew. Just like Lucy herself knew that both Irene and Hannah would come running if she ever called needing them. They were a family.

A warm rush of appreciation flooded her being. She had a family, and soon it would be one person larger.

Trying to cover the uncharacteristic mushy feeling that enveloped her, Lucy asked, "So what's new with Irene? Last time I talked to her she was heading to a belly-dance-athon. Did you hear how she did?"

"She placed second in the senior division."

"That's great."

"Well, not according to Irene. The winner was eighty, and she's rather put out that a senior citizen beat her."

"But Irene's a senior citizen."

"Not that senior," Hannah said, doing an imitation of Irene's voice.

The squeeze intensified, and Hannah groaned. "Whoo, whoo, whoo," she panted.

Abel checked his watch. "Ten minutes. It's been ten minutes since the last one. They're getting further apart, not closer together. Something's wrong."

"Nothing's wrong," Hannah gritted out between pants. "We're just here way too early. I could be at this all day. Heck, we could be at this two days."

"I don't know if I can make it all day, much less two," Abel said weakly.

Lucy didn't know if he could make it either. "Abel, really, Hannah knows what she's doing."

"And just what is she doing?" Woody asked in a booming voice.

Lucy's heart gave a funny little leap at the sight of him striding down the hall. "Woody, what are you doing here? You didn't bring all the kids, did you?"

Lucy could only imagine what sort of mischief they could get into in a hospital.

"Lucy, give me a little credit. Right after you left, I called in one of my foremen and left him in charge."

"Did you arm him?" Abel asked.

Woody laughed, as if what Abel asked was a joke, but Lucy wasn't so sure it was.

"He came bearing tools, but no power tools." Woody grinned at Lucy. He was referring to their conversation last night, and she knew it. It was a private reference, just for them. There was an intimacy in that sort of thing that made her nervous.

Without missing a beat, he continued, "So I think they'll behave. I briefed him on the clubhouse infatuation, and he's going to help them go over the blueprints. That should leave him relatively safe."

A small dark-haired woman bustled down the hall. "Hey, is there a party and I missed my invitation?"

"Woody and Lucy, this is Meghan Maloney. She's the midwife who's filling in for me at the practice."

"Where's Rick? I thought he'd be here?" Woody asked.

"Having Rick deliver my baby was just a bit too...well, personal," Hannah said. "Meg was gracious enough to offer. Meg, this is Woody Pembrooke, Abel's partner, and Lucy Caldwell, my sister."

Lucy loved hearing Hannah call her a sister. Though they weren't related by blood, Hannah was the sister of her heart.

Tears would flow, if she'd let them, which she wouldn't. The idea of Hannah having a baby had simply made her overly emotional, and she wasn't going to give into the tears.

Lucy Caldwell wasn't a crier.

"Nice to meet you," Meg said. "And, speaking of gracious—Hannah, how about if I graciously offer to check and see how you're progressing?"

"Why don't you two have a seat? I'll send Abel out when we're done," Hannah said before she shuffled off down the hall, Abel and Meg trailing behind her.

"Come on, let's find someplace to sit down," Woody said.

"Woody, I can't thank you enough. I've only been on the job a little more than a week, and yet you juggled everything so I could be here with Hannah and—"

"Shush. I know how close the two of you are. She's the one who talked me into hiring you, remember? I got glowing reports on Lucy-this and

Lucy-that ever since I met her. Plus, I love Hannah. I knew you had to be here.''

"Well, thanks anyway."

"Anytime."

They sat next to each other on the couch, and Lucy suddenly realized she was holding Woody's hand. Or Woody was holding her hand.

Yeah, Woody was definitely holding her hand, because Lucy didn't hold men's hands. She should rip her hand away.

But no, that would be rude. He wasn't kissing her, after all. He hadn't even mentioned kissing her today. She felt…well, whatever it was it certainly wasn't disappointment. She didn't want to be kissing Woody Pembrooke.

And obviously, he didn't want to kiss her either.

There. That feeling that definitely wasn't disappointment was back, but she ignored it.

Abel walked into the waiting room.

Lucy jumped up and ripped her hand away from Woody's. "What happened?"

"Meg's sending us home. I said, hell no, but of course Hannah took Meg's side and said there was no reason to stay at the hospital all day."

"Sending you home?" Woody repeated, his frown said that he wasn't any more pleased than Abel at the thought.

"Yeah. Hannah's still only one centimeter. She hasn't budged since we got here, and her contractions are slowing and getting weaker. Meg says it could be tonight, or it could be a day or two. Even a week. There's no reason to wait. That's what they're saying. But what if she delivers in the car, or at home or—''

Lucy suddenly realized she was squeezing Woody's hand again. She dropped it as she approached. Abel smiled. "I'm sure Hannah knows what she's doing."

Abel's expression said he wasn't as sure as Lucy.

"I can't get a hold of Irene," he said. "She must already be somewhere between here and Florida. I should have waited before calling her like Hannah asked."

"Oh, don't worry about that. Irene had wanted to come earlier, but didn't want to butt in," Lucy assured him.

"Butt in? I don't think so. I need someone to help me deal with Hannah. She's unreasonable. I mean, she wants to go home and take a walk. A walk! In her condition? She could end up delivering on the sidewalk. Can you imagine what that would do to our poor baby's head? He'd have a flat head like Herman Munster on that old TV show. They'd call him Flat-headed Kennedy. Or—''

"Abel, Hannah's a midwife, remember? If she delivered on a sidewalk—which she isn't going to do—she'd know how to handle the situation," Lucy said.

Poor Hannah, having to deal with Abel's worry. And yet, even as she thought it, Lucy felt a stab of longing. She'd gone through Cain's birth on her own. She could have called Hannah or Irene, but had needed to prove to herself that she could handle things by herself. She never had anyone worry about her like Abel was worrying about Hannah.

"Hannah knows what she's doing," Lucy said again. "And she'd never do anything to put that baby at risk. I don't think I've ever seen a baby that was so wanted."

Abel didn't looked soothed. "I—"

"So humor her. Take her home," Woody said. "Pregnant women should get anything they want."

"Hey, I'd get up in the middle of the night to get her pickles and ice cream, or something, but she won't sit still and—"

A fully dressed Hannah walked into the waiting room. "Abel, let's go. Woody and Lucy have better things to do than listen to you carp."

"I don't carp," Abel said.

"Yes, you do. Lucky for you I like it. Come on, you can take me for lunch." She turned to Woody and Lucy. "Thanks for coming you guys. Next time, maybe it will be the real deal."

"Call me as soon as you want me," Lucy said. "And I'll be here."

"I never doubted that."

They all said goodbye in the lobby. Lucy headed out into the drizzle, and realized Woody was following her. "Did you need something?"

"I was hoping I could hitch a ride home with you.

J.R. gave me a ride down here after he dropped off Hump to watch the kids.''

''Hump? You let a man named Hump baby-sit my son?'' Lucy asked, deciding it was better to worry about who was baby-sitting Cain than to worry about riding home with Woody. She'd thought she'd have a few minutes respite. She hurried through the parking lot, wishing Woody would just go away.

Instead, he simply matched his gait to hers and said, ''Well, I don't know that a name makes a man, but it if will make you feel better, Hump isn't his real name. It's Ray Humphrey. On the site it's just Hump, but the kids are calling him Mr. Hump.''

Lucy wished she could think of a way to not give him a ride, but she couldn't.

''Does the name Hump bother you?'' he asked, as they reached her van.

''No,'' Lucy said, with a bit more force than was necessary. ''Why should it?''

It wasn't that the word hump made her think of sex, or that sex made her think of Woody, because she definitely wasn't thinking about sex and Woody in the same thought. Despite the fact she couldn't shake her disturbingly erotic dreams, she wasn't thinking about what it would be like to kiss Woody Pembrooke, or even worse, have sex with him.

She clicked the button on her key ring that unlocked the doors and climbed in.

Woody followed suit. ''Well, if it's not Hump's

name that has you all hot and bothered, is it giving me a ride home? I promise to stay on my own side of the van.''

''Why would I think you wouldn't stay on your own side?'' She fumbled trying to get the key in the ignition.

''Because you've been thinking about kissing, just like I have. And since you're thinking about kissing,'' Woody continued, ''you're worried that we'll be alone in the van with no kids or friends to act as a buffer, so you're worried about me staying on my own side, because you don't really want me to.''

He smiled a knowing smile, as if he'd worked out everything in his tiny little male mind and was satisfied with his conclusion.

''That was a convoluted sentence if I ever heard one, and I don't need a buffer.'' Lucy tried to make the idea of needing a buffer sound like a scoff, but was afraid it didn't quite pass muster. Instead, it sounded sort of breathy, and maybe even wistful, to her ears.

Breathy and wistful weren't good…not good at all.

She fumbled with the key, wondering why it wasn't sliding into the ignition with its normal ease. That was Woody's fault. He'd flustered her with all his talk of kissing and buffers, making her sound all breathy, even though she wasn't wistful in the least.

She didn't want to kiss Woody Pembrooke. She

was just a female wanting to kiss a male. Any male would do.

Hormones. A basic biological imperative.

"Oh, we definitely need a buffer," he said in that low, rumbly voice of his. "Because the idea of kissing you has been growing on me."

The key finally hit home in the ignition and the engine turned over. She floored the accelerator, making the Lumina scream its readiness to move.

"But we agreed that kissing wouldn't be wise," she said as she glanced in the rearview mirror.

"Whoever said I was wise? I have four kids. That fact alone might make some people question my wisdom."

Lucy didn't say a thing. She slid the car into reverse and tried not to glance at the grinning idiot man sitting next to her.

Buffer?

Kissing?

She'd rather kiss a toad.

She drove out of the parking lot and out onto the street, wishing every puddle she hit was Woody Pembrooke's big, fat, egotistical head.

"Are you going to just sit over there and stare at me the entire drive home?" Lucy suddenly snapped.

"I was thinking about it. Why? Does it bother you?"

"Of course it bothers me." Lucy turned off Third Street onto State with a little more umph than necessary. And noted with a small degree of pleasure that the force of the turn shifted Woody farther away. "I mean, who wants to have someone stare at them? You're creeping me out."

"Creeping you out?" he asked with a chuckle.

There it was. The proof that Woody was making her lose her mind. She was reduced to using an eight-year-old's vernacular. Instead of admitting defeat, she chose to ignore her momentary slip. "It's one of Cain's favorite phrases. It's hip."

"Ah, but I don't think hip is a *hip* word anymore. And we weren't talking about current slang, but about kissing. How about kissing? Does that creep you out?" he asked softly.

"What?" His sudden question almost had her careening into the back end of the big truck ahead of them. She forced herself to take a deep breath and concentrate on driving.

"What is it with you and this kissing thing?" she asked, rather than answer his question, because truth be told, the idea of kissing him didn't creep her out in the least.

"To be honest, I have no idea why every time I look at you I automatically think of kissing. I don't want to think about kissing you. Oh, it's not that I don't like kissing. Don't get me wrong, I like it just fine. But there are a hundred reasons why I shouldn't want to kiss you."

"Yeah. Same for me. Maybe even more."

The drizzle gave way to full-fledged rain, so Lucy switched her wipers on high. She wished she could turn off and on the mental image of Woody kissing her like she could the wipers.

"I mean, you work for me," Woody said. "There's that entire sexual harassment thing. And kids. There are five reasons right there. When we're together, there are almost always five kids around. That makes six reasons right off the bat why we shouldn't kiss."

He paused, then added, "Of course, we're together now and there are no kids."

"But I'm driving a car. And driving a car and kissing don't go very well together. So, that's seven reasons." Lucy switched on her lights and concentrated on maneuvering through the rain-slicked streets. "And it's raining, so I need to concentrate, and I can't concentrate when you talk about kissing, so that's eight reasons."

"There was last night on the stairs," Woody's voice got softer and deeper.

It sent vibrations that wiggled in the pit of Lucy's stomach.

Softer still, he said, "There's something to be said about kissing in the moonlight."

"But, like you said, I'm driving now. And there is no moonlight. There's not even sunlight. There's just rain."

"So kissing isn't advisable." He sounded disappointed.

And if she was honest with herself, Lucy would

admit that she was disappointed as well. "And there are those hundred reasons why we shouldn't."

"But the only reason I can think of is that you're driving. I seem to have forgotten the other ninety-nine," Woody admitted.

Lucy sighed. "Me too."

"If you weren't driving, do you know what I'd do right now?"

She slid to a stop at a traffic light and glanced at the man sitting just across the van. Every time she looked at him, her pulse skyrocketed, but this time, it just about went into orbit. "What would you do, if I weren't driving? Which I am."

"I'd reach across the space between our seats. It's not that far. I wouldn't even have to lean."

He demonstrated, but stopped short of actually touching her. "And then, I'd brush my fingers through your hair. Have I ever mentioned that I like your hair? It's not quite curly, not like Cain's is anyway. It's more wavy. And it looks soft. So soft. I'd reach across and just run my fingers through it, to sort of see if it's as soft as it looks."

A car beeped its horn and Lucy realized the light had turned green. Swallowing compulsively, she slowly eased the car forward glad to have the road to concentrate on instead of Woody Pembrooke.

"And then—" He stopped.

"There's more?"

"Honey, I'm only getting started. After I'd satisfied myself that your hair is indeed as soft as it looks,

I'd bring my hand to the back of your neck, and gently pull you toward me. We'd meet in the middle and…'' He paused.

''And?'' she asked, her voice little more than a breath.

''And that's when I'd do it.''

''Kiss me,'' she said.

''Yeah,'' he agreed. ''I'd start sort of slow and gentle. I'd want to be sure that you wanted to be kissed. I'm not the type of man to take what isn't offered. Would you?''

''Want to be kissed? If I wasn't driving, and if I didn't remember the other ninety-nine reasons why we shouldn't, and if the kids weren't around, then yes, I'd want to be. But that's a lot of ifs.''

''Well, I'd do my best to make sure neither of us remembered the other ninety-nine reasons, and I'd kiss you slow and gentle, until I was sure, and then I'd pull you even closer, and kiss you harder and more intimately. I'd want to memorize your lips. I'd want to see if you really taste like sunshine. And while I was doing that, my hand—''

''Woody!'' Lucy pulled the van over to the side of the road and sucked in a huge gulp of air, but it didn't help her catch her breath. The darned man had used up all the oxygen in the van with his talk.

She exhaled. ''That's enough.''

''You think so? Because I was thinking as hot as it was talking about kissing, I think it could be even hotter trying it. And you're no longer driving. And there are no kids around. And for the life of me, I can't think of a single reason in the world why I shouldn't kiss you. Can you?''

Desperately, Lucy searched her mind, sure that she could think of at least one, but she couldn't think of anything except this man beside her. ''No. Not even one.''

Slowly, Woody reached across the expanse between their seats and lightly ran his hand down the length of her hair.

''It's as soft as I imagined,'' he whispered.

''It's my shampoo,'' she said, striving for humor, but neither of them laughed.

His hand ran under her hair and rested lightly on the back of her neck, gently guiding her toward him. Slowly, tenderly, his lips met hers. It was a delicate touch. A featherlight caress.

He stopped and pulled back only enough to ask, ''Are you sure?''

''No, but I don't want to stop.''

This time she kissed him. No longer content with gentle introductions, she kissed him with all the pent-up need that had built within her from the moment she'd met him. She kissed him with a hungered, wild frenzy that surprised her. She couldn't remember feeling such need.

She kissed him and—

A knock on the window sent Lucy shooting back to her own side of the van. She tugged on her shirt, and nervously tried to pretend nothing had happened.

Woody unrolled the passenger window. "Is there a problem, Officer?"

A slightly soggy police officer peered in the window, a stream of water trickling off the brim of his hat. "That's just what I was going to ask, folks. Do we have a problem here?"

"No problem, sir," Woody said.

"Ma'am?" he asked, poking his head into the van, looking at Lucy as if he thought perhaps she was being held hostage.

And maybe she was. Somehow Woody had made her forget everything but his kiss.

Lucy Caldwell did not go around parking in downtown Erie with a man she'd only known a week. She didn't go parking with men she'd known for months.

She just didn't go parking.

"No problem." No problem except she'd totally forgot herself, and was necking with her employer on a public street. Not just a public street, one of the busiest streets in downtown Erie.

"We have five kids," Woody said, as if that would explain it.

"Well, I guess I can understand why you and your wife might stop for a little…er, recreation if you've got five kids at home, but I think you should be moving on. Or get a hotel room. My wife and I used to do that every now and again when the kids were little. There's a hotel downtown that rents rooms by the hour.''

''Thank you, but that's not necessary,'' Lucy said. ''We're not married and…'' She stopped short.

The officer chuckled. ''Well, whether or not you're married is your business. And the hotel? It's a better idea than necking on State Street.'' He gave a little wave and started back down the street.

Woody rolled up the window, and Lucy put the car in gear and merged into traffic.

''About that kiss…'' Woody started, then paused.

''What kiss?'' she asked. She wasn't sure how to deal with what had just happened, so she was opting to forget it happened.

''Lucy.'' Exasperation tinged that one word.

''I don't want to discuss that…incident. It never happened.''

''You're asking me to forget the most amazing kiss in my life?'' he asked.

''I'm telling you I don't know what you're talking about. We went to see Hannah and Abel in the hospital and then we went home to the kids.''

''That's your story?'' he asked.

''And I'm sticking to it.''

''Fine.'' He was silent a moment, before he added, ''You know, when you first moved in, I was impressed. Here's a woman who's not afraid of anything, I thought. But now, I see I was wrong. You're a coward.''

''Not a coward,'' she assured him. She'd met

every obstacle in her life head-on. "No. I'm a realist. And realistically, nothing can develop between us. I might have momentarily forgotten that, but I remember those other ninety-nine reasons now."

"Such as?"

"I'm independent. I want to stand on my own two feet. I don't want to depend on anyone, on any man. And I have a son to think of."

"I didn't forget Cain," Woody said. "I understand that children take precedence. I have four of my own—"

"Cain's my priority. He's all that matters to me. And what time I have to spare, I'm using to start my own business. You, more than most, should understand how much time and energy that takes. Between Cain and the business, I won't have time for anyone else."

"I see," was his flat response.

Lucy glanced across the car, but couldn't read his expression.

"You're a nice man, Woody," she said.

"I've heard that before. Last time it was just before my wife packed up her stuff and moved out. She said she was sorry, that I was a nice man, but she just couldn't cope with four kids anymore. She said she wanted more than a nice guy like me could give her."

"I'm sorry," she said softly. She couldn't understand how anyone could ever leave this man.

"Don't be. Things hadn't been good between us

in a long time. It wasn't the kids, they simply magnified the problems that were already there. And you're right, it was just a kiss. Strike that. It wasn't even a kiss. Nothing happened. We went to see Hannah and Abel, then went home.

"Straight home," he said with emphasis.

"Yes," she agreed. "We went straight home. Nothing happened."

6

"LUCY, HONEY!" a gray-haired woman in a pair of hot-pink stretch pants and an oversized T-shirt that read Belly Dancers Wiggle While They Do It, cried as Woody and Lucy walked into the kitchen.

"Irene," Lucy cried as she rushed into the older woman's open arms. "When did you get in?"

"My flight landed about an hour ago. I called the hospital and they said Hannah had gone home. False labor and all that. I'm betting it was that Abel who made her go to the hospital at the very first twinge. I decided to let her calm him down. He's had her in a tizzy for months, and I imagine he's a little edgy right now."

"A little? That's the biggest understatement I ever heard," Woody said with a chuckle, as he stepped forward and extended his hand. "Woody Pembrooke, ma'am. It's a pleasure to finally meet you. I've heard a lot about you."

Irene shook his hand with gusto and a smile. "All lies. These girls insist on telling people stories, none of which are true."

Lucy just raised an eyebrow at her foster mother

and Irene relented. "Well, most of them aren't true."

"I'd like to hear their stories and decide for myself," a big burly man, with male-pattern baldness that had left him just a sprinkling of grey hair fringing his head, said.

"You must be Ray." This time it was Lucy extending her hand. "I can't thank you enough for staying with the kids."

Woody noticed that she didn't call him Hump and smiled. She was all manners and primness now, but a few minutes ago, she'd been as wildly uninhibited as he'd been. At least until the cop showed up.

Wasn't it just his luck? Always a police officer when he *didn't* need one.

"Have you looked outside?" Hump asked. "If I hadn't come here, Woody would have had me out there in that rain doing something, I'm sure. He's a slave driver. So, it was my pleasure."

Hump looked pointedly at Irene and repeated, "My pleasure."

Irene blushed.

Woody wondered just what Hump had been up to, because he suspected it wasn't just baby-sitting the kids. The man was past an age when most men had retired from the business, but Hump swore he'd never retire. And physically, as well as mentally, he was in great shape. Better, in fact, than most of the men half his age.

"I should be going now," Hump said. "I'll head back to the site."

"I'll be there soon," Woody called after him. "Tell the guys I said thanks."

"Sure thing, boss." The big man waved, and headed out the kitchen door.

"What was that all about, Irene?" Lucy asked.

Her foster mother's look of innocence intensified. "What? What was what about? You know, Lucy, you should be more specific. You have a habit of asking vague questions that no rational human being could answer. What was that about? What kind of question is that?"

Lucy wasn't buying it. She knew Irene better than that. "You want succinct? What was that blush about, Irene?"

"I don't know what you're talking about. I have rosacea, you know. My skin is always a little on the pink side, and it's very rude of you to comment on it, Lucy. I brought you up better than that. Why I—"

Sensing that Irene wasn't going to give up any good information, Lucy simply asked, "So, how long can you stay?"

She'd get Hannah to help her tag-team their foster mother later. When the two of them worked together, no one was safe. Not even Irene.

Lucy smiled. It was so good to be home. She hadn't realized how much she'd missed it until now. For the first time in years she truly did feel at home.

"I'm staying for as long as I'm needed. Maybe

longer. I called Jean…you remember Mrs. Allue from next door at the old house. Well, I'm moving into her spare room for the duration. She says she's got more room in that house than any one person and their five cats can use. Five cats? Can you imagine? It's so stereotypical. I mean, get a few grey hairs and buy a cat.'' Irene shook her head, as if the idea of falling into a stereotype was foreign to her.

And it probably was. Irene would never do anything that was expected. At a time when single parenting was unheard of, Irene Madison had opened her door and her heart to Hannah and Lucy and a parade of babies. She'd never married, said she'd never seen the sense. She didn't want to have anyone dictate to her, and that strength was just one of the many gifts Irene had shared with Lucy.

"So you're here—"

"For as long as it takes. Hannah needs someone to help her keep Abel calm. And I'll confess, I'm a little bored with the Florida senior scene."

"Why don't I go check on the kids?" Woody said. "Then I have to go check in at the site."

Lucy gave him what she hoped was an absent-minded wave and turned back to her foster mother. Concentrating on Irene was easier than thinking about that kiss in the van.

A kiss she was bound and determined to forget.

"WHATCHA LOOKIN' AT, Daddy?" Brandon asked that night.

Woody dropped the curtain, and turned back to

his son. "I'm looking at you. You're supposed to be going to sleep."

"You were lookin' out the window again."

"No, I wasn't. I just noticed that the blinds were crooked when I went to put your shoes in the closet. I've told you about leaving stuff lying all over the floor. You're going to get up in the middle of the night and fall."

Woody flipped off the light on Brandon's dresser, leaned down and kissed his son's forehead. He hurriedly left the room before he was tempted to look out the window again to check that Lucy was still sitting on the stairs.

"Hey, Dad, now that the little kids are in bed, wanna watch a movie with me and Shane?" Robbie asked as Woody came down the stairs.

"Thanks, guys, but the rain finally stopped so I thought I'd go out back and get a breath of fresh air. Maybe when I come in though, okay?"

"Sure."

Woody hurried through the kitchen toward the backdoor. The house was stifling. That's why he was in a hurry. Fresh air, fresh air. It had nothing to do with bumping into Lucy out on the stairs again tonight.

Nothing at all.

But as he opened the door and saw her sitting there, in the shadows, he couldn't help but feel a stir of excitement.

''Oh, Lucy, you're out here,'' he said, hoping he sounded as if finding her there hadn't even crossed his mind.

''Yes,'' she said. ''And I was hoping to see you.''

''You were?'' Now that was a surprise.

''I think we need to talk.''

''That sounds ominous.'' He took the same seat he'd occupied the night before. ''I like Irene, by the way.''

''So do I. I'm glad she's here. Hannah will be, too.''

''She seems nice.'' Smooth move, Woody. So eloquent. What he wanted to say was he'd been hoping to find Lucy out here again tonight. That he wanted nothing more than to sit with her and talk with her.

No, that was a lie. He wanted to kiss her again. And he wanted more than that. He'd been haunted by mental images of *more than* that all afternoon.

He was studying her mouth, thinking about kissing and more, when it suddenly hit him that her lips were moving, she was talking to him.

''...kissing,'' was all he caught.

''Kissing?''

''Are you paying attention to me, Woody?''

''If you're talking about kissing, I am.'' He was suddenly all ears.

LUCY LIKED TO think of herself as confident and fearless, but this once she was feeling uncertain and nervous. "I'm talking about *not* kissing. I owe you an explanation. It's not that I don't like your kisses. It's been years since I..." She could feel herself blushing.

"There hasn't been any man since Cain's father. Oh, a couple dates, but nothing more. And I don't have time for more now."

"Do you want to talk about him?" he asked.

"What's there to say? We were together, then he left. There hasn't been time, and I'll confess, there simply has been no inclination, since."

"Even if there's not much, I'd like to hear it," he said.

Normally she avoided talking about the past, but she wanted to tell Woody. And she refused to explore why she wanted to share it with him.

"We were in college and thought we were going to be together forever. But when I found out I was pregnant, forever didn't even last until Cain's birth. My boyfriend wasn't ready for the responsibilities. He's never even seen his son. He signed away his rights without blinking an eye."

"Were you ready for the responsibility?" Woody asked softly.

"I had to be. And the moment that I saw Cain, I knew that he was the greatest achievement in my life. I finished school and have worked ever since trying to be give him everything he deserved. That's what this summer was. For him. And selfishly, for me. I wanted one perfect summer together. I wanted to let him be a part of a family. Sometimes I think he's missed out in that area more than anything else.''

"What about you? You finished school, you worked, even this summer—it's all for Cain. What about you, Lucy?''

"There wasn't time left over for me. There still isn't. But…'' She wanted to touch him, but didn't. She didn't know how to reach out to him. "…I'm telling you to make you understand why today…''

Gently he reached out and ran his hand through her hair. "You didn't owe me any explanation about the past, but I'm glad you told me. You're a brave woman.''

"Don't try to make me some kind of hero. I'm not. I've been paralyzed with fear so many times. Fear that I'll fail Cain, just like my parents failed me. Fear that I'll fall on my face trying to get this company off the ground. I've made mistakes… sometimes big ones. But today…kissing you. That didn't feel like a mistake, but I didn't think Cain's father was a mistake until afterward. I don't trust myself to think rationally when I'm so overrun with hormones.''

Woody didn't say a word. Lightly, he kissed her cheek.

The sweetness of that soft kiss almost stole her breath away. "Could we just…I don't know what I want.''

"Then why don't we let it go for now and simply sit here on the stairs and enjoy the quiet evening."

"There's not much quiet during the day, is there? Not with five kids around. Oh, and did I tell you about this afternoon with the worms?"

"Worms?"

Lucy glanced at Woody. They hadn't resolved anything. She should tell him flat out that this—friendship—was all she had to give him. Instead, she simply sat on the stairs and pretended that she was young and optimistic once again, that she believed that she could have anything she wanted—even this man sitting next to her—as she launched into her daily recital...

"They asked me to make worm omelettes for Irene and..."

THE NEXT AFTERNOON, Lucy balanced a precarious load of laundry as she walked down Woody's stairs, studiously not trying to analyze what was going on between her and her boss. Nothing was going on. They'd cleared everything up last night, and maybe had the start of a friendship, but nothing else.

She was going to concentrate on the laundry and nothing else. Who would have thought five people could wear so many clothes, especially when four of them always looked so ragged around the edges? Add her laundry and Cain's into the equation, and she knew she'd never catch up. But she didn't dare lose too much ground. So, she tried to keep at it.

The kids were all sitting at the kitchen table.

"What are you guys up to?" she asked as she carried the last basket of towels through the kitchen toward the basement.

"Just getting a snack," Robbie said.

"Fruit," Cain hastily added. He knew how Lucy felt about between-meal snacking.

"Fine. But before you do, would you all go check your rooms for dirty clothes? Just toss them on the stairs and I'll get them."

All four kids scurried toward their rooms, with Cain tagging along for good measure. Lucy smiled as she lugged the heavy basket into the basement. It was Friday. Her second week was almost officially over, and other than the first day, the kids had been good. Very good.

Too good?

No, there was no such thing as too good.

She was just a great baby-sitter. That's all. All those other sitters Woody had gone through just didn't know how to handle kids. She must have picked up more from raising Cain than she thought.

Or maybe after dealing with corporate types for so long, she was just capable of anything…even handling demon-spawn.

"Lucy, here you go," Robbie called. She heard the thud of clothes hitting the basement stairs, and then the door being slammed shut.

She went and collected the clothes off the stairs. The thump was a sneaker that had come down, too.

She left it sitting on the stairs, and then carried the last of the dirty clothes to the washer and started a load of towels.

Humming, she picked up the sneaker and walked up the stairs and opened the door.

Tried to open the door.

It didn't budge.

"Hey, you guys, the door is stuck."

There was no answer.

Lucy pounded on the door.

"Robbie? Shane? Cain? Would one of you come check the basement door? I can't open it."

She could hear them through the door. The low murmur of children's voices and a feeling of foreboding crept over her.

Maybe there *was* such a thing as too good.

"Open this door right now, you guys, or you're spending the rest of the day in your rooms."

She used the sneaker to thump on the door for added measure, but it appeared all the adding in the world wasn't going to get her out of the basement.

She walked back down the stairs and scanned the basement for an avenue of escape. A prisoner of war had a duty to escape. And it appeared that the truce was over. This was war. And she had to escape in order to get out and kill the kids.

Oh, not literally.

But she was going to make them suffer.

Oh, yeah. They were going to suffer all right.

There was no phone extension in the basement.

What was Woody thinking? With kids like his, there should be a phone in every room of the house, just for such occasions.

Actually, if Lucy had been thinking, she'd have bought a cell phone straight off, and never have made a move without it.

Well, Woody didn't, and neither did she, so she was going to have to figure something else out. It was only three o'clock, and Woody wasn't due to come home until five. So she had a couple hours in the basement if she didn't think of something.

Windows.

There were smallish basement windows. Lucy wasn't overly endowed, so she could probably make it through. She had always felt a certain kinship with Olive Oyl. Long and straight.

She pushed a box over toward the window. Yeah, she could do this. The opening was probably bigger than it looked.

She unlocked it and opened it.

The opening didn't look bigger. As a matter of fact, it almost looked smaller.

But she boosted herself up, and ducked her head through. Her shoulders slid through easily enough.

She slid her arms around her, and grabbing onto another of Woody's hydrangea bushes, she pulled and wiggled.

Wiggled and pulled.

Her waist went through just fine.

Pulled and wiggled, and shimmied until even her hips made it.

It was when she reached the area just below her hips that her trouble started. It seemed that maybe she wasn't shaped like Olive Oyl. From the front, she'd always thought so, but obviously she should have checked out her back.

She pulled, and wiggled and shimmied some more, to no avail.

No, she definitely wasn't long and straight.

She tried pushing her way back into the basement, but something was caught. She reached around and felt. Her jeans' pocket had snagged on a nail. Awkward as it was, she tried to de-snag it, but that wasn't working.

She couldn't go forward. She couldn't go backward.

A huge splat of rain whacked her on the head.

She was wet, the kids were alone in the house doing heaven knows what and she was stuck in a window.

Things were bad.

But worst of all was the realization that she had a huge butt.

A mountainous region on her backside that she'd never noticed.

And it was stuck.

Things couldn't get any worse.

Then Woody's truck pulled into the drive and she realized they could.

Oh, she was saved. But in order to be saved, she'd have to call him. And then he'd see her stuck and know what a huge, mammoth-sized hiney she had.

It would be embarrassing.

Or it would be if she was out to impress the man, but she wasn't so what did it matter if he thought she had a big butt?

It didn't.

She heard, rather than saw the truck door open, and then spied Woody's work boots on the other side of the truck.

"Woody?" she called. "Uh, Woody, I need your help."

"Lucy? Where are you."

"Come around to the other side of the truck."

He came around, all dusty and sweaty and damp-ish looking.

Lucy had never seen such a beautiful sight. Not that she thought Woody was beautiful in a feminine sort of way. No, he was all man. A magnificent, gorgeous man. But they were just good friends. Last night, sitting on the steps had been comfortably friendly…nothing more as long as she forgot how sexy he was.

"What on earth are you doing?" he asked.

She craned her head so she could see him better. Maybe his stupid question had reduced his attractiveness.

Nope. No such luck. He still looked mighty good. Sighing at the injustice of discovering a big butt and a guy who just couldn't stop looking good, all in one day, Lucy said, "Just checking to see how many escape routes you have in the house, so I know just where the best place is to lock up your children and my son."

"And do you think this is a viable escape route?" he asked, kneeling so she didn't have to crane her head quite so much.

"For the kids? Yes. For big-butted women? Obviously not."

Woody had the nerve to chuckle, and rather than irritating her enough so she forgot how good he looked, it simply twisted something in her gut and made her want to kiss him all over again.

Wanting to think of something other than kissing, she thought of the demon-spawn and said, "The kids locked me in the basement and are doing something in the kitchen. So, if you're done standing there and smirking, could you give me a hand so we can go check what sort of havoc they've wreaked?"

He moved closer. "Why don't you back out of the window and return to the basement? I'll let you out that way."

"I can't. I'm really stuck. Going backward doesn't seem like much of an option. Maybe you should just pull." She was starting to feel a little claustrophobic, and that was enough to make her think about something other than kissing.

Almost. But not quite.

Darn, the man had great lips. Why on earth had

she ever suggested he shave his beard? At least his lips had been hidden from view beneath it.

"What if I hurt you?" he asked.

"Woody, I'd rather have you pull me out than have to call the fire department. Because if you can't get me out of here, I'm going to have to really exact a horrible revenge on the kids. Right now I'm just thinking moderately awful."

"They locked you in the basement?"

"Woody, we can discuss this when I'm not hanging in a window frame? Just pull."

He took her hands—and if she wasn't worried about being stuck, she might have let herself notice how much she liked the feel of his work-hardened hands in hers, but she was worried, and wasn't noticing, she assured herself—and he rocked back on his heels and gave a gentle tug.

Lucy didn't budge.

"Come on, Woody, you sling building supplies around all day. I'm sure you can do better than that."

He braced his feet, leaned back farther on his heels and gave a hard, sharp tug. Like a cork coming out of a bottle, Lucy shot out of the window and the momentum sent her tumbling right on top of Woody who landed flat on his back next to his hydrangea bush.

"Thank you," she said, flustered, and trying to climb off the top of him.

He grabbed her hand and held her in place. "Don't go yet."

"Why?" she asked, looking down at him beneath her.

"Because I had a dream about this." He reached around her and gently massaged her back end.

"A dream where you pulled me and my big butt out of a window?" she asked, her voice husky.

"A dream where I cupped my hands around your perfect butt, and then did this…" He leaned up and kissed her.

Her only coherent thought as his lips touched hers was that his lips were as perfect as she remembered, even more perfect than his chin. As soon as the thought flashed through her mind it evaporated and all that was left was feeling.

Excitement.

Tenderness.

Wonder.

Lust.

The feelings swirled, knocking against each other, and mixing around until Lucy had no real sense of anything but the kiss.

No, not the kiss, in lowercase letters, but THE KISS. It was even better than their earlier kiss because there was a certain knowing, a certain sense of expectation linked to this one. It was forever destined to be THE KISS in her memory.

For a memory was all this could be, she thought with regret as she pulled away from him.

"Woody, there are a thousand reasons why that shouldn't have happened."

"I thought we decided there were only a hundred?"

"Well, we can add a big one right now. The kids are in the house, unsupervised, thinking I'm locked in the basement."

He released his grip on her. "That's a good one."

She stood. "And neither of us has time for a relationship. You have the kids and your company. I have Cain and a business to build. We both have other obligations."

"And kissing will make us forget all of them?" He stood as well and shook his head. "I don't think so."

"But this is our second kiss of the week, and if we can kiss twice in just one week, think what it could lead to. It could lead to so much more."

"Oh, yeah, it could do that."

"And more than kissing could make us forget." Lucy couldn't afford to forget herself. Cain was her priority, and nothing could get in the way of her remembering that.

"I can't imagine either of us would forget for long. Kids, even more than real life, have a habit of reminding you they're around."

"I'm your employee. Kissing me could be construed as sexual harassment."

"Lucy, I think you're reaching. We both know I need you more than you need me. Even if you tell me no, your job isn't at risk. And I don't think it can be sexual harassment without some repercussions if you say no. And I'm not firing you."

"Well, maybe you should. I mean, the kids locked me in the basement, and now I'm sitting in the rain, kissing their father. That doesn't sound like a very responsible baby-sitter to me."

"Point—my kids are…rambunctious. I've never seen anyone, except Hannah, handle them this well. And since Hannah's a bit busy these days, you're definitely top pick for baby-sitting, even though you were locked in the basement.

"Point—I was sitting in the rain kissing you, so I could hardly fire you for it.

"Point—I'd like to kiss you again, but I'm willing to wait for you to want me to, so let's get out of the rain, and deal with the kids."

She smiled shyly, relieved that he was going to forget this kissing nonsense until she wanted to kiss him again, because though she might want to kiss him again, she didn't plan on letting him know about it. "I'd appreciate it if you'd let me deal with them in my own way."

"You have a plan?"

"Yes. And if you don't mind, could you watch Cain for a while so I can go make arrangements without him working as an enemy spy? He didn't unlock the door either, and I'm not going to forget that. All five of them are going to feel my revenge."

"Sure. Are you going to let me in on the plan?"

"Maybe. But you have to understand, it's my counterattack. I'm the general. You're just an assistant. I'll let you get them in position for me."

Woody saluted. "Yes, ma'am."

"And, Woody?"

"Yes?"

"About the kiss."

"No. Don't say anything more about it right now. When and if you'd like to try it again, let me know. Because though I might admit that you're right about why more kissing might not be advisable, I have to tell you, I'd throw caution to the wind in a heartbeat if you'd ask me." He helped her up. "Now, come on. You're a sorry, muddy sight. Let's get in out of the rain."

7

SATURDAY.

Lucy stretched in bed and didn't even open her
eyes to look at the clock. It didn't matter what time
it was. She didn't have to get up. She could stay in
bed all day. She could—

"Mom," Cain said from the other side of the
screen. "Mom, you up?"

Lucy sighed. Staying in bed all day was a fantasy
best left to those with no kids. "Morning."

"Can we go get breakfast? Mr. Pembrooke was
going to help us start framing the clubhouse today."

"And if I say no, go back to sleep?"

"Ah, Mom, it's after seven-thirty."

Seven-thirty was the deal she'd started when Cain
was little. He couldn't get up on weekends until after
that, and now she found herself wishing she'd made
it at least eight o'clock. But she hadn't, so it looked
like it was time to get up.

"Okay," she said, admitting defeat.

"Great. Can we have pancakes? I need a big
breakfast because Mr. Hump is coming over too, and
they're going to help us frame in the clubhouse, but

we're going to do all the sides ourselves. Woody, he said that he had to inspect the job and if it isn't up to specs, then we'll have to redo it. I mean, it wouldn't be good for a guy who builds houses to have some ratty clubhouse in his backyard, so we have to carry on the Pembrooke tradition of quality.''

Lucy swallowed her laughter. ''Pembrooke tradition of quality?''

''That's what he says his business motto is. I said, but I'm not a Pembrooke. And he said, anyone who lives with him or works with him is an honorary Pembrooke, so I have to carry on too. Cool, huh?''

If Lucy hadn't already decided against kissing, she'd be tempted to kiss Woody for making her son feel as if he was a part of the *Pembrooke tradition.*

She cleared her throat, trying to budge the uncharacteristic lump.

''Yeah, it's cool, honey. And since you've got such a big day, what if we make some of our cinnamon muffins and take them over to Woody's for everyone. I mean, you need something filling to sustain you.''

''Hey, cool. The kids have never had our cinnamon muffins. I mean, I'm the best stirrer around. And they'll like 'em, don't you think?''

''Yeah, I think.''

''Hey, Mom?''

She pushed a strand of hair off her face. ''Huh?''

''I'm sorry about yesterday. I mean, locking you

in the basement and all. We would have let you out. We were just goofing around on the phone. We only locked it to be sure you didn't come up. We thought we'd finish before you were done with the laundry anyway. I mean, the kids threw even their clean clothes down there to take you longer. But we would have let you out, honest.''

She messed up Cain's already bed-headed hair. ''That's okay. Woody already handled the punishment, but remember what I said. I'm not mad, but I am getting even.''

''Is it going to be bad?'' he asked.

''Yeah, real bad.''

He grinned. ''Can I warn the kids?''

''Sure, because there's nothing you can do to stop it. I could strike today, or tomorrow. Whenever you least expect it, I'll be there and I'll get you all.''

Cain's eyes widened with delight. ''Cool.''

''Yeah, it's going to be cool, all right.''

''DAD. DAD. DAD. DAD.''

Woody Pembrooke carefully pried open his eyes and looked at his youngest son sitting on the edge of the bed.

''Come on, Dad. It's time to get up.''

''If it's not noon, it's not time. It's the weekend, and it's my day to sleep in.''

''Not today. Today we're framin' the clubhouse. Remember? Mr. Hump's comin' and Cain's comin', and I got my hammer all ready. I'm good at nailin', you said so, so I'm gonna nail all day, and saw and—"

"You're not going to let me go back to sleep, are you?" Woody asked, resigned to his fate.

Brandon shook his head. "Nope."

"Are the other kids up?"

"Yep. So come on."

"I've got to get my coffee and a shower before we do anything else."

"Ah, Dad," Brandon whined. "You're taking forever."

"Not quite forever."

"Almost. I wanna nail."

"How about you come help me make my coffee? You can scoop. You know it always tastes better if you scoop."

"Okay."

Woody padded barefoot after his son, and snagged a T-shirt on the way out of the room. Paired with his boxers, he was presentable enough to sneak downstairs for his coffee before heading for the shower.

"Dad. Dad. Come on, Dad," Brandon urged.

It was going to be a long day. Woody was going to need all the fortification he could get.

"If you don't stop Dadding me—" It wasn't Brandon who stopped, but Woody—dead in his tracks.

He looked at Lucy, sitting at his kitchen table,

then down at his boxers, and pulled at the hem of his T-shirt.

"Good morning. I was just coming down to make coffee before I took a shower, and—" He stopped, knowing he sounded like a raving lunatic. "Uh..."

"I made the coffee," Lucy said. "Help yourself. There are fresh cinnamon muffins, too, if you're interested."

He poured his coffee and said, "Maybe after my shower," as he hurried from the room.

"Okay. I'll set a couple aside for you." Lucy paused a moment and then said, "Oh, and Woody?"

He turned. "Yeah?"

"Nice legs."

A warm rush flooded his cheeks as he hurried out of the room and into the bathroom.

So Lucy had seen him in his boxer shorts? There was nothing to be embarrassed about.

He'd like to show her a whole lot more than that. After yesterday, he hadn't been able to think of anything else. And he'd like to try kissing her again. Hell, he'd like to do more than kissing.

But she'd said no.

But she'd also said she liked his smile.

He looked in the mirror and forced his cheeks into a smile. Well, it certainly was more visible without the beard, but it didn't look all that special to him.

He spotted a pink Post-it note stuck to the wall next to the mirror.

Another Lucy memo.

He'd grown accustomed to finding them stuck all over the place.

Close the refrigerator.

No muddy shoes beyond this point.

No wet shoes in the oven.

The last couple days of rain were to blame for the shoe memos. Lucy swore if she never saw a wet sneaker again it would be too soon.

He looked at this memo. *If you are male, please lift the seat before you pee. Lynda and I don't like sitting on a wet one.*

You could take the woman out of the office, but you couldn't take the office out of the woman.

He laughed, and caught a glimpse of his expression in the mirror. Well, it still wasn't all that spectacular, he thought, but Lucy liked it. The thought made his smile even bigger.

And today she'd admired his legs.

He looked down. They weren't bad, as far as legs went, he guessed. They weren't overly hairy, though if he were a woman he'd definitely be in need of a shave. But he wasn't, so no worry there.

He flexed his foot. Yeah, there was a nice muscle back there. No flab. Women weren't the only ones who worried about flab. He patted his stomach. His line of work definitely helped keep him in shape. That and trying to keep up with his kids.

And if Lucy thought his legs were okay, maybe he could get another kiss. Oh, legs and kisses didn't seem to go together. But she hadn't minded his kisses at first. As a matter of fact, she'd actively participated in them.

It was only after they stopped kissing that she'd minded.

So, maybe the trick to more kissing was showing off his legs, and catching her off-guard. And once she was off-guard and his lips were on hers, the trick had to be not stopping, that way she wouldn't remember to protest.

Yeah, that might work.

Whistling off-key he tried to think of ways to get Lucy Caldwell alone and off guard.

A COUPLE HOURS LATER, Woody was helping the kids use a square to check the beam for the clubhouse when Lucy began her preparations for her upcoming attack.

"Locked, and loaded," she muttered, as she trained her sites on Robbie. Oh, yeah, Robbie was the oldest, and he was the first one she was taking down. He'd been the ringleader yesterday, of that she had no doubt.

She was sure it had been his idea to lock her in the basement while they made crank is-your-refrigerator-running-you-better-go-catch-it calls. She knew the idea came from the infantile movie they'd watched the other day, but she was sure the idea of trying it themselves was Robbie's.

Of course, he hadn't counted on the phone company's call-back option, nor had he counted on the three people that had called Woody to report the prank calls.

But Robbie's most fatal mistake was he hadn't counted on Lucy's revenge.

She'd warned them all. But they hadn't listened. Well, it was time for the demon-spawn to reap their just reward. Woody had grounded them for the incident. No phone for a month.

Oh, yeah, that was a tough punishment.

But what she had in mind would be a lesson they'd never forget. The kids prided themselves on their mischief-making capabilities, but they were about to learn they weren't the only ones able to wreak havoc.

Havoc was her plan, and she was starting with Robbie.

The boy brought his hammer back for a blow, when she made her move.

Splat!

"Hey," Robbie screamed as he whirled around to see what had happened.

The other four children turned around as well and Lucy ran from her bedroom window, down the stairs to her next position. She had carefully mapped out her strategy and prepared a plan.

Guerilla warfare was the only way to deal with demons. Hit 'em when they couldn't see you coming and then move before they found you.

She grabbed another water balloon, and lobbed this one at Shane.

Splat!

"Lucy, what are you doing?" Woody hollered.

"I'd distance myself, Woody. I'd hate to have you taken out in the cross fire." She lobbed another balloon and whacked Lynda.

Splat!

"Did I ever mention I was pitcher for my high-school softball team?" she yelled, as she reached for another balloon.

"This is for yesterday, for locking me in the basement," she hollered as she raced from the garage to the small oak tree in the center of the backyard. She hefted a smaller balloon at Brandon.

Splat!

She stepped out from the behind the tree, one last balloon in her hand. "Oh, Cain, honey."

"Mom, don't. I'm your son. You're only son. You love me." He shot the other kids a smile that said his mother would never shoot a water balloon at him.

"Sweetheart, you are my only son, and I do love you." She smiled at the demon-spawn and added, "And I'll confess, that though you're not my kids, and though I've only been here a couple weeks, I love you guys as well. But," she took a couple steps closer, "you crossed the line locking me in the basement. A commander can't let her troops mutiny. So you must be dealt with."

"Get him, Lucy," a dripping, grinning Robbie yelled.

"Yeah, get 'im," Shane echoed.

All four Pembrooke kids started chanting, "Get 'im, get 'im," as Lucy continued her approach.

"So, here you go, honey," and she lobbed the last balloon at her son's abdomen.

Splat!

"There," she said, wiping her hands against her shorts. "I think you've all learned your lesson. Don't lock me in basements."

"Yeah, you got us" Robbie agreed. "But, um, Lucy?"

"What?"

Robbie looked at his siblings and Cain, then back to Lucy and said, "There's five of us, though, and there's just one of you."

"You think you can take me?" she challenged.

Robbie's grin said he did. He cried, "Come on, guys, get her."

All five kids charged toward her, but Lucy was prepared. She hadn't expected the demon-spawn to go down without a whimper. She sprinted for the front of the house, and as she rounded the corner, grabbed the hose she'd set up earlier and took aim.

As the kids rounded the corner, she squeezed the handle and they were met with a stream of freezing water.

"Ah-ha! I've got you all now," Lucy cried. But the kids didn't stop, they kept right on coming and Robbie tackled her.

"Get the hose from her," he hollered.

Lucy was laughing so hard that the hose was quickly pried from her hands. Cain held it, pointing it at her.

"Hey, Mom?" he asked.

"Yes, honey?"

"I love you, too," he said with a wicked grin as he pressed the handle.

Lucy screamed right along with the kids.

Woody just stood at the corner of the house and watched Lucy play with the kids. The battle was long and wet. If asked, he wouldn't have been able to name a winner. But this was the type of battle where everyone won.

They were turning his front yard into a swamp. They were soaked and covered with mud. But his kids were laughing and carrying on, just being kids and having a ball. Cain fit right into their midst.

Gone was the quiet boy who had shown up at Woody's doorstep that first day. In his place was...was yet another demon-spawn. Woody grinned, warmed at the thought.

And Lucy?

Hannah had told him that she was a corporate executive. And every now and again, he saw evidence of that past life. Post-it memos. Negotiating terms.

But right now, in her cut-off jeans, water-logged T-shirt with a soaked ponytail plastered to her neck, he didn't see any evidence of that past occupation. What he saw was the most attractive woman he'd ever met.

Something warm and totally unexpected flooded through him with more force than his garden hose exerted.

Lucy Caldwell wasn't just attractive, she was beautiful.

She loved his kids. That's what she'd said. The words had meant more to him than she could ever imagine. His kids were the center of his existence. He'd stayed in a loveless marriage for their sake, and he'd picked up the pieces when his wife had left, for their sake. He'd spent the years since trying to make up for what they'd lost.

He'd do anything for his kids.

The thought that Lucy cared for them warmed him, even as it made him jealous. She loved his kids, but how did she feel about him?

She'd said she liked his smile and his legs. And she obviously liked his kisses, at least she liked them while she was involved in them, and not thinking about them. She might say they shouldn't, but they had more than once. There was a constant sexual awareness between them.

But he wanted more.

He wanted her to—

"Hey, Woody. Are you going to hide back there forever, or are you going to help me deal with these miscreants of ours?" she called.

Ours.

He liked the way that sounded.

Wanting to sweep her into his arms, but settling

for joining her in a water fight, he slogged into the midst of the battle.

"Daddy, Daddy, help us get Lucy," Brandon called.

"Sorry, Bran, but I've sworn my allegiance to Lucy. And you're all going to get it now."

The kids shrieked and ran in various directions. He winked at Lucy.

"Hey, Woody, I've got another stash of water balloons under your hydrangeas." She pushed a wet strand of hair off her face, smearing even more mud across it.

At that moment the warm feeling in Woody's chest exploded. It may have only been a couple weeks, and way too soon, but he realized what he was feeling wasn't just a physical attraction. It was more.

It was something he never thought he'd experience again.

"Pembrooke? Did water shoot through your ear into your brain, or what?" Lucy asked. "Go get the balloons. I'll cover you with the hose."

He grinned and kissed her muddy cheek. "Aye, aye, ma'am."

He loved her.

There were a hundred reasons why kissing her wasn't a good idea, and there were probably even more reasons why loving Lucy Caldwell was a worse idea, but he couldn't remember one of them.

He loved her. That outweighed any other concern.

"Well, go get them."

He raced across the lawn for the balloons, dodging kids as he went, but no longer able to dodge his feelings.

He loved Lucy Caldwell and anything that stood between him and that feeling could simply go soak itself.

8

———

"'THERE'S SOMETHING about Harry,' Julia's mother said.

'Yeah. She knows about building clubhouses, she knows how to speak French...and she knows how to be a friend,' Julia said. 'And I think I know about that now too.'

"The End," Lucy said with flourish.

"Can we read it again?" Lynda asked.

"I thought maybe we'd start something new tomorrow. There are so many wonderful books out there."

"But I like this one," Lynda insisted.

"Maybe you'd like to try something else out and then reread this in a few months. I could lend it to your daddy for you."

"I want you to read it," Brandon said. "You do Julia and Harry's voices just right. Daddy would make them sound like boys."

"Yeah, we want you to read it," Shane seconded. "We can read some other stuff, but maybe this fall, you'll read it again."

"Yeah. I mean, I'm old enough to read it myself,'' Robbie said. ''But the kids like the way you do it, and I'd help keep them quiet for you.''

''You guys, Cain and I will be moving into our own house when school starts.'' Saying the words out loud tore at Lucy. It had only been a few weeks, and already she had a hard time picturing her life without the four Pembrooke kids in it.

''Why are you moving?'' Lynda asked.

''Because I'm just here for the summer. Your daddy's looking for a new sitter to start after school starts.''

''But we don't want you to leave,'' Brandon said, looking as if he was on the verge of tears.

Lucy wanted to throw her arms around him, around all the kids, and promise to never go, but she didn't have the right. She had plans, and Woody certainly hadn't asked her to change them. He might enjoy making out with her, but he'd never hinted at wanting her to stay beyond summer vacation.

Not that she wanted him to.

''You guys, the apartment is fine for the summer, but I think it would be too small to stay in for more than a few months. That's why we need a new place. But it's not like Cain and I are leaving Erie. We're here to stay. So, you'll see us. Why, when we get our new house and have more room, we'll invite you all for a sleepover.''

''This house is big enough. You could move in here. Cain can stay in our room,'' Shane said. ''I have a bunk bed.''

"Hey, that's a great idea. It would be easier for you to watch us if you lived here," Lynda said.

"And where would Mom sleep?" Cain asked. "There aren't any other beds and no other rooms."

"She can sleep with Daddy," Brandon said.

"Yeah, he's got a great big bed," Lynda said. "We all fit, so I know your mom would fit with Daddy."

"Let's ask him if you can sleep over." Brandon ran over and threw his arms around Lucy's neck.

Her heart just about melted as she hugged him back and listened to the kids' excited plans to move her and Cain in.

"And let's tell Dad you're not moving," Shane said.

"Kids," she said, her voice sounding tight to her ears. "Maybe Cain can sleep over sometime soon, but I think I'll just stay at my place. And I'm so glad you want us to stay, but when the summer is over, we'll be moving. But I promise, we won't move too far away, and you all are welcome to come visit any time."

"It won't be the same," Brandon said.

Lucy could feel the excitement drain out of him, so she hugged him even tighter. "You're right. It won't be. But maybe it will be better."

"I don't think it can be better if you're not here," Lynda said.

"Honey, I can't stay."

"Maybe Daddy will marry you and then you can stay forever," Brandon said.

"Brandon, I like your daddy, I really do, but I don't want to get married. Not ever."

I DON'T WANT TO get married. Not ever.

Woody had stood in the doorway, listening to Lucy finish reading the story, and had stayed there quietly listening to the conversation. He shouldn't have. He'd heard more than he wanted to.

He almost stepped out right after Brandon offered to let Lucy move into his room and add his support to the idea. But he'd stayed hidden until Lucy made her proclamation.

I don't want to get married. Not ever.

He glanced out the window for about the hundredth time. She still wasn't on the apartment stairs. It was after nine. Maybe she wasn't coming out to sit on the stairs tonight.

He'd give her ten more minutes, then he was going to her place to get her. He wanted to talk...

The problem was, he didn't know what to say. *Lucy, watching you toss water balloons at my kids today made me realize I love you, but then I heard you say you're still leaving at the end of the summer and don't ever want to marry, and I wanted to say...*

"Dad, what are you looking at?" Robbie asked.

Embarrassed to be found out by his son, he dropped the curtain. "Nothing."

"Wanna play a video game with us?" Shane asked.

Woody shook his head. "I'm going outside for some—"

"Yeah, we know, air." His sons exchanged a look that said they weren't buying his story.

Woody didn't owe them an explanation, and couldn't have explained even if he did. So he just said, "Well, it's been a long day," then hurried out the backdoor, feeling like a guilty schoolboy sneaking away for some evening tryst.

Not sure what to do, he had just started up the stairs when the apartment door opened. Lucy walked through it and stopped in her tracks.

"Woody," she said.

He thought maybe he heard relief in her voice, but decided he was just hearing what he wanted to hear. "Nice night, isn't it?"

"I was just listening to the crickets. I love summer nights."

Summer. The word reminded Woody that Lucy's time here was finite. Woody needed to remember that.

LUCY MOVED OVER to make room for Woody. "Sit down."

Woody folded his large frame onto the small step. "I didn't think you were coming out tonight," he said.

"It took me a while to get Cain settled. He went on and on about…"

"About what?"

Lucy wasn't about to admit that Cain had spent the evening pestering her about staying here, about not moving when the summer was over. She simply said, "About his big plans for the rest of the summer."

"He seems to be enjoying the kids."

She gave a little laugh. Everything out of Cain's mouth was Robbie this or Shane that. "Oh, you don't know the half of it."

"And you?" Woody asked. "Are you enjoying the kids, Lucy?"

"More than I ever thought I would. You've got fantastic kids, Woody. Creative on occasion, but fantastic." She hesitated and then before she could think better of it, confessed, "I'm enjoying this as well."

"This?"

"Here, on the stairs at night with you. It's becoming quite the ritual." He didn't say anything. Something was wrong, Lucy could sense it, but she wasn't sure what.

"I must have checked the window a dozen times. I couldn't decide if I should be the first one out again, or if I should come out after you."

"So you waited," he said.

"No. I came out the minute Cain was settled. I couldn't wait."

"Just like you can't wait for the summer to be over." There it was again. Something different in his tone.

Lucy didn't understand what was wrong, but she knew something was. "What are you talking about?"

"I heard you earlier, reading to the kids."

"You heard the end of the story?"

"I heard them ask you to stay..." he paused a moment and then added, softly, "...and I heard you say no."

"The summer. That's what we agreed on." That something she sensed in Woody felt like anger, but she couldn't decide why he would be angry. "I didn't lead them on, if that's what you're worried about."

"I know you didn't."

"I wish you'd come in when you heard them. I didn't know what to say when they suggested I move in...into your bed. I almost died of embarrassment." She laughed, but the sound was brittle to her ears.

"Why?" he asked.

"Funny, Pembrooke, real funny. Like either of us would share a bed with our kids in the house."

"People share a bed all the time with kids in their houses."

"Married people," she clarified.

"And we're not married." There was a finality in his tone.

Lucy was becoming more and more confused. "Right."

"And you don't want to get married, ever."

She'd forgotten she'd said that. But she nodded, slowly. "That's right. I'm in the middle of building my dream. I've got an entire summer with my son and I'm going to make a new life for both of us, build my own business, something I can be proud of."

"On your own," he said.

"Yes, on my own."

"It's your dream, doing it on your own, isn't it?" he asked.

"Yes. It's been my dream for a long time." She wasn't sure what was wrong with him, or why this was bothering him, but she tried to explain. "I need to prove to myself that I can make it on my own. I need to do it for Cain, so he can see what I can accomplish and know he can accomplish even more."

"I see."

"What do you see, Woody?" she asked.

"I've got to go in now." He stood and started down the stairs. "I'll see you tomorrow."

"Woody, what do you see?" Lucy asked again.

"Hey, Dad, whatcha doing out there, Dad?" Robbie called out the kitchen window.

"I've got to go in now," he said. "The two older boys are still up and I need to check on them."

"Dad and Lucy sitting in a tree," Robbie and Shane chanted. "K-I-S-S-I-N-G. First comes—"

Woody was striding down the stairs. "Shut that window now, boys."

Lucy had never heard him talk so sharply to the kids, not even after they'd locked her in the basement.

Obviously neither had the boys. The window slammed shut with a hard thump.

"Woody?"

What is it? she wanted to ask. *Are you regretting our stolen moments? Have you finally seen that they can't lead anywhere?* Instead, she simply repeated his name. "Woody?"

"Maybe it would be better if we don't meet out here any more. You know how much trouble my kids can get in even with an adult in the house." He opened the kitchen door and called, "I'll see you tomorrow, Lucy."

"I'M HERE," Irene called Sunday morning as she poked her head into Lucy's bedroom. Her neon orange T-shirt read Belly Dancers Shake, Rattle and Roll. "It's after seven. Why aren't you up?"

Lucy sat up and wiped her sleep-blearied eyes. "Because it's Sunday morning and I don't have to work, so I foolishly thought I'd sleep in."

She'd spent a restless night trying to decide what happened between her and Woody. She was no closer to a solution now than she was right after he left last night.

"Well, then go back to sleep. I don't want you anyway, I want Cain."

At the sound of his name, Cain poked around the screen. "Hey, Grandma Irene."

"What on earth are you still doing in bed?" Irene asked. "Any boy worth his salt would be up and at it already. Why, it's summer vacation. Sleeping in is only for school days. Summer vacation means you should be up at the crack of dawn, ready to cause trouble."

"Gee, thanks, Irene," Lucy muttered. "I seem to remember someone who enjoyed sleeping in on weekends."

"Who?" Irene asked, innocently.

"I'm not allowed up until after seven-thirty," Cain said. "That's the deal."

He came around the screen and hugged Irene.

She messed his already messy hair. "Well, we have to hit the road, so I need you up and dressed now."

"Where are we going?" Cain asked, excitement in his voice.

He and Lucy both knew that adventures with Irene were always a great time.

"We're driving to Marineland."

"Great. I want to see the whales and the—" he stopped short. "Hey, Grandma, can I ask my friends?"

"Well, not until you're dressed. Tell the kids I want everyone to eat, get dressed and be in the driveway by eight o'clock. That's only forty-five minutes from now, so you don't have any time to waste."

"All right!" Cain pulled open dresser drawers, grabbed clothing and sprinted for the bathroom.

"Irene, what are you doing?" Lucy asked.

This was supposed to be her morning to relax and wake up slowly. Instead, a whirlwind had blown into her room and she knew slow wasn't in the cards.

"I'm bored," Irene said. "I think I'm going as crazy as Abel—and that's pretty crazy—waiting for this baby. So, I decided to do something to distract myself. And can you think of anything in the world more distracting than five kids at Marineland?"

Lucy could. Being around Woody Pembrooke was more than distracting. "I don't know if you can handle all five of them yourself. At least not in a place that big, and with as much potential trouble as Marineland has. I mean, I can just imagine one of them jumping in a pool of sharks. And you know, it's not the kids I'd worry about. No, I'd feel sorry for the sharks."

"Oh, I don't have to handle them by myself. Hump's coming too. We're borrowing your van, okay? My car won't fit everyone. It's only a few hours to drive there, but we'll be back late."

"Hump?" The borrowing the van part didn't bother her. Lucy heard Hump's name and sort of stuck there. "Hump?" she repeated.

"Oh, he's aptly named, let me tell you," Irene shot her a self-satisfied smile. "And he is impressed with my skills."

"Irene!" Lucy gasped.

"You've got a dirty mind, little girl. My belly dancing skills."

"Oh." Lucy sank back against the pillow.

Irene sat on the corner of the bed. "But I'm sure I'll share the rest of my skills with him soon. He's a special man. And you might live like a nun, but I'm not very good at it. After all, life's too short at my age."

Lucy didn't feel very nunnish lately, at least not around Woody, but she was wise enough not to mention it to her foster mother. "But Irene, weren't you seeing someone?"

"Ancient history. Why it's been months since I've had a decent date. I think I used up all the good men in Florida, which is why coming back here was such a great idea." She grinned. "Now, are you going to lie there and talk about my love life all day, or are you going to crawl out of bed and come see us off?"

"You're crazy, you know that?" Lucy grinned.

"Yeah. But that's why you love me."

"That and about a million other reasons." She leaned forward and kissed her foster mother's cheek. "Are you sure you're up to an entire day with five kids?"

"Do you remember the triplets we kept for a

month while they were cleared for adoption? I handled them, and you and Hannah just fine. So today will be a piece of cake. After all, this whole group is potty-trained. Let me tell you, diapers times three was no picnic.''

"Tell me about it. I still have nightmares.''

"So, get up and make me some coffee. You know I can't stand my own.''

Irene didn't actually make coffee. She made colored water. No matter how many times Lucy tried to get her to add more coffee, Irene never managed better than hot, coffee-colored water.

"Better yet,'' Irene said, "you get dressed, and I'll head down to Woody's and I'll try the coffee at his place. Maybe he already has a pot going. If not, I guess we'll see if I do better at his place.''

Lucy groaned, but it wasn't the idea of having to drink Irene's coffee that did it. "You can't just barge in on him like you do on me.''

Lucy remembered catching Woody unaware in boxer shorts. His legs had moved right up there on her list of sexy-Woody-Pembrooke-body-parts.

"Honey, the day any man doesn't let me into his house with open arms is the day you might as well bury me.'' Irene stood and walked toward the door.

"But—''

"Get out of bed, you slug. I'll expect you down there in ten minutes.'' And Irene whirled around and slammed the door behind her.

Lucy flopped back against the pillow. So much

for a peaceful Sunday morning. But the day would certainly have possibilities when the kids were gone.

A whole day to herself? What, oh what would she do?

Maybe she'd take a two-hour long bubble bath with a good book. Or go to the beach. Or take a walk down on the dock and eat ice cream for lunch while she fed the seagulls. Or—

The possibilities were endless.

She snuggled a little further under the blanket, but then bolted upright as she realized that Irene was heading to Woody's. The poor man had met her foster mother, but had never had to deal with Irene on his own.

Lucy suddenly had visions of Irene bursting into Woody's room and shaking him awake. For a moment, she was stuck on the mental image of Woody, one sexy leg snaked out from under the blankets as he slept. His untamed hair even more wild from his tossing and turning. And that very sexy chin would be covered with early morning stubble.

She groaned at the mental image, and tried to erase it as she threw back the sheet and climbed out of bed.

"DAD. DAD. DAD. DAD."

Woody pulled the pillow over his head, but a small hand lifted up the edge.

"Dad. Dad…" the chant continued.

Sighing, knowing that he wasn't going to get to

sleep in on this particular Sunday, Woody faced the inevitable and pried his sleep-gritted eyes open.

"Yes, Brandon?"

As his eyes focused, he saw it wasn't just Brandon in his room. There were three other children and Cain as well. And they were all grinning from ear to ear as they stared at him.

Woody sat up. "So what's up at," he glanced at the clock and groaned, "seven thirty-one in the morning?"

"Mr. Pembrooke," Cain said.

"I thought we decided I'd just be Woody?"

Cain grinned. "Woody, my Grandma Irene is here, and she wants to take us to Marineland today with Mr. Hump, and we could see the whales—"

"—and penguins," Brandon said.

"And they've got dolphins, Daddy. You can even pet 'em," Lynda added.

"I'll help Mrs. Madison," Robbie said, drawing himself up to his full preteen height. "We won't get into any trouble, I swear. Right kids?"

Shane waved his newly bandaged-free arm. "Yeah, we'll be so good they'll hardly know they have kids with them."

"Cain, I'm not sure your Grandma is up to five kids. I don't want her put on the spot."

Irene herself waltzed into his room, and Woody pulled the sheet higher.

"I've seen a naked chest before," Irene hooted with laughter. "And I wouldn't have asked your demon-spawn if I didn't want them to come. And before you tell me that one old lady can't handle them, let me remind you, this old lady has handled more children than you can imagine. Plus, I'm bringing Hump and he's coming armed with a mallet, in case they forget to behave."

"But—" he started to protest.

Irene interrupted him. "Oh, shush. You didn't have any plans, did you?"

"We were going to work on finishing the clubhouse," he tried.

"Well, that can wait until tomorrow. It's almost done anyway. Me, I'm going to Marineland today, and unless you come up with a better argument, so are they."

"Please, Dad," the kids pleaded.

"Well, if you're sure," he said.

Irene interrupted their screams of delight. "Well, if you're all going, you'd better be out in the driveway by eight o'clock, dressed, fed and ready for a day, because I'm not waiting."

All the kids scrambled. Irene grinned at Woody. "I'll take good care of them. I've never seen Cain so happy. The boy needed a family."

"He does fit in with them, doesn't he?"

"That little boy has always been too good. I'm glad to see a little of their demon-ness is rubbing off on him. Now, you put on a shirt—or not—and come tell us goodbye. We won't be home until late tonight."

"Thanks so much."

"No thank-yous are necessary. I like kids. I like spoiling Cain. But, more specifically, I like your kids. So thanks for sharing."

She walked out of his room and shut the door.

Irene liked his kids. As a matter-of-fact, so did Lucy. It had been a long time since someone noticed how great his kids were.

He remembered their conversation from yesterday. Lucy might like his kids, but she was still leaving at the end of the summer. He'd be foolish to think he could convince her to stay when her mind was obviously made up.

He pulled the covers entirely over his head just as someone banged on his door. Brandon called, "Come on, Dad. I need breakfast before I can go, and you said I can't pour my milk for cereal anymore since I dumped a whole thing last time."

Woody remembered the spilt gallon and was glad Brandon had remembered to have someone else pour.

"Okay, I'm coming."

"Hurry."

Woody pulled on his jeans and despite Irene's offer, a shirt, and padded barefoot down the stairs, wondering what he was going to do about Lucy Caldwell.

LUCY WATCHED IRENE back her van out of the driveway. The noise level was every bit as loud as that first day when Woody's truck had pulled in the drive.

"Well," was all she could think of to say.

"Do you think they'll survive?" he asked.

"The kids, or Irene and Hump?"

"Irene and Hump," he said with a grin. "I know my kids can survive just about anything."

Lucy seemed nervous around him. She turned and headed back toward her apartment, but Woody stopped her.

"Why don't you come inside? We can have a quiet cup of coffee. Irene made a pot before she left."

"Have you tried it yet?" Lucy asked.

When he shook his head, she laughed. "If you'd said yes, I'd have accused you of wanting me to share it just because it was so bad and you didn't want to drink the whole thing. Your chances of survival would be bleak, to say the least."

"Speaking of chances." He stopped in the middle of the drive.

There was something in the way he looked at her that made her breath catch. "Chances?"

"Yeah. What are the chances that you might want to do something with me today?"

"Something like what?"

Oh, she knew what she'd like to do. She'd like to strip him naked and have her way with him. She'd like to memorize his body from his sexy lips right down to his sexier legs. She'd like to—

"Well, it's been two weeks, and other than late-night chats on the stairs and a childless visit to the hospital, we're always surrounded by the kids."

She nodded slowly. "Between the two of us, we have five kids, so I guess the fact that we're always surrounded makes sense."

"Sure it does. But since we're not going to be surrounded for an entire day, I thought..."

He paused and raked his hand through his hair and then took a long breath in and said, "Well, hell, Lucy. I know you're leaving at the end of the summer, and I know you said you don't want any more kissing. I'm an adult, and I'll learn to live with that. But I like you. Just you the person, and it's a rare thing to find someone you truly like. So, I'm putting that other stuff behind us. What I'm trying to say is I want to spend time with you. Just you. I don't care what we do. We could head for the beach, go see a movie. I'll take you out to eat. I'd even go to the mall, if that's what you want."

"You'd go shopping on purpose, just to spend time with me? Even shoe shopping?"

"Yeah. I wouldn't like the shopping part, but I suspect I'd really enjoy the spending time with you part."

She felt uncharacteristically choked up. "That's probably the nicest thing anyone has said to me in years."

"You like that, well how about this? Since my wife walked out on me—on us—I've dated a couple times, but I haven't... What I mean to say is, I'm a man with impulses, but there hasn't been anyone that I *impulsed* with, no one I wanted to take a relationship to the next level with. But with you..."

He took a deep breath and dove right back in. "I'm not asking for a lifetime commitment. I know you're leaving at the end of the summer, but I wanted... I'm making a mess of this. Every time I'm around you, I feel like an untried schoolboy. What I'm trying to say is I can't get you off my mind. I dream about you. As much as I'd like more, I'd give about anything for just one more kiss, I want your friendship more and—"

"Pembrooke?" she asked softly.

"I'm sorry. You weren't ready to hear—"

She cut off his sentence with a kiss.

He was right. She didn't want to hear more. But she wanted more. So much more. More kisses. And more of what might come after.

She tried to put all of that in her kiss. All her sexual desires. All her admiration. All the friendship she thought they were developing. All that and more.

"Wow," Woody said when they finally drew apart.

"I love the beach," she said as soon as she'd caught her breath. "And I'll confess, I'm even fond of shopping, but I have a much better idea about how we can spend today."

She took his hand and led him toward his house. "And I think we should take it inside, because otherwise your neighbors will be scandalized and call the cops. That one police interruption was enough for me.''

They walked into the kitchen, and slowly, deliberately, she shut the door and locked it.

"Lucy, are you sure?" Woody asked.

"No. I'm not sure. This could be a big mistake, but I am sure I want you, and that if you're willing to take a chance, so am I.''

She still wasn't sure what happened last night. Woody had seemed so distant. And now, all this talk about just friends, and leaving... She just wasn't sure what there was between them. What he wanted.

Lucy wasn't sure of so many things, but she was absolutely sure of this one thing right now. "I want you.''

"If you want me, then you'll have me." As soon as they opened the kitchen door, he scooped her into his arms.

"Woody, put me down, you fool. You'll break your back.''

He chuckled as he continued to walk. "I think my back can handle carrying you. I'm not letting you go in case you change your mind. I need you.''

"I need you too, and I'm not changing my mind, but I can walk to your room on my own.''

"No." He set a light kiss on her forehead. "You've been on your own for too long. Today you've got me.''

Today.

He wasn't promising more than today, Lucy realized.

She told herself that she felt relief. She didn't want him to read more into this than just a physical thing. That's all it was, after all, she assured herself. Simply physical.

9

WOODY PLACED LUCY in the center of the bed. She'd been in this room before, but how had she not noticed how large the bed was?

She felt small and nervous.

She wondered if she should take off her clothes. If he was going to take off his. What did a new-millennium woman do now?

It wasn't as if she'd never had sex—she was a mother, after all. It's just that—

He sat on the bed next to her and ran a finger across her brow. "That dimple is back. What are you worrying about?"

"I'm not worried." That was a lie, so she added, "Well, not really. It's just I don't want to disappoint you."

Woody chuckled again.

Lucy let the sound of his laugh wash over her. It relaxed her. How could a man's voice affect her so strongly? She could feel every word, every laugh, vibrating in the center of her soul.

"Lucy. Just you being here with me. This would be enough to keep me happy. Do you know how much I like looking at you? That first day, I watched you stubbornly drag a huge suitcase up the stairs— unwilling to ask for help, unwilling to stop until the job was done. You were tired, hot and sweaty, and I don't think I've ever seen anyone look better to me."

He wanted nothing more than to strip her naked and bury himself in her warmth. Hard and explosive. That's how she made him feel.

But Lucy deserved more than that. So, despite the fact he'd never thought of himself as a romantic man, he set out to seduce her, to take his time and make this moment magic.

"Tell me what you like," he whispered.

"Kissing you. I really, really like kissing you."

She reached for him, and he happily obliged. As he let his lips show her his longing, he slid his hand under her T-shirt. He groaned as his skin grazed hers, and thought he would die of pleasure when he realized she wasn't wearing a bra.

He broke off their kiss long enough to slip the T-shirt over her head. Needing to get closer, he started to kiss her again, but she shook her head. "Fair is fair. I don't have a shirt, and neither should you."

In all his thirty-three years, Woody had never stripped a shirt over his head so fast. He tossed it on the floor, and returned to kissing her. His cal- loused hand stroked her body. He couldn't remem- ber ever feeling anything so smooth. So soft.

Her small hand toyed with the light hair that covered his chest. Such a simple thing, and yet it made his heart race even faster.

"Have I mentioned I like the way you feel as much as I like the way you look?" she asked.

"I'd like to think of something romantic to say, but all that comes to mind is me too."

"Me too?" she asked with a small laugh.

"Yeah, you feel as good as you look, too." He tried to come up with something more romantic.

"That's plenty romantic enough for me."

"Well, then let me try this. We've got too many clothes on. Let's get naked."

This time it wasn't a small laugh, Lucy actually giggled. "*Let's get naked* is definitely the most romantic thing I've ever heard."

Woody stood and started to peel off his jeans. "Honey, whenever I'm around you, all the wonderful things I say to you in my dreams just evaporate. I can't think straight when you're around."

Lucy wiggled out of her pants and faced him. All her nervousness had evaporated and all that was left was desire and something more. Something big. Something intense.

She put that big intense feeling aside until she could examine it later. All she wanted to think about now was how much she wanted this man.

"Woody, having a man tell you he can't think when you're around is just about as romantic as anything Shakespeare ever wrote."

She stared at his hard, chiseled form. "You have to be one of the most beautiful men I've ever seen."

"Hold that thought." He reached in the night-stand drawer and pulled out a foil packet. "I don't want you to think I keep these around because I have…that there are…I mean, other women, or I expected…because I didn't expect, but I hoped and I already have four kids, and you have one and I didn't—"

He stopped and took a deep breath. "Well, hell, Lucy, it seems like I've wanted you forever, and I wanted to be prepared so I bought these the other day."

He was so…well, cute, sitting naked on the edge of the bed, blushing like a schoolboy.

"Thank you," she said. "That kind of consideration is sexy, too."

"I broke the moment, didn't I?" He sighed. "Maybe there's a sexy, romantic way to talk about birth control, but I couldn't think of one. Even if you were…well, using something, we would have needed, I mean I would have needed a condom and I—"

"Woody," she interrupted. "The only thing that could possibly break the moment for me is if all our kids came running into the room now."

"But they're on their way to Niagara Falls."

"That's right," Lucy said, running her hand down his chest in what she hoped was a sexy, siren sort of way.

"And we have the whole day."

"Do you think we could possibly spend the whole day in here?"

He grinned. "We could try."

He reached out and ran a finger across her jawline, down her chin, and then slid the hand behind her neck, and pulled her toward him.

His lips touched her and Lucy would have sworn under oath that she could feel desire coursing through her bloodstream. The feeling went beyond anything she'd ever experienced. Need. Craving. Yearning.

Like a starving man presented a meal, she feasted. She explored Woody's body with unabashed curiosity. Surprised by her boldness and daring.

He was work-hardened—she traced the muscles in his abdomen with her tongue. And then kissed each callous on his hands. She wanted to taste, to touch every inch of him, but before she'd covered every inch, he stopped her.

"My turn," he said.

Despite the evidence of his strength, his gentleness almost brought her to tears. His caresses were so soft, as if he was afraid she'd break, and in reality, Lucy wondered if she would if he continued to caress her much longer.

Her need to be connected to this man, to cease to be just Lucy, but to merge with him and become something new and incredible, grew so big that she truly thought she might shatter with the need.

"Please," she asked, when the need grew too much to bear. "Now."

"So beautiful," he murmured. He kissed his way up her body and pressed himself against her. "So beautiful."

"Please," she said again.

He obliged her, sliding into her, soothing the ache, a gentle joining of two souls.

A dance as old as time itself, and yet new and wonderful because it was Lucy and Woody. Woody and Lucy. They were joined and ceased to be separate entities, but were made something new and wonderful.

Their rhythm was slow at first, but as the heat grew, the tempo increased until they both burst into flames, one after the other. Beautiful, burning, blazing heat.

And with it came the knowledge that the something growing in the center of her chest—the something she didn't want to identify—was too big to be ignored, and yet scared her just the same.

This feeling...

She wouldn't name it. All she wanted was to bask in the afterglow of making love to this man, to melt against his heat.

She didn't know what to do, what to say. And was thankful that he simply pulled her into his arms. That he didn't talk. Didn't ask anything of her. He just held her.

She surrendered to the warmth and strength of his

embrace. There would be time to worry about what to do with Woody Pembrooke. All she wanted today was to enjoy this...whatever this turned out to be.

She must have dozed because the sound of a phone made her jump. Woody wordlessly kissed her, then disentangled himself and rolled over to pick up the phone on his nightstand, Lucy felt a tangible sense of loss.

"Hello," he said in the gruff voice that gave her the shivers.

She'd just made love with this man. What would that mean to their relationship? Did he see what they had as a relationship, or was it just a momentary mutual need that had brought them together?

The fire that had consumed her was gone, and Lucy was left with her cold doubts and fears.

There was a long pause, and Woody said, "Yeah, she's here and I'll tell her. We'll be right there."

He slammed the receiver down on its cradle. "It's Hannah. She's in labor, and it's for real this time."

"How far along is she?"

"Abel said the contractions are every four minutes, and strong. He wants us to hurry."

Lucy sprang from the bed and started pulling on her clothes. "About what just happened," Woody started, one leg sliding into his jeans.

Lucy pulled her own pants into place and snapped them. "It was nice. I want to thank you for a lovely afternoon."

"Nice?" That warm rumbly tone that had attracted her from the first, was replaced by an angry growl.

"Very nice. I just don't think it would be wise to let it happen again."

She didn't look at him. Not that sure what she'd see reflected in his eyes, but sure whatever it was, she didn't want to see it.

"I mean," she continued nervously when he said nothing, "it's not likely we'd actually have a chance for a repeat performance. After all, five kids kind of put a damper on... Well, let's just say it's for the best. You're a nice man, Woody, but like we said before, there are a hundred reasons why we shouldn't do this again."

"One of them is you're leaving at the end of the summer, right?"

"Why do we keep coming back to this? Yes, I'm leaving. That was the deal. I asked Abel to help me find an apartment for Cain and I, just like you wanted me to."

"You asked for his help, but only after I guilted you into it. Lucy Caldwell doesn't like relying on anyone, does she?"

"No, I don't. What's wrong with that?"

"You don't know? You can't figure it out?"

"No, I can't. Relying on myself, being independent. That's all I know how to be."

"You're afraid," he said bluntly.

"Afraid? Listen, I've been standing on my own

two feet for my entire life.''

Lucy had already confessed to being afraid of failing Cain, failing at her new business. But she wasn't going to confess that the fear of trying and then failing to build a relationship with this man who touched her soul was even greater. She'd learned long ago that pretending you weren't afraid was the next best thing to being fearless.

She glanced at him. It wasn't anger that she saw in his eyes, but disappointment.

Somehow that was worse.

He shook his head. "You're afraid of this—of what's going on between us because it means trusting someone else, learning to depend on someone. This could change our lives, if you let it."

"I like my life just fine. I'm doing great on my own."

"*On my own.* That just about sums it up, doesn't it? I mean, I just mentioned helping you with your business but you nixed the offer. This need to stand on your own two feet isn't independence, but fear."

"I am perfectly capable of getting my business off the ground without your help. I want to do this on my own. It has nothing to do with being afraid." She looked in his mirror, and ran her fingers through her hair, trying to smooth it back into place.

"You might be capable, but there's no sin in leaning on someone. There's nothing wrong with needing someone." He paused a moment, and then added, "I need you."

"To baby-sit your kids for the summer," she clarified, more for her sake than for his. He couldn't want anything more. They'd only known each other for a few weeks.

"And I'm not suggesting I'm not going to baby-sit for you, just that doing this again wouldn't be wise, even if we could find an opportunity, which I doubt we will."

"But you don't want anything more than a professional relationship?" he asked.

"Woody, the sex was great, I just don't think—"

"It wasn't sex," he said, firm and sure of himself.

"No? Then it was a pretty good imitation." She tried to laugh, to turn this conversation into something lighter, easier to set aside, but the sound was too brittle, even to her own ears.

"I made love to you. You made love to me." He spun her away from the mirror so she was facing him. "I love you. You deserve poetry, romance, but the best I can come up with is saying, I love you."

She'd worried about whether he'd thought about this as simply a one-night, or rather day stand, or a relationship. But she was even more worried to hear the word *love*. That wasn't what she'd wanted.

Was it?

"We've only known each other a couple weeks," she reminded herself as much as him. She'd tried the quick infatuation route with Cain's father, and wasn't up to trying it again with Woody. "You can't—and I don't—and—"

"And?"

She pulled from his grasp and headed toward the bedroom door. "And Hannah needs me. We have to go. I don't want to talk about this anymore."

"We're not through with this," he said, grabbing her hand and pulling her onto the bed. "Hannah will be fine for five more minutes."

"I don't know what to say."

"Well, that's a start. It seems to me you were doing a lot of talking a few minutes ago, but you weren't saying anything that made sense."

"This doesn't make sense," she said, sliding away from him, needing some distance. "That's my point. And I don't know if I want to try and figure it out."

"Why?" Woody slid closer, crowding her.

"Because maybe you're right, I'm afraid. I don't understand relationships like this."

"Define this?" he asked.

"Sexual. Totally sexual, chemical attraction."

"And that's what you think this is? Just sex?"

"Yes." She nodded. That's all she wanted this to be. Just sex. She could handle that. But if it was more? She didn't know.

"And if I said I thought it could be more? If I said that having you in my life has changed everything I thought I wanted?"

"Then I'd say I'm sorry if I led you on."

"Oh, you didn't. You said it all the other night to the kids, remember? *I don't want to get married. Not ever.* I heard you, but I didn't really listen, I guess."

"Married? Who said anything about marriage?" she asked.

"No one. And I guess, no one's going to." He stood. "Let's go."

Lucy wanted to say something, but didn't know what. Woody loved her? What on earth was she supposed to say to that?

"BITE ME."

Lucy couldn't believe her soft-spoken friend had just said *bite me* to her husband. But Hannah didn't sound overly soft-spoken at the moment, she sounded stressed.

"Hannah," Abel Kennedy said to his wife, with more than a little exasperation in his voice, "I'm not biting you, but you are going to listen to me and breathe your way through this contraction. Come on. Eee. Whoo. Eee. Whoo. Inhale, exhale. Breathe. You know how to do it."

"Bite me long and hard, Kennedy," Hannah growled. "Eee. Whoo. Eee. Whoo."

"I don't know, Hannah," Lucy said. "You've always struck me as pretty tough to gnaw on."

Hannah took a long, cleansing breath. "I'm glad you're here. You can tell Abel here to bite me because he won't listen to me."

"Um, Abel, Hannah said you're supposed to bite

her. But Hannah, I'm a good enough friend to point out that you're already in enough pain. I don't think you need Abel to chomp on you. Plus, I seem to remember giving you a nip or two during a fight when we were growing up. You don't taste good at all.''

She smiled at her friend. Glad to have something to preoccupy her from the long awkward silence that had enveloped the car as she and Woody raced to the hospital.

"It's his fault I'm here." Hannah flopped back against the pillow. "This hurts."

"Yeah, but just think, you're going to have a baby soon."

Abel looked pale and worn out. Lucy offered him a smile. "Abel, Woody's out in the hall. Why don't you go say hi to him for a minute," she said, offering him a break. The poor man looked like he might fall over at any moment.

"Call me if you need me, sweetheart." He kissed Hannah's cheek, grabbed Lucy's hand and gave it a squeeze. "I'm glad you're here. She needs you."

"I'm glad I'm here too," she said.

"Where's Cain and the demons?" Hannah asked when the door shut.

Lucy sat on the edge of the bed, still holding Hannah's hand. She remembered this point in her labor with Cain. All of a sudden it had hit home with a bang—she was going to be a mother. Someone was going to be totally dependent on her. For someone determined to be as independent as possible, the thought was frightening.

Lucy wanted to give Hannah an opportunity to think about something else. And what could be more distracting than the demon-spawn?

"Irene and Hump took them to Marineland for the day," she said. "I can only imagine what kind of mischief they're going to get into there. I mean sharks, huge tanks of water...And it's not just the kids. You know Irene can be just as bad. She's going to be extremely put out that you had the baby while she was gone."

Hannah laughed. "Irene's never known the meaning of the word *fear*. But I do. I'm scared, Luce. I mean, I've delivered hundreds of babies, but what if I can't handle having one of my own?"

Fear.

Lucy knew all about that emotion. She thought of Woody, pacing out in the hall. He was right. She was afraid. He'd said he loved her, and all she'd given him was excuses why he shouldn't.

But love?

She pushed her worry aside and concentrated on Hannah. "You're going to be a great mom," she reassured her.

"You think so?"

"No. I know so."

"I—"

Lucy saw the contraction begin. "Now, I'm not Abel, and you can't browbeat me. So do your breathing exercises now, or I'll kick your pregnant hiney.''

Hannah didn't even argue, she simply nodded and started breathing.

''Inhale, breathe out. Inhale, breathe out. Inhale…'' Lucy talked her friend through the contraction. ''There. Now that wasn't so bad.''

Hannah smiled weakly as she took a large, cleansing breath. ''Out with it,'' she said suddenly.

''What?'' Lucy asked.

''Honey, we've been friends for too long for me not to know something's bothering you.''

''The fact that my best friend, the sister of my heart, is about to give birth isn't enough to make me worry?''

''No.''

''Hey, you want to say hi to Woody?'' Abel hollered through the door. ''He says he'll just wait out here in the hall, but I said I was sure you wanted to see him.''

''Of course I want to see him. Tell him I'm decent.''

Woody peeked his head through the door. ''You're sure it's safe?''

''Has Abel been telling you stories? Don't believe a word he says.''

''You told me to bite you,'' Abel protested.

''I've told you that before and you haven't minded.''

"But—"

Lucy couldn't take her eyes off Woody as he walked into the room and planted a huge kiss on Hannah's cheek. There was so much unsettled between them, and she knew she'd hurt him with her response after they'd—he was right, it wasn't sex—made love. Somehow she was going to have to set things right, but she wasn't sure how.

She caught Hannah's eye and saw the dawning of understanding in her friend's expression.

"So, what were you two up to today, since all the kids are gone?" Hannah asked, casting a sly glance at Lucy.

"I was just enjoying the solitude," Lucy said at the same moment Woody said, "We were just hanging out together."

"Luce, it was just that kind of hanging out with Abel that got me in this condition."

"We weren't…" Lucy started to protest, but Hannah's look froze the protest on her lips. "Isn't it time for another contraction?" she asked.

"Oh, that was low. So low—"

At that moment, Lucy could indeed see another contraction grip Hannah.

"Oh," Hannah cried.

"Breathe with me," Abel said, all the joking forgotten.

As the contraction ended, Hannah started to cry.

"Hey, what's wrong?" Abel asked.

"Nothing." Hannah gave a big sniff. "Nothing's wrong. I'm just so happy."

"Happy?"

"You're wonderful, and we're going to have a baby, and Lucy's home and I know she's going to be happy, and now Irene's home and—" She stopped and sniffed again and a look of concentration came over her face. "I feel the urge to push."

Lucy pressed the button and the nurse light blinked off and on. "Come on, Woody. We'll be right outside." She kissed Hannah's cheek. "You're going to be a great mom."

"If I'm half as good as you, I'll be satisfied. And I just want you to be happy. Don't let anything stop you." Hannah gave a little wave and Lucy heard her whispering to Abel as they walked out the door, "I didn't mean to yell at you. I don't want you to bite me, really. I love you and—"

He kissed her. "I know that, and it's going to be fine."

"I have to push."

Meghan Maloney ran past Lucy and Woody into the room.

"I have to push," Hannah said again.

"Don't until I check and…"

Lucy watched the door slam shut. She stood and just stared at it.

"Wow, I'd forgotten what it was like," Woody said.

She turned and looked at the amazing man who'd stumbled into her life.

"It shouldn't be long now," she said, staring at the closed door.

"Let's sit down. Because you look like you might just fall over. Are you all right?"

All right?

She let Woody lead her into the waiting room and took the seat he indicated.

All right?

How was she supposed to be all right when she'd spent her afternoon in bed with this amazing man who'd touched more than just her body, he had touched her heart.

He said he'd made love to her.

And despite her claims that it had just been sex, she'd made love to him as well. Because…

Oh, for crying out loud, she thought as she realized the truth of the matter.

She loved him.

How on earth did that happen?

She might not have admitted it before, not even to herself, but it felt like she'd loved Woody Pembrooke for a long, long time.

Maybe it had started that first day, watching him with his kids. Or when her son had spouted off about being part of the Pembrooke tradition. Seeing how Woody was with her son…how could she not love him?

Or maybe it was simply how he made her feel. He was the other half of her whole.

In her life she'd only loved three people. Irene, Hannah and Cain.

Three people who she knew she could count on. Three people she knew would never let her down, and who she'd die trying to never let down.

She figured her heart was full enough for two lifetimes.

And now she loved Woody.

And his kids.

How was she supposed to deal with that?

"Lucy, are you okay?" he asked, concern etching his face.

She nodded, not willing to say anything because she knew the minute she did, she'd have to blurt out how she felt, and she wasn't sure she wanted to do that.

She had plans. Loving Woodrow Pembrooke wasn't one of them. She tried to concentrate on nudging that love aside.

It wouldn't budge.

Darn it. It just figured.

"Woody, I—"

"Don't say anything. Not until later. After this, we'll go and we'll talk."

"But—"

"No. Don't say it."

"Fine." He didn't want to hear she loved him? She'd wait, but he was going to hear it today.

She hadn't planned on falling in love. But she had. She wasn't sure what would happen, but she wasn't going to turn away from love just because it frightened her.

She was going to face it head-on.

10

"IT'S A GIRL," Abel said as he skidded to a halt in front of their couch.

"Ten toes, ten fingers, and the most gorgeous blond hair, just like her mom. She's absolutely perfect." He puffed his chest out with pride. "You remember when you told me what great babies you made, Woody? Well, I think you'll have to agree that I don't do too bad in that department."

"Ah, well, now, you've managed one pretty baby, but you come to me when you've had four, and we'll talk. I mean, anyone can manage one pretty baby, but four?" Woody laughed as he stood and clapped his hand on Abel's back. "Congratulations."

"How's Hannah?" Lucy asked.

Abel hugged Lucy. "Just fine. She doesn't want me to bite her anymore. The nurses said if you give them a few more minutes you can come back."

"Are you sure? I mean, I thought just family—"

She didn't get to finish the sentence because Abel interrupted, "You are family. I mean, you and Woody are going to be little Eileen's godparents."

"Oh." She wanted to cry, and it was all Abel's fault.

Lucy hated to cry. It didn't fit the tough image she wanted to project, but there it was. So when the urge to cry hit, she sniffed it back. Like, every time she watched *The Champ,* she ended up snuffling like crazy. She felt like an anteater run amuck. And sometimes even Hallmark commercials could do it to her. If those things could choke her up, being a godmother certainly put her over the top.

"I would be honored," she managed between sniffs.

Abel loped an arm over her shoulder and led her, sniffing like crazy, back to Hannah's room.

Hannah was holding the baby when they walked in. "Isn't she beautiful?"

Lucy stared at the little girl, the newest member of her family, and was suddenly no longer just sniffing, but was crying like crazy. "She's absolutely beautiful."

"Do you want to hold her?"

Lucy nodded and Hannah handed her the baby. She'd almost forgotten what it was like to hold a newborn. She was so small, so dependent...so beautiful. "Woody, would you like a turn?"

Her heart almost melted when she saw the big giant of a man cradling the newborn.

How could she have let fear keep her from answering his declaration of love with one of her own?

How could she imagine, even for a second, that she could live another day without him?

Well, she couldn't. She watched him staring at the baby and couldn't remember a time she didn't love this man. She couldn't remember even one of the reasons they shouldn't be together.

It was time to tell him so.

Past time.

IT WAS TIME TO have it out.

Woody glanced at Lucy. She sat quietly on her side of his truck. Too quiet.

They needed to clear the air.

"Lucy," he said, unsure what he'd say next, but knowing he needed to make her understand.

"You didn't want to talk while we were at the hospital, and I don't want to talk in the truck. Just wait until we get home, Woody."

"Like hell I will." He pulled the truck over and threw it into park. "I have a few things I have to say to you."

"And they can't wait until we get home?"

"No."

He took a deep breath, and started, "When Ashley walked out on me and the kids, I knew that I'd never remarry. She said that she couldn't cope with being a mother to four children. She wanted more. Not more kids, but more of a life than she could have here with us. So she left me and left her kids without a backward glance. She's not a bad person, but it was too much. She couldn't cope.''

"But she left you here, expecting you to cope," Lucy said softly.

Woody shrugged. "For me it wasn't coping. Oh, there are the ever-present baby-sitter woes, and the logistics of caring for four children, but it's not coping…it's a joy. I love being a father. I love my kids. But I didn't expect to ever find a woman I could love, one who not only accepted my children, but loved them enough to deal with all the logistics in order to get to the joy.

"And then you showed up. You and Cain. Lucy, I love you. And whether you love me as well, doesn't matter. You fill up a place in me I never knew was empty. It's so full, that I feel as if I could simply burst apart with the enormity of it.''

"Woody, I—"

He leaned across the bench seat and placed a finger softly on her lips, those lips he knew so well. "Don't say it. I'm not asking you to say you love me too. I'm just asking for a chance. Don't go at the end of the summer. Stay with us. I know you want to start your business, that it's important to you to do it on your own. I swear I won't interfere, we'll hire someone to help with all the kids. I'll do anything you want, only don't leave.''

He took a breath and continued, "I know you

don't want to get married. I won't push you, I swear. I just want—''

Gently she kissed his finger, then pulled it away from her lips. "You know, Pembrooke, if I didn't love you I could get seriously annoyed with you trying to shut me up. If you think I'm going to change and be some mealymouthed little woman for you, well, you've got another think coming. I mean, if I'm going to deal with five kids—''

What she had said hit him all of a sudden. He wasn't sure if he'd heard what she'd said, or what he so desperately wanted to hear. "Wait, go back a minute. What did you say?"

SAY? LUCY DIDN'T want to just *say* anything. She wanted to shout it, so the entire world could hear. "I said, I don't like you telling me to shut up," she hedged, smiling.

"No, before that."

Though she'd prefer shouting the words, it appeared she was more apt to cry over them. She blinked back the tears that suddenly filled her eyes and repeated, "I love you."

"Yeah?" he asked with that smile that she found so endearing.

"Yeah."

He unsnapped her seat belt, and pulled her across the seat. "So what are you going to do about it?"

"Marry you, you big doofus. And build a life with

you. And raise our kids with you. And fight with you and make love with you and…'' She paused and looked at this man who filled her heart to overflowing. "Oh, just shut up and kiss me."

"My pleasure."

They made magic together. A rare sort of magic that even five kids could never dim. Lucy knew that all her life she'd been looking for this man, and that she'd found him and that he loved her…well, that was magic, too.

"When you were reading to the kids, you said you never wanted to get married," he said.

Lucy ran a finger down Woody's strong jawline to his ultrasexy chin. "I didn't. Not ever. I wanted to be independent and not rely on anyone. Until I met you. You changed everything. I want to lean on you, but only if you lean on me in return. I want to spend the rest of my life with you. It took me a while to admit how I felt about you. I think I fell in love with you that first day, watching you deal with Robbie's daredevil tendencies and Shane's injured arm and even Cain peeing on your hydrangea bush. On some level I think I knew then that I loved you."

"How long will it take you to plan a wedding?" he asked. His voice was that quiet bearish rumble that made her knees go weak.

She laughed and stroked his chin…that stubbly, sexy-as-sin, chin. "How soon do you want it?"

"Tomorrow?"

"I don't think I can manage it that fast, but how about before school begins. We'll do something small and intimate out in the yard—"

There was a loud rap against the passenger window. Lucy turned. "Oh, no."

"You two again?" said the officer. "Did you check out that room? Because I'm going to have to cite you for public indecency, or...well, I'm not sure if that charge would work, but I'll think of something."

"What if I told you that I just asked her to marry me and she accepted?" Woody asked.

"Well, you said you had five kids, so I'm thinking it's about time...past time."

"You're right. It is. But don't you listen to him, officer. I asked him. And since you've been present at two of the most significant moments of our courtship, maybe you'd like an invitation? Not that I'm trying to bribe you into not thinking up a charge, or anything."

"Well, now," said the officer. "I guess if I'm a guest, I can't really write you a ticket, now can I?"

Lucy grinned. "I think it would be bad form. The wedding is going to be just a small ceremony, only family and loved ones, and..."

Epilogue

It was a beautiful August day when Lucy and Woody's friends and family gathered in Woody's backyard.

Woody, wearing a suit for the occasion, and Lucy, dressed in a simple off-white sundress with a wreath of flowers in her hair, stood under a trellis with roses and streamers woven through the wooden lattice.

Irene, dressed in her formal belly dancing outfit, including little bells that jingled every time she moved, clasped Hump's hand, dabbing tears from her eyes. She'd promised a special wedding dance, at the reception.

Officer Ericson and his wife stood next to them.

Abel stood next to Hannah, who also dabbed while cradling little Eileen.

A group of Woody's employees and their families filled out the guest list.

The minister said, "Do you, Lucy Ann Caldwell, take this man, Woodrow Wilson Pembrooke, to be your lawfully wedded husband?"

Lucy looked at Woody. How on earth had she gotten so lucky? To have found him, the other half of her heart, when she wasn't even looking?

"I do," she said.

"And do you take his children into your heart and into your home?" the minister asked. "Will you treat Robbie, Shane, Lynda and Brandon as if they were yours?"

"They are mine in every way that matters. Families are made in the heart, not just by blood," she said, grinning at the four of them, lined up behind their father.

That she'd gone years not knowing she had four more children was a mystery, because she couldn't remember a time when they weren't a part of her. "And I will be the best mother I know how to be."

The minister turned to Woody. "And do you, Woodrow Wilson Pembrooke, take Lucy Ann Caldwell to be your lawfully wedded wife?"

Woody squeezed her soft hand in his large calloused one. He'd thought that he'd never find anyone who could tolerate his kids, much less anyone who would love them as much as he did. But to have found that person, and to have fallen so deeply and madly in love with her...well, it was a miracle that he planned to celebrate every day for the rest of his life.

"I do," he said.

"And do you take her son, Cain, into your heart and into your home? Will you treat him as if he was yours?"

Woody grinned at the boy who was as much his son as Robbie, Shane or Brandon was. "I will."

"Then, by the power vested in me by the state of Pennsylvania, I now pronounce all of you a family."

"You may—"

No one waited for permission. Lucy found herself enveloped in arms. It was hard to tell whose arms were whose, but it didn't matter. This was her family.

She was home.

And she was never leaving again.

The wonder of it all hit her time and time again as the afternoon celebration went on.

After they cut the cake and mingled with the guests, Lucy spied all five of the kids on the clubhouse's flat roof.

"Hey, Mom and Dad," Robbie called down.

Lucy thought her heart would melt. He'd called her Mom.

She took Woody's hand and he squeezed hers. She knew he understood.

"We—the kids and me—we just wanted to say we're happy you're married. And it's not just the family honeymoon to Disney World. Me, Shane, Brandon and Lynda, well, we want to call Lucy

'Mom,' if that's okay.''

"I'm sure she'd like that," Woody called up to the not-so-demonish-spawn on the clubhouse roof.

"I would love it," she said, trying not to cry.

"And Woody, I've never had a dad," Cain called down. "So if you don't mind, I want you to be mine, too. Okay?"

"Cain, I'm honored to be your dad."

"And there's nothing we can do to chase you away, is there Lucy?" Robbie pressed.

"Nothing in the world. Not naked pizzas, or overflowing toilets, or locking me in the basement." She heard all their guests laugh and couldn't help but chuckle herself. "I might get even, but I'm not leaving."

"Hey that rhymed," Shane yelled.

"Even," Robbie said slowly. "Yeah. You taught us all about getting even."

"Robbie, what are you thinking about?" Lucy called, suddenly suspicious. The kids looked innocent. Too innocent.

"Well, you know how you got even with us for locking you in the basement?" Robbie asked.

"Yes," she answered slowly, even as she scanned the yard, looking for whatever they were up to.

"You got more than a little even. I mean, you got us even better." All five of the kids were nodding and adding their *yeahs* to what Robbie had said.

"Well, you won't lock me in the basement again. Will you?"

"Nah. But you know how you're supposed to throw rice at weddings?" Robbie asked.

Slowly, Lucy nodded.

"Well, we decided rice wasn't as much fun as—"

"Water balloons," Shane yelled, as he reached into a big box, grabbed a balloon and lobbed it at his father.

Splat!

That was all it took.

Water balloons rained down on Lucy and Woody, and pretty soon went beyond them. Abel caught one right in the chest.

"Oh, this is war now, you dognapping demonspawn," Abel cried. "Come on, Woody. It's time we breached their defenses."

"I'll get the hose," Lucy yelled.

Hannah handed Eileen to Irene. "Take her back a safe distance while I help Lucy."

Irene and Hump stood in the kitchen doorway and watched the ensuing melee.

Half an hour later, the backyard was a mire and Woody pulled his soggy bride against him. "Well, that wasn't quite what we had in mind."

"But I wouldn't change a thing," Lucy assured him.

"Neither would I. I love you and our kids."

They shared a secret smile as they walked with their family into the house and into a new life together.

*   *   *   *   *

WARNING:

HOLLY JACOBS HAS BEEN BUSY!
Don't miss Holly's Silhouette Romance,

DO YOU HEAR WHAT I HEAR?

published November 2001

If you enjoyed what you just read,
then we've got an offer you can't resist!

Take 2 bestselling
love stories FREE!
Plus get a FREE surprise gift!

Harlequin Romance®

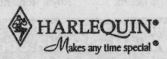

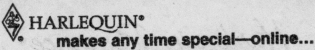